The Diamond Bearer's Secret

The Unaltered Series: Book Five

Lorena Angell

License Notes

Books by Lorena Angell

The Unaltered Series

A Diamond in My Pocket, Book 1
A Diamond in My Heart, Book 2
The Diamond of Freedom, Book 3
The Diamond Bearers' Destiny, Book 4
The Diamond Bearer's Secret, Book 5
The Diamond Bearers' Rising, Book 6
Books 7-10 coming soon!

The Lost Crown Series

Royal Refugee
Royal Resistance
Royal Redemption

This book is for:

The brave souls in my life who are true to
themselves and stand firm even when the
deck is stacked against them.
I respect and love you.

Contents

Chapter 1 – Dissention in the Ranks

I'm in heaven. Being held in Chris's reassuring arms, cocooned in his jacket, with the romantic setting of a moonlit lake in front of us, well, there just can't be anything better. Chris tucked his jacket around me to cover my recent injury. When the diamond shard left my body and joined with the portion of the diamond residing in Jonas Flemming, my clothing ripped, and my blood stained the fabric. My skin has healed, but I'm still cold. Chris's body heat next to mine is helping, though. Helping a lot.

Moments ago, Chris asked me if I wanted to go on a date. A date? We can see our future and the generations we'll create together, yet he wants to go on a date? The thought makes me shiver with excitement.

Chris pulls me closer. "Feeling better?"

"Yes. Just a little cold. You know, I've never been asked on a date before. Unless you count Brand's attempts to ask me out."

"Brand asked you out?" he asks, sounding displeased.

"He tried. I said no. So, I guess this is the first time I've been asked out by a guy I *really* want to be with." I look up into his eyes and smile.

"How did you make it to nineteen without being asked out? Why haven't you had any boyfriends? I had two girlfriends before I was sixteen."

"Really?"

"They weren't actually girlfriends," he says, downplaying his comment. "They were girls I could point to and say to my buddies, 'See that girl over there, I'm goin' with her.' "

My eyes roll automatically. "I watched some of the kids at school do that. I thought it was the most ridiculous thing ever. But maybe it was because I didn't have someone pointing at me and claiming me as theirs."

"We can go back to the group and I'll point to you from across the way, if that would make you feel better."

"I think I'd like that," I say, wondering who he'd tell he was "going" with me. Brand? Jonas? Amenemhet? Brand and Jonas would probably respond with, "Yeah, we know." Amenemhet would probably be confused and say, "Where are you going?"

He leaves his jacket around me, stands and looks down at me. "I can't brag about you being with me if I haven't even asked you to be mine." He pauses and repositions himself so he's standing a little bit further away. He seems so shy as he asks humbly, "Will you be my girlfriend?"

"Yes!"

I know the whole scene would look silly from anyone else's viewpoint, but to me it's incredibly sweet.

He sits back down and kisses me slowly. I feel our deep connection, his happiness, his gratitude, and his deep emotional issues concerning his father's recent death. He ends his kiss and pulls me into a hug. With his mind he says, *I love you.*

I love you, too.

"We better go back to the others or they'll start wondering about us," he says.

"Is that bad?"

"No. Not at all."

He doesn't add to his comment. He takes my hand and begins walking back to the group.

I think about how only one month ago I celebrated my nineteenth birthday with my parents and began my "internship" with Dr. Janice Johnson. I'd had no idea I was embarking on what would be the final leg of my journey—the reuniting of the diamond shards. So much has happened; it doesn't seem possible to have accomplished everything. Many people have died, some of whom didn't deserve that fate. Those who did should have seen it coming.

I never thought I'd find Chris behind the door at Justin's compound, completing the vision I'd seen earlier. Now, he walks beside me—as a fellow Diamond Bearer. He'd worried on the flight back from Alaska that we might not have a future together. Nothing could be further from the truth. Crimson considers us to be the strongest Diamond Bearers because of our love for one another. Frankly, I don't understand what she means.

First, I need to let Crimson's recent words sink in. She just told me she's protected me throughout my life. She basically let me know my life has never been my own. The more I think about what she said, the more I feel like a slow-motion bomb is going off in my head, like in one of those action movies where a huge explosion is shown from six different angles—six different shots, over and over again.

My heart rate increases and a knot forms in my stomach as I contemplate my life. Have I ever done any-thing for myself? Deus Ex's words come into my mind: *"What makes her so special? Why does everyone coddle Calli?"* At the time she said this, my life was in danger because of the diamond shard in my heart and Freedom's control over the shard. Maybe Deus saw something else. Maybe she could see my life for what it is: controlled, managed, directed.

I died on the stone alter. Maetha saved me. I nearly

drowned in the river. Chris saved me. Crimson told me about several near-miss accidents I didn't even know about where she'd saved me. When have I ever saved myself?

Memories of the two creepy men who tried to kidnap me come to mind. I saved myself then. Or did I? I used the powers of the diamond to save myself. The knot in my gut relaxes a little and I wonder why I'm even questioning this. I've had a great life! I have two wonderful parents who love me completely. I've been able to travel with them, learn from them, and develop into a strong individual through their support.

Or maybe that was all preplanned too.

Chris and I approach the group, hand in hand. One week ago, I was sulking at my parent's cabin in Maine, feeling Chris was further away from me than ever before, spending my time worrying our future wouldn't come true. Yet, here we are today, stronger than ever.

What a difference a few days make.

Chris tightens his grip. I glance at him and take in his moonlit profile. He's been through so much lately. His own father thought nothing of risking Chris's life in his pursuit of ultimate power. Then, earlier today, Chris witnessed his father's murder. He still needs to deal with that, among other things. For instance, what about all the years of parental neglect and emotional abuse at the hands of his father—his now deceased father? How does he overcome that?

What about Brand, growing up with a father who never loved him? Or Jonas? His case is even more depressing. His father killed his younger brother while Jonas hid in a closet. The burden has followed Jonas, haunting his psyche. Beth and Anika just lost their parents to General Harding's thugs. They're orphans!

Why did my life have to be so perfect?

I've never dealt with loss, never had heartbreak. Oh sure, I had one serious injury from Suz's firecracker in middle school, but other than that, I've sailed through life without a scratch. Up to now, I've felt like one lucky girl. I've felt fortunate for having such a peaceful life. Now I know different. I wish I didn't. I wish I could turn back the clock and erase the knowledge I just received. I'm not a lucky girl. I'm protected. If I was to walk in front of a speeding train, Crimson would—

"Are you okay?" Chris brushes the side of my cheek with his fingertips.

I hadn't realized we'd stopped walking. I look ahead to the group in front of us. "Yeah, I am. Just a lot to take in over the last little while."

"I know," he says, almost whispering. "You shouldn't feel like you do. You didn't choose to have your life controlled. So, don't feel guilty about it."

"I'm sorry, Chris. I've really got to work on controlling my thoughts and keeping them to myself. It's stupid of me to feel this way and worse that you have to deal with my whining." That's not the first time Chris has read my mind or heard my thoughts since he received the diamond. I'll have to be careful what I think about.

"You don't have to apologize." He pulls me into a tender hug, then delivers a quick kiss to the top of my head. "Come on. Let's join the others. Cheer up." My stomach warms. Chris is relaying some of his healing power.

I rest my cheek on his chest and wrap my arms around him. "Thank you." After being intertwined with him for a few precious seconds, absorbing his energy, I pull back and say, "Hey, where are you going to take me on our date?"

"I have a few places in mind. Let me think on it."

Turning toward the group, I find several faces staring

at us, having witnessed our intimacy. Others are deep in conversation, celebrating General Harding's death, ironically. Our arrival seems to have dampened the excitement, but Chris doesn't hesitate to add fuel to the boisterous exclamations and soon others follow his lead.

I could learn a thing or two from Chris, I think. He has every right to be sad and sullen, yet he puts his emotions aside because he sees the bigger picture of what has been accomplished. Sheez, it wasn't long ago *I* was lecturing *him* about the "bigger picture."

Chris squeezes my hand lightly and says, "I'll go get us some food." He leaves me standing near the edge of the group.

Others' thoughts start infiltrating my mind, slowly becoming louder than my own. I can't determine whose thoughts I'm hearing. I can't even tell if they are male or female. The words flow through my mind like words on the air. My mind translates them into my own voice. It sounds like I'm thinking them, but I know I'm not. How do I know? Because they're talking about me.

This is a joke, a voice says. *Especially thrusting Calli on us.*

Another says, *We've followed everything she's asked, yet they are hailed as the new heroes.*

Her mind is inaccessible and that concerns me, the first voice says. *Something is amiss.*

A different voice adds, *There's no possible way the youngsters will replace us.*

The second voice asks, *Have you decided? Are you with us?*

I freeze in my spot, not knowing for sure if they're talking to me directly. I don't even know who's talking to whom.

A fourth voice says, *Yes, I'm with you.*

I conclude being able to hear other Diamond Bearers' thoughts is a rather unpleasant experience. My eyes roam the crowd. As I've noticed before, the Bearers all seem to appear middle-aged. Crimson looks like she could be in her mid-forties. Some, like Mary, Duncan, and Ruth, are on the older end of the spectrum, appearing to be in their early sixties or so. Because they appear older, the rest of us younger people look quite young.

Mary's blonde hair moves against her pink floor-length robe as she talks animatedly to Jie Wen. As his mouth curves into a slight smile, his eyes narrow even more. He looks happy. They are joined by Chuang. He carries a platter of vegetables and hummus. Chuang and Jie Wen are dressed in long Chinese robes with side slits and ornamental buttons. Both robes are dark in color with bright-colored circular designs and high collars. I glance in the other direction and see three men laughing: Duncan, Kookju, and Fabian. They've chosen to wear long robes in dark colors similar to Mary's. Duncan and Fabian have more grey hair than brown. Kookju's is jet black.

These observations do nothing to help me figure out who had been talking.

"Calli, how are you holding up?" Maetha pulls my attention away.

"Oh, um, I'm okay." I return my gaze to the sea of possible suspects in search of the disgruntled Bearers.

"It's no use, Calli."

"What?"

"I know what you're doing. It's hard to figure out who goes with which voice unless you see their face at the same time, and even that's not a definite." She takes our conversation to mindspeak. *You're picking up on the dissenters in the group. They haven't completely gone against nature, but if the line were any thinner, they'd be on the other side.*

Do you know who they are?

For the most part. You already know as well, I suspect.

Yeah, I think so. But shouldn't we compare notes? I ask.

No. You need to draw fresh conclusions based on your instincts. Mine are tainted with too many years of past actions and thoughts. I might paint an inaccurate picture of someone in your mind. Remember, just because someone has a low moment and doubts Crimson's rules doesn't mean they are going against nature's will. Emotional ups and downs are human traits and we are all human.

Thank you, Maetha.

She brings our conversation back to verbal. "I know you're struggling with what you've recently learned. Try not to let everything overwhelm your thinking."

"Easier said than done," I quip.

Chris returns, holding two plates full of assorted goodies. "I grabbed a little of everything. Let's go sit with the others." He motions in the direction of where Brand and Beth sit by Jonas and Anika.

We walk over to their table. The conversation halts when we sit.

I say to Jonas, "Are you feeling better?"

He smiles. "Yeah. It's not every day you get a diamond slammed into you."

"Can you believe it's been two weeks since you got the diamond?" I ask.

"No."

Anika's voice is shaky as she says, "I wish I could have been there to see Freedom die."

"No, you don't," Jonas assures her.

Beth joins her. "Yeah, we do. Even though our families hadn't been destroyed yet—"

Anika bursts into tears. Beth puts her arm around Anika's shoulders and pulls her close.

The entire gathering quiets down and focuses on our table. I sense calming vibes being sent to Anika from several Bearers. I also hear more thoughts.

She's too emotional to be one of us.

What do you expect? She's just a child who has lost her parents.

All the more reason to not give her a diamond.

I doubt Crimson will give her a diamond soon anyway. What is the progress with the informant? Have you heard back?

Yes. We'll discuss it later. Not here. We don't know for sure she can't read our minds.

Chris pulls my attention back. "What's wrong, Calli?"

"Just a lot on my mind, that's all." I continue by speaking to his mind. *Let's talk about it later.*

All right.

Brand changes the subject. "So, Anika, how long do you think it should take to charge these topazes with Repeating?" He pulls his shirt collar down to expose several bandages holding what I assume to be topaz nuggets against his skin.

"I don't know. A day or so." She wipes her eyes.

"Okay. Is that how long it took to charge Calli's healing topaz?"

"The weaker stones took a whole day. The Imperial topaz was only a few hours. You'll know when they're filled."

"Oh. I get it. These will be ready by tomorrow then."

I'm excited to try out Brand's power. I know Crimson is as well.

I glance around the table at the faces of my companions and slip into their minds easily, except for Brand's. I find sorrow. I feel angst and loss. Once again, I'm reminded how easy my life has been. I don't feel I can relate to anyone.

Yes, you can, Crimson says to my mind. *You can experience their emotions with them.*

I glance around to find Crimson and locate her on the other side of the gathering. *That's not going to help them feel like they can relate with me.*

Why do they need to?

I don't know.

Beth says, "Calli, are you going back to college for the fall term?"

"Crimson told me I should."

Jonas says, "What about the convenience store robbery? What ever happened with that? Aren't you two still in trouble?"

"I don't think so. We are only persons of interest."

"That doesn't mean you're off the hook. That means the police want to question you. This isn't going away that easily."

"I'll talk to Crimson about it." I sound less than enthusiastic, I realize.

"I wish I had such a personal relationship with her." Beth dips a celery stick in some hummus. "You're lucky!"

Jonas says, "I'll look into the situation with the police when I get back to the island. I know my way around the Internet and can access internal computers."

Chris scoots forward in his chair. "You're a hacker?"

"No, well, not really. If there's something to find concerning you two and the robbery, I'll find it."

Brand says, "So you're an Internet Guru or some-thing?"

"We'll call you Guru, for short," says Chris.

"How is that shorter than Jonas?" Anika laughs and wipes her eyes again.

"If I find anything on you two, I'll let you know, A.S.A.P."

"What about you, Chris? What are you going to do?" Beth asks.

"I'm going to see if I can get a job at the Pentagon. I already have low-level clearance. Merlin says he might be able to pull some strings."

"What kind of job?"

"No idea."

"Well, that kind of sucks for you two, being so far apart." I see Brand elbow Chris's arm. Chris doesn't respond.

Instead, Chris changes the subject. "Anika, when is your parents' funeral? Calli and I would like to come support you."

Her eyes brighten momentarily, then darken again. "The day after tomorrow, but you don't have to go to the trouble."

Brand says, "That's soon. Why so soon?"

Chris elbows Brand this time.

I say, "We want to come, Anika. Where will it be?"

Anika writes down an address and gives it to Chris.

Chris turns to Beth. "What about your parents' funeral?"

"Oh, you really don't need to come." Her eyes shoot downward to her hands as she twists a napkin mercilessly. *Please don't come. Please don't come,* her mind pleads.

Beth is embarrassed. She doesn't want us to learn more about her family life. I wonder what could be so bad that she wants to keep it hidden.

Beth flips the conversation back on Chris. "When is your father's funeral?"

Chris's shoulders stiffen and he sits a little straighter. "There won't be a funeral." His voice holds no emotion, his expression shows no sadness. "Who would go? Anyway, he'll have been cremated by now."

Everyone is quiet. I figure they are unsure how to respond. I say, "Everyone grieves in their own way. Beth, if you don't want us to come, we won't. Anika, it's no trouble to show our support. And Chris, I'm sure we can all get together later and help you scatter some ashes, if you want."

Crimson comes over to our table, bringing a welcomed change of subject. "Maetha has arranged rooms for everyone tonight. She has the keycards. Tomorrow morning, Maetha's plane will depart for North Dakota to take Anika home. Jonas, you will be going with Mary back to Bermuda. The rest of you can go with Anika if you wish."

Jonas's expression turns downward.

Crimson adds, "Jonas, you must learn immediately how to harness the full diamond's power now that you have it. Besides, the only reason you are here instead of on the island already is because Rolf knew where the island was located. He could have directed a military attack to that location if you remained in place."

Brand says, squeezing Beth's hand, "Beth and I will go with Anika."

Beth nods.

I ask Crimson, "What are you going to do?"

"I'll be going wherever you and Chris go. We have some training to do."

Chris says, "We're going to North Dakota."

Crimson smiles. "Great. I'll meet you there."

"You aren't going to fly with us?" Brand asks.

"No. I don't use airplanes."

Brand is intrigued. "Then, how are you gonna get there?"

"I'll let Calli know when I have arrived. Good night, everyone."

As Crimson walks away, her voice enters my mind. *Calli, always keep your topaz charged with mind-control power in the event you're around obsidian and need to appear invisible. Tell Chris to keep a topaz charged with running. Oh, and tell Chris to take the battery out of his cell phone when not in use. Cell phones can be activated remotely if the battery is inside.*

I ask, *Crimson, what do you think about the other Bearers who are unhappy? I'm sure you heard them grumbling.*

Yes, I heard them. Their futures are not clear. Remember to keep this ability of reading Bearers' minds to yourself.

Okay. I will.

After Crimson is far enough away, Brand wonders aloud, "What did she mean when she said she doesn't use airplanes?"

Jonas responds, "I think you're on a need-to-know basis, Brand, and you don't need to know."

Everyone laughs. I enjoy hearing the laughter, especially in this dark moment of life for Beth, Anika, and Chris. The adage is right—laughter is the best medicine.

Chris speaks to my mind. *I'd say it's the second-best medicine. Your kisses are number one in my book.*

His words cause me to blush. I've really got to work on blocking my thoughts.

Chris accompanies me to my room after Maetha gives me my room key. He walks inside first, checking for anything or anyone out of the ordinary. I follow him into the room. When he's satisfied, he closes the door.

I take off Chris's jacket and lay it on the bed next to a bag full of clothing Maetha has provided. She probably had one of her many connections go shopping. I suppose someday I'll have access to her long list of helpers and be able to snap my fingers and have someone purchase and deliver whatever I need, too.

Chris walks over and stands behind me. "Earlier, you said you had a lot on your mind. What did you mean?" He places his hand on my back. A million nerve endings fire simultaneously and a shiver wracks my body. He pulls away as if he's hurt me. "Sorry."

I turn to face him, feeling bashful. "You startled me, that's all."

"How about you change into something that's not ripped and bloodied?"

"Good idea." I look through the assorted clothes in the bag and find a pair of sweat pants and a tee-shirt.

Chris eyes the clothing choice with one eyebrow up. I resist reading his mind.

"I'll . . . um, change in the bathroom." Not waiting for a response, I hurry to the bathroom and strip out of my torn running suit. As I do so, the tinkling of the twelve clear crystals sliding around in my front pocket pull my attention away from the possible intimate situation on the other side of the door. I'd forgotten Chris and I had removed them from the machine at his father's government compound. I decide to leave the crystals in the zipped pocket where they'll be safe for now.

Exiting the bathroom, after changing into my decidedly non-formfitting clothes, I walk past Chris to the two chairs by the window and say, "Let's sit down."

Chris doesn't follow. Instead, he sits on the bed with his back up against the headboard and his legs crossed at his ankles. He pats the bed beside him, indicating he wants me to sit by him.

Flutters of excitement speed through my body. I walk over to the side of the bed and sit carefully on the edge near his feet. He's taken his shoes off, exposing his feet. Strands of light-brown hair peek out from under the hem of his jeans. My eyes travel slowly up the length of his ideally designed Runner's body, past his narrow waist and across his flat stomach, up to his broad shoulders. I blurt,

"I can hear the other Bearers' thoughts."

"I know." He smiles seductively.

"I was hearing them talk about us, earlier. That's what was on my mind."

"They were talking about me and you?" he asks.

"No, yes, all of the younger people. Some are not happy with Crimson for picking us to be Bearers."

"I didn't get 'picked.' And neither did Jonas. So, what's their problem?"

"My thoughts exactly. I'm not sure who's against us, though. I can't tell who's talking when they communicate. I could only tell there were four different individuals."

"Jie Wen, for sure," Chris assumes. "He's got an attitude a mile high. Probably Kookju and Chuang too. They seem to group together. And we shouldn't leave out Yeok Choo. There. That's four." Chris acts proud of himself.

"Now you're just being racist."

He pulls his head back slightly and brings his brows down. "Why do you say that? They all hang out together, they happen to be Asian. That's not racist. Look at our group. We sat together tonight: you, me, Brand, Beth, Jonas, and Anika. We're all white. You said the Bearers' thoughts were against the younger group. Well, we all happen to be white Americans. Does that make them racist for grouping us together?"

"I get your point, Chris. But I think we should be careful about drawing conclusions. Besides, none of them have gone against nature yet. They're not really helping nature, but they're not against nature either."

"That's good, at least. Did you happen to pick up on the regions where the different Bearers are stationed?"

"Huh?"

"Maetha said the Bearers are stationed all around the

world. So, I looked into their minds to see where."

"Oh, I hadn't thought of doing that. You're clever, Chris."

He ignores my compliment. "Marketa is stationed in the Czech Republic and Alena is nearby in Russia. Jie Wen and Chuang cover China, and Kookju's in Korea. I had a hard time reading Yeok Choo's mind at first, but then I found she's stationed in Malaysia. That's all I figured out."

"Well, we know Maetha is basically over the U.S., and Amenemhet and Mary seem to be joined at the hip with Maetha. Neema too, before, well . . . anyway, Merlin is definitely stationed here. Who does that leave?"

"Amalgada, Duncan, Ruth, Avani, Aernoud, and Fabian."

I'm a bit surprised he's picked up on everyone's names so quickly. "Well, Duncan told me he's from Romania originally, but I don't know if he's stationed there. Fabian sounds Spanish, but that could place him in Spain or Central America. Amalgada's Irish lilt is pretty cool, however that doesn't necessarily mean he's stationed in Ireland. Avani looks like she walked right off the cover of a Taj Mahal travel brochure."

"Aernoud is a little harder to place. His accent is European, but I don't know if he's Swiss, or Dutch, or German. Maybe Danish."

My hands instinctually clasp together. "Ooh, Danish. That makes me hungry."

"You didn't eat much tonight," Chris reminds me tenderly.

I ignore him and ask, "So why do you suppose there aren't any Diamond Bearers in Africa or the Middle East?"

"Or Australia? Or the Pacific Isles?" he adds before I can.

"Or Central or South America?" My competitive side

surfaces. "Oh wait, Fabian might be."

"I know there are Runners in those parts of the world. There are probably representations of all powers in the other countries. Maybe the answer is simply that there aren't enough Bearers to cover every region. They probably go where the most trouble is occurring." Chris pats the bed again and says to my mind, *Come here. I want to hold you.*

I move up to his side and sit next to him. He pulls me into a hug and I rest my head on his shoulder. He inhales a large cleansing breath and lets it out slowly. "We've been through a lot today," he sighs.

I think about pointing out it's 2:00 a.m. so, technically, everything happened yesterday, but decide against it. Instead, I say, "Everything has changed for you. You're an Unaltered and a Diamond Bearer now."

"And right where I want to be . . . next to you."

"Me too." I wrap my arm across his chest and snuggle my head further into his shoulder.

Chris rests his hand on my shoulder and asks, "Why do you think Beth doesn't want us to know more about her parents?"

I'm surprised with his subject change. "I'm not sure. Probably for the same reason as you. She wants us to look at her as she is today, not where she came from."

Chris tenses up. "That's not the same as me at all, Calli."

"What do you mean?" I lift my head off his chest and look up at him.

"Everyone already knows about my father and that I was spying for him. It's common knowledge. I'm not trying to keep my past a secret. I just want to forget about my past, that's all."

"That's what I just said. You and Beth want everyone to see you as who you are today, not where you came from."

"I disagree." Chris pushes off the bed and starts to pace, obviously agitated.

"Then tell me how you'd explain it."

"I think . . . well, first, look at how Anika is reacting to the loss of her parents. She loved them, and they must have loved her or she wouldn't be so broken up. Beth isn't visibly upset like Anika. I think Beth had a different home life than Anika and me. Beth probably hasn't had much love in her life from her parents. She doesn't want us to know that. She probably thinks that makes her weak in our eyes. She's in mourning because she just lost the two people who define who she is—rebellious, strong willed, and independent. As for me, my mother loves me and has done the best job of raising me that she could. I loved what I thought my dad could have been if he hadn't been so power-obsessed. The man Deus shot was the shell of the man I wanted to be my father. I have no reason to pay any respect to his passing. I don't plan on scattering his ashes, except for maybe down the toilet."

"Okay, I think I understand your point of view." I pat the bed next to me, hoping he'll relax and put his anger aside.

Instead, he says, "It's late and we have an early start. I'll see you in the morning."

"All right," I say, let down. "Good night."

He opens the door to leave and says, "Make sure you flip the latch after I leave."

"I will. You do the same on your door."

He doesn't respond. The next sound I hear is the door closing.

I get up and flip the latch. My mind keeps replaying our conversation, wondering if I should have said things differently. I didn't mean to upset Chris. I wanted to give him companionship and support, which I know he needs in his vulnerable state. His father's death is definitely a touchy subject, no matter how much he tries to convince himself it isn't.

I decide I'll keep my opinions to myself and give him support and try not to read too much into the conversation we just had.

Chapter 2 – Cautionary Counsel

The next morning, I change into fresh clothes and gather my others off the bathroom floor. The crystals jingle as I open the front pocket to remove them. I take an elastic band and bind them together so they won't rattle around. Then I try to stuff the bundle into my pocket, but they're too bulky and my pockets are too small. Instead, I bury the crystals deep in the clothing bag, thinking I'll keep the bag close to me. The last item I pick up is Chris's jacket from the night before. I bring it to my nose and inhale his unique scent. It has lessened without the wearer nearby, but . . . oh no! Chris is Unaltered now. He shouldn't have a unique scent anymore. His jacket still holds what may be the last of his amazing smell. I'll never wash it, ever.

I really must be in love to be thinking this way. I don't know whether to be happy about that or not. I'm reminding myself too much of the giggling girls from high school. Perhaps I was too hard on them.

I find the rest of the group in the breakfast room of the resort. When I enter the room, my eyes seek out Chris. He's not here yet. I grab a plate and load a blueberry muffin and sausage links on it. I pick up a small carton of milk, then sit down with Brand and Beth. They're snuggled intimately close to each other, making me uncomfortable.

I look around the room as I take small bites of sausage. At the door, Mary is receiving orders from Maetha. Anika and Jonas sit alone in the corner, holding each other's hands. Anika's lips reveal she's saying good-bye. Jonas is incredibly kind and compassionate. I'm pleased he has been able to continue living and develop into such an awesome guy. It's what I wanted for him from the moment I first detected his cancer at Cave Falls.

"Why are you staring at Jonas?" Chris asks from behind me, making me jump.

"Oh, Chris, I didn't see you come in. I'm thinking about when I detected his cancer for the first time."

"Oh." He sits beside me and clears his throat to get Brand and Beth to break up their lovey-dovey fascination with each other. It works.

Wait a minute. Chris was able to sneak up on me because I didn't smell his aroma. Dang. It's true. He has no scent. I can't help but feel let down.

Standing next to Maetha's private plane as our luggage and boxed information from General Harding's compound are loaded into the cargo hold, I inhale a deep breath of Indiana air to try to clear the cobwebs from my mind. So much has happened in the last few days. It's hard to keep everything straight in my head.

Brand walks over and holds his hand out to me, topazes cradled in his palm. "I don't think these topazes are charged, Calli."

I take the stone he offers me and confirm his suspicions. "You're right. They're empty. That's too bad. I would guess you can't charge topaz with power stored in quartz. I'll have to be sure and pass that along to the group."

"Yeah," Brand adds, "Crimson will be bummed. She wanted to test out my power."

Captain Rutherfield gives the okay to board the plane. Anika claims the bench seat. She wants to read in peace. I catch a glimpse of her book title and see the words "death" and "what happens."

Brand and Beth are situated across from us, cuddled up close. Not much has changed since breakfast.

Chris seems distant. He hasn't said much.

The plane engines begin building speed and the plane rolls forward. We slowly make our way to the end of the runway. When the nose of the plane turns to face the runway, the plane accelerates forward without pause, pushing me back into my seat with the force needed to leave the ground.

Once we're in the air, I figure I better try to talk with Chris about the awkwardness between us. I say, "I'm sorry if I said anything upsetting last night."

His frustrated expression and tone of voice draws Beth's attention. He says, "Are you kidding me? Why are you apologizing when I was the one to screw up?"

Sheez, I really wish I had more experience with relationships. I feel my cheeks heat up as if I'm in trouble. Frankly, I don't really know where I stand at the moment. My head has been buried in books for so long, ignoring the conversations on the lips of others that I'm now communication-challenged.

"I'm sorry, Calli. See, I did it again." Chris takes my hand and gently squeezes it.

"You know, Chris, we don't have to talk at all." I switch over to telepathic words. *Maybe you need some healing kisses.* I smile, hoping to lighten the mood.

"I get a little snappy and defensive when I'm stressed. That's why I left your room last night."

"Oh, that makes more sense. How about next time you're feeling that way you tell me?"

"Okay. I was also nervous."

"Why?"

"Well," he leans his head next to mine and whispers,

"I couldn't get that invisible kissing session from the compound out of my head. I really wanted to . . . I was hoping . . ."

His warm breath on my ear and his topic cause my cheeks to warm rapidly.

Brand chuckles, "What's going on, Calli?"

"Mind your own business," I reply.

Beth playfully smacks his arm. "Leave them alone. Come on, we're moving." She pulls him out of his seat and leads him away.

Once we're alone, I ask Chris, "If you were hoping and wanting, why did you leave?"

"I was afraid."

"Of what? I don't bite . . . often." I nudge my shoulder against his, letting him know I'm joking.

"You've never been in a relationship before. My past relationships didn't last, obviously. I don't want to scare you away like everyone else." He looks down to the floor. "Sorry. I'm rambling."

I listen to his words and think them through.

He brings his gaze to mine and continues. "Listen, I want to date you, Calli. I don't want you to feel you were cheated out of experiencing first-love. Hopefully, I'll be the only boyfriend you'll ever have. I'm not a pro either, so we can go slow."

"I'm kind of relieved, to be honest." I touch his hand and let out an exhale of relief. "I don't know the first thing about having sex. We have decades and centuries ahead of us. There's no point in rushing to the finish line."

He pulls his hand away and turns in his seat toward me. "I wasn't talking about sex. Is that . . . is that what you thought was going to happen last night?"

"No . . . maybe. I don't know." I'm officially embarrassed. Even my toenails feel like they're blushing. "I guess I thought that's how things would go."

"I think you've been watching too much television. I'm not your stereotypical, chick-flick kind of guy." Taking both my hands in his, he says, "Calli, I want to clear the air here. I don't ever want to put you in a situation that makes you uncomfortable. Like I said, I don't want to lose you."

"I don't watch television," I mutter defensively, then look at our clasped hands. "I guess I thought because we saw the vision of our future, you'd want to—"

"Someday, when we have sex—and we will, obviously, because you've seen our grandchildren—it will be when *you're* ready, and not because you think we're supposed to."

I ponder on his words and wonder how he understands my mind better than I do.

He continues, "I know you don't fully understand the difference between guys and girls."

"Sure, I do," I correct him. "I've read about the male body in my parents' medical books."

He smiles. "That's good, at least. You understand the mechanics of the male body. I doubt those books explained what it feels like to have raging male hormones."

"No, they didn't. But, when I extracted your mind at Maetha's I didn't see anything like that."

"You were searching for other topics, thankfully. I want you to understand that when we're close, like when we kiss, our bodies react."

"That's nature's will in its simplest form. Moving the species forward, procreating." I can't help but feel like I'm the narrator of nature-themed documentary.

"Yes, but just because our bodies react doesn't mean we have to have sex. It's not your fault or your responsibility to help me out, either. I can assure you I won't die because of being turned on, regardless of what other less-respectful guys might say."

I ask, "Do you think a couple should be married before becoming intimate?"

"Do you?"

"I asked you first." I grin.

"Are you asking if I have religious views?"

"I guess so."

"No, I don't have beliefs that dictate how I behave. I have only my conscience and my desire to do my best. As for being married before sex, I think there are extremes on both ends. I've watched friends jump directly to sex and have one-night-stands, then regret it. I've also seen kids right out of high school get married just to have 'God-approved' sex, only to find out later they have nothing in common. My own parents waited till marriage. They had a short engagement in the hopes of staying 'pure.' My mom didn't get to see the real side of my dad until she was his wife. I've heard her talking to other people, saying how she regretted not getting to know him better before they got married. I think she meant she wished she'd dated him longer or had a longer engagement. She might have been talking about sex, I don't know. I decided long ago I didn't ever want to have regrets because of jumping in too fast. I became determined to be in a committed relationship and in love before going there."

"So, have you ever been in love?" I regret asking such a personal question the moment the words leave my lips. "Sorry. You don't have to answer."

He stares at me for a moment. "You know, Calli, if you want to extract my mind you can."

"I don't want to. I might see more than I want."

"That's a good point. Well then, yes, I thought I was in love once."

"I'd be lying if I said I didn't feel a bit jealous."

"I didn't know you yet, Calli. I hadn't seen the vision.

Do you want to know who?"

"No," I say. His answer confirms his only love wasn't Kikee. I don't need to know more.

He asks, "What are your religious beliefs, and how do you feel about intimacy before marriage?"

I'm happy he's directing the subject away from him. I say, "You really went out on a limb by telling me your views, Chris. What if I was someone who firmly believed in waiting till marriage?"

"Then I'd compromise and try my darndest to make things work."

I think I love him even more for that comment. "Well, don't worry. You and I have similar beliefs. My parents are not religious. Nor am I, unless there's a religion that follows the scientific method."

"I think that's just called being a scientist."

"My mom always talked openly with me. She's one of those matter-of-fact people who don't mince words or beat around the bush. She taught me I should wait to have sex until I met someone I wouldn't mind being a co-parent with. Someone who would be a responsible parent and pull his share of the load. My mom taught me lust can be confused with love and when we make decisions based on how we feel, we sometimes make bad ones. Logic should always come before feelings. That's what she says anyway."

"Now I know how your mom feels toward sex. But what do you feel, Calli?"

I snuggle close to him. "I feel very much in love with you. I know what lust feels like, too. I think when we're ready to move to that level, it will feel right to both of us."

"So, you don't believe we should be married before then?" he presses.

"Not given what we know about our futures. Besides, my mom would freak out if I got married soon. She'd be more like, 'Oh, you only had sex? You used protection, right?' Instead of 'Married! What in the bleep, bleep, bleep were you thinking?'"

Chris chuckles. "My mom would freak out if she thought I had sex before I got married. She's traditional that way. My dad . . . I don't know what my dad would have said." His expression falls.

I touch his arm. "Chris, I feel marriage is about love and commitment to another person. Devotion. I value *that* level of connection. It's what my parents have."

"I hope we'll have that, too."

"I know we will."

Crimson speaks to my mind, letting me know she's arrived in North Dakota already and has rented a car. She'll be waiting for us when we get off the plane.

As I inform Chris about Crimson, Brand walks by and asks, "How did she beat us here if she doesn't fly in airplanes? Does she run super fast or something?"

"Or something."

◇ ◇ ◇

Like she promised, Crimson is waiting for us when we step off the plane in Bismarck, North Dakota.

Brand scoffs, "A minivan? She rented a minivan?"

Beth asks, "Why is that a big deal? Do you have something against minivans?"

"Well," I say, "there's seven of us in total, plus our luggage and boxes. What did you expect her to choose?"

Brand grumbles, "I just don't like them, that's all."

She greets us as we load into the van. Anika sits in the front with Crimson. Chris and I move to the back-bench seat and Brand and Beth sit on the middle seat.

"Anika, direct me where to drive you," Crimson says

peacefully. I sense she's giving Anika calming strength. Now that we're in Anika's home town she's probably feeling the heavy weight of reality.

We drive through the streets to a rather large home with a metal security gate. Anika gets out and walks around the front to the security keypad. She enters a code and the gate begins to slide open. Turning to Crimson, who has her window rolled down, Anika says, "I'll just take my bag and go from here. You don't need to drive in."

"Are you sure?"

"Yes."

I've already grabbed Anika's bag and hand it forward to Brand before Crimson asks. Brand opens the door and passes it to her. He says, "We'll see you tomorrow, Anika."

"Thank you," she responds meekly. I notice an older woman has come out the front door and is walking to greet Anika. "Bye everyone." She waves and leaves.

Crimson drives away. No one says a word. In my mind I'm thinking about how difficult this must be for Anika. Her life will be so different now with her parents' deaths.

Brand clears his throat. "Crimson, how do you travel? Do you run . . . you know, like a Runner?"

"I can if I need to." Crimson keeps her voice level, almost bored sounding.

"But Runners can't out-run an airplane, so how were you able to get here before us? I know you didn't drive."

"I fly."

"But you said you don't like flying."

"Not in planes."

I can't see Brand's face to see his reaction, but the gasping, choking sound he makes paints a good picture in my mind.

"No way," he says, instantly doubting her. "Seriously, how do you travel?"

"I click my heels and wiggle my nose. What do you want me to say, Brand?"

Beth nudges him with her shoulder, as if to get his attention. "She said she flies." Beth's mind opens and allows me to see she's a bit embarrassed with how casually Brand talks to Crimson. She feels he's not showing Crimson the respect she deserves.

Crimson says, looking out the window, "Perfect. There's a shopping center across from a hotel." She pulls into the hotel parking lot. "Chris, will you secure us two rooms?"

"Adjoining?"

"Close together, but they don't need to be adjoining."

Chris extends his hand to me, which I take, to accompany him into the lobby. The place is nice and clean, like most hotels I've stayed in. The female receptionist welcomes us and more than willingly fulfills Chris's order for two rooms. Not surprisingly, she's apparently smitten with Chris's good looks. He kind of comes across rude, in my opinion. And yet, she seems undeterred. Her persistence might have something to do with the fact she's checked out both our left ring fingers.

Chris takes the keycards and we go back out to get the others.

I ask, "Do you get tired of girls coming on to you?"

"Yeah."

"I can tell."

He turns his head as if he's about to say something, but we arrive at the van, so he doesn't.

Chris and Brand put their belongings in their room and follow us to ours. I set my bag on one of the beds and

Beth adds hers.

Crimson walks over to the table and sets the box down she's carrying. Then she points to the second bed. "Beth, you can have your own bed. I'll be out on errands tonight."

Beth picks up her bag and sets it on the other bed, then does a belly flop onto the center of the mattress and rolls over on her back. "Nice bed," she says.

Brand asks, "What kind of errands? Are you going to go 'flying' around?" He makes air quotes with his fingers.

Crimson sits in one of the extra chairs in the corner. She doesn't answer.

Brand says, "Did Calli tell you I wasn't able to charge a topaz with my Repeating quartz."

I note the change of flow in Brand's conversation right away. He must have repeated.

"I already know. That's unfortunate." Crimson lets out a sigh. I imagine she's let down that she won't get to experience the repeating power. "Are your powers still fully functional?" she asks Brand.

"Yes. I'm worried they're going to disappear. Do you think they will?"

"I don't know."

He scrunches his brows together. "Can't you look to the future to see?"

"No."

"No?"

She looks at different papers from the box while responding, "Humanity isn't dependent on you keeping your powers."

"So, I'm just a fun little experiment or something?"

She sets the papers down and looks directly at Brand. "No, you're the result of government experiments. It's harsh, I know, but that's the truth of the matter."

Crimson's shortness with Brand indicates to me she's getting tired of his incessant questions. However, she's not heartless. She adds, "Don't fret over it, Brand. I like you. In fact, if repeating was a cosmic power, you'd be my chosen leader of the Repeaters. It's just not important in maintaining the human race."

"Oh, well, okay," Brand trips over his words. "I guess I'm like a side-kick then. Not really useful."

"I didn't say you weren't useful, Brand. Look what your power has brought to pass already. I'm not going to switch my focus just to find out if you will keep your powers."

I jump into the conversation. "I, for one, looked forward to trying out Brand's power. Too bad the topaz didn't take."

Jonas and Mary bi-locate to the room without warning.

"Hey everyone," Jonas beams proudly.

"Jonas," I say, "did you bi-locate on your own? I haven't been able to figure out how to do that."

"No. I had Mary's help. Where's Anika?"

"With her family," Crimson says. She extends her arm in front of her and slowly moves it in a half-circle, from her left to her right. As she does so, the blue, glittering, secrecy mist surrounds our group. "Let's get started with the first Task Force meeting. I've gone over the files from General Harding's compound and separated them for you to investigate." She looks at Brand and Beth. "The two of you will be investigating individuals, searching for the level of knowledge they've amassed while working at General Harding's compound. We need to know who knows too much."

Beth asks, "What do we do when we find someone who might be a threat?"

"You'll discuss as a group how to handle the individual. If I feel I need to interject, I will. Jonas has been set up with a complex computer system on the island. He'll do his part from there. If you run across someone who you think needs to be tracked, pass the name along to Jonas."

"You know how to do that kind of computer hacking?" Beth asks Jonas.

Jonas smiles. "Oh yeah. If there's information to be found, I'll find it."

I ask, doing a little math in my head, "Are you already in Bermuda, Jonas?"

"No, we're still traveling. Right now we're stopped, so we can bi-locate with you."

Crimson hands the files to Beth, "You two take these and go to the other room and look them over. I need to talk to Chris, Calli, and Jonas."

"Okay," says Beth. She takes the room key and they leave.

Crimson turns to us. "Come sit at the table."

We each take a seat. Jonas and Mary stand nearby. The blue mist floats with us, keeping our conversation private.

Crimson says, "The first thing I want to teach you is how to block your minds as a Diamond Bearer. Calli, I want you to close your eyes and imagine the checker board analogy Maetha shared with you. Jonas, Mary will explain this with you when you two leave the meeting. This is a mental exercise. Keeping others out of your mind is all a mental game. So, Calli, imagine the checkerboard and your game pieces set up, except place your front row game pieces on the red and black squares. Now take your remaining pieces and pile them on top of the others to create a wall."

I shake my head. "That sounds too simple."

"Duncan taught you to mentally decide what you do

and don't want others to know—which is one way to block your mind—but that isn't working with you. I'd like to build upon the checkers example because you were able to master that one while the diamond was in the pouch. Are you placing your mental game pieces in place like a barricade?"

"Yes, I'm imagining that."

"All right. Chris, try to read her mind."

Chris says, "I can't. Good job, Calli."

I open my eyes, feeling quite proud of myself.

"Wait." Chris holds his hand up. "Now I can."

A frustrated grunt escapes my throat.

Crimson tilts her head to the side and smiles sympathetically, giving me the impression she understands how hard it is to master this ability. "Jonas," Crimson says, "do the same exercise and let Mary test your walls. I want a report from Mary that you've mastered the blocking ability. Now, you two, go."

Jonas and Mary bow their heads and vanish.

"Calli, when you're thinking to yourself, or sending your thoughts to Chris, you're an open book to the others. This is not a good situation, especially because I want to control who knows you carry the blue diamond. I have carefully monitored and protected the information bleeding from your thoughts."

"You've had to babysit my thoughts?"

"Don't think of it like that, Calli." Crimson straightens her back and says, "Keeping the transfer secret for now will give us both the opportunity to root out the dissenters of the group. If we don't discover and replace these individuals, then the future doesn't look as optimistic. The Bearers need to feel confident enough around you to slip up and expose themselves. The sooner you learn how to block your mind from the others, the better."

"Okay." I exhale and look down.

Chris says to me, "Try building a virtual wall in your mind."

"Okay." I close my eyes and imagine the seven-foot-tall brick privacy wall in my parent's back yard. Tall trees on both sides of the wall create the illusion the wall is taller than it is.

Crimson says, "Try to read her mind again, Chris."

"Her mind is blocked."

"Open your eyes, Calli." Crimson's voice is gentle.

I look at Chris, expecting him to say he can access my mind. Waiting for him to say so. He doesn't.

"Very good, Calli," Crimson praises. "Now think about something you and Chris have done together like delivering the diamond together, or healing his legs. But think of something other than those two examples to see if Chris can read your mind.

I think about the day I first saw Chris walk into Clara Winter's office, and the look on his face when he realized I was sitting on the couch as a Runner, not a Healer. I don't know why that is the first thing that comes to mind.

Chris stares at me with his smoldering, steel-blue eyes. I return his stare, cherishing the opportunity to just look and gaze. I daydream about looking into his eyes for endless years to come.

He says, "I can't get through her wall, but she's projecting her thoughts into my mind."

"What? I am?"

Crimson asks, "Are you purposefully communicating with Chris?"

"No. I mean, I don't think I am."

"Calli, think of another time you and Chris were together, but this time I want you to move that thought behind your virtual wall. Mentally place your thoughts behind it."

I do as she says and think about the day at Cave Falls when I accidentally read his mind and found he'd been shown a vision of me. I remember feeling incredibly shocked. I hadn't expected to find that in his brain.

Chris shakes his head.

"What? Really? I'm still projecting?"

"No, you're not. That's why I shook my head."

Relieved, I rub my temples.

Crimson says, "I want you to continue these exercises, Calli. And Chris, I want you to let her know when you're able to read her mind or if she's unknowingly projecting her thoughts."

"Why is it so important I close my mind off to Chris?"

"Because when you're sending him your thoughts, other Bearers can hear them too, if they're nearby, and if they're trying to hear. If you've protected the conversation by using the Blue Diamond, that's different, but otherwise, your thoughts are open. I don't want the other Bearers to know what you know, what you're going to learn, and what you're going to do. You overheard thoughts of others at the gathering who do not understand everything, some of whom may never understand my reasoning. The next year is going to be enlightening and I want you to be as safe as possible by protecting your mind."

I can't even form a proper question for the ambiguous things she's just said. What in the world is she talking about?

Crimson continues. "You and Chris need to use the diamond's Seer powers so you can be aware of your surroundings to protect your lives. I do not want you taking public transportation. Taxis are okay, but planes, buses, trains, are out—unless it's Maetha's plane. Never put yourself in a position where you are not in control of your future. And remember Diamond Bearers can die in other ways besides decapitation and having their hearts blown out. If the body is injured severely, like from a plane crash, you won't be able to heal yourself. Get caught next to a bomb, well, I don't need to explain that's deadly. These types of deaths haven't occurred yet because Bearers have avoided trouble of that kind. Maetha risks her life when she puts it in the hands of Rodger Rutherfield, but sometimes there are no other options. Rodger is a capable pilot, but even the best can find themselves in situations out of their control."

I ask, "What about all the flying we've done lately?"

"I've been watching the future for incidences concerning Maetha's plane. Make no mistake, I don't like my Bearers flying, but sometimes there's no other way to get from point A to point B quickly."

Chris asks, "How do we look for our futures? I've been struggling with how to do this."

"The diamond is new to you, Chris, as is the familiarity of the Seer power. Try asking yourself if you're going to die today."

"Oh, okay."

"Crimson," I say, "why didn't anyone ever teach me to protect myself? In fact, why was I taught to *not* look for my future?"

"If you'd looked to your future you might not have been strong enough to handle viewing the events that still needed to happen for you to get the full diamond. The other Bearers who received their diamonds in a similar fashion were instructed to avoid looking for their futures too. Chris, on the other hand, has a whole stone in the pouch, and Calli, you have a whole diamond now. You both need to care for your lives by becoming aware of potentially deadly situations. However, I don't want you to confuse looking for danger with looking for answers."

Chris asks, "What do you mean?"

"Think of dwelling on the future, or looking for answers, like snooping at a Christmas present. If you sneak a peek at a present before Christmas morning, the magic will be gone when you open it because you already know what's in the box. Some things in life are one-shot deals. The magic and excitement surrounding these moments are what infuse us with happiness. Don't deprive yourself of the happiness in the here-and-now by dwelling on future events that may or may not happen. That's my job. You two should only look for your immediate death or injury. Or the black fog of obsidian. You already know your long-range future and what it can be."

Chris asks, "How will I know if I'm looking too far or for answers? I mean, how far do I look for my death?"

Crimson glances back and forth between us as if she's considering something. Then she says, "If you were to look far enough for your death, Chris, you'll find it happens when Calli inserts the diamond into your chest at some point in the future."

"What? I'll die?" he cries out.

I'm just as shocked to hear the news as he is.

She puts her hand up to calm him. "Right now, that is the moment when your heart will stop beating . . . when you'll die. I don't want you searching out that moment, Chris. Look only for today or tomorrow. Ask yourself if you'll die soon. If you still see events playing out in your mind, you'll know you're not going to die right away."

"But you're saying my heart will stop when I get the diamond inserted?"

"Yes. If Calli doesn't start your heart again, you'll remain dead."

I try to reassure him. "Don't worry, I'll heal you. Just

like I did with Jonas."

"But Jonas didn't die," Chris asserts. "He was still breathing."

Crimson says, "That's because Calli's quantum entanglement with that particular diamond prevented him from dying. She was healing him without even knowing how she was doing so."

"But you're saying I'll be completely dead. Has Calli brought someone back to life whose heart has stopped?"

I look at him and reach out with my hand and take his. "You restarted my heart after I drowned, Chris. I won't let you die."

Crimson says, "Try not to stress out about this, Chris. Wait until you're ready . . . and if that day never comes, well, that's your choice too."

My eyes shoot over to Crimson. Does she know something we don't?

Chapter 3 – Wise Healers

Crimson reaches into one of her bags. "I'm going to give the four of you some money to go across the street and purchase some nice clothing for the funeral tomorrow. Dressing appropriately shows respect to those who are mourning."

Chris accepts the money. Once we're out in the hallway, he stops and says, "Calli, I know you'll start my heart. I didn't mean to sound like I doubt you. I guess my mind did a couple flips when she said I'd die when I receive my diamond."

"I wasn't offended, Chris," I say as I reach up and give him a hug, just wanting to feel his body and his strength.

When I pull back and look up into his appreciative eyes, he says, "Thanks, Calli." His mouth descends the short distance to mine, emphasizing his words in a most agreeable way. I really like the way I feel around him—fiery, impulsive, and tingly all over.

Some distant nudging thought reminds me we're standing in a hotel hallway—hardly a private spot. Not really wanting to, I break away from his kiss. I whisper, "We'd better get Brand and Beth."

"Yeah," he says, resting his forehead on mine.

❖ ❖ ❖

The four of us go across the road to the nearby shopping center. Chris gives Brand half of the money. Beth promptly snatches the money from Brand and stuffs it in her pocket, which I find interesting. They take off and go their own way.

Chris takes me by the hand.

"I don't like shopping," I say, volunteering my thoughts. "I wish I could just pick up some of my clothes from the dorm. My friend, Pamela, helped me load my closet recently."

"How many pairs of shoes do you own?" Chris asks.

Strange question, I must admit. "I don't know, like three. No wait, five, if you include the two pairs Pamela picked out."

"You are so different than most girls, Calli."

"Bad different?"

"No." He pulls me in the direction of the women's section. "At least I won't have to work a night job to support your shopping habit."

"So, I'm different because I don't like to shop or have a lot of shoes?"

"Yes, and because you're not self-absorbed or artificial." He raises our clasped hands to his warm lips and kisses the back of my hand.

"Thanks. All right then, let's get this done." My mind continues to consider that owning several pairs of shoes or liking to shop doesn't make someone self-absorbed or artificial. I think a person could be self-absorbed with only one pair of shoes.

We shuffle through the racks and find a few things to try on in the dressing rooms. My choices of dresses look horrid, so I don't step out of the dressing room to show Chris.

"Come on, how bad could they be? Anything would look good on your body," he compliments, or at least he tries to.

"I'll keep looking for a dress. Try your clothes on. If

you like them, come show me."

I don't expect I'll see him, so I continue scanning the dress section. After a few minutes, I've selected two more dresses. My attention is grabbed as Chris walks out of the dressing room.

He looks amazing in his dress slacks and button-up shirt. The deep blue of his shirt emphasizes his eyes and enhances his blond hair. I find it hard to take my eyes off him. I'm reminded of when he entered the room with the rest of the Runners just before we began the delivery journey. My memory of that is movie-like: slow motion, mystical mist, spotlight shining down on him. Oh yeah, he looks great!

"What do you think?"

"You have to ask?" I fan my face with my hand.

He looks at what I'm holding. "The green one will work perfectly. Put the other one back."

"What?"

"I've seen you in this dress already."

"Like a vision?"

"Yes."

"Well, why didn't you tell me that earlier? We could have saved time."

"The vision just happened."

"Oh? What happened after that?" This feels strange for me to be on the other end of vision-receiving, wondering what he saw.

"I'll let you know when it happens. Let's find some shoes."

We purchase our outfits after choosing appropriate shoes and then take a seat at the small eatery just off the main walkway.

"Now I own six pairs of shoes . . . probably more than I've ever owned at one time in my life."

Chris seems a bit preoccupied. Nodding his head in the direction of the food vendor, he says, "Are you hungry, Calli?"

"A little."

"What would you like?"

"I could sure go for a burger, fries and a Coke. It's been a long time."

He gets up and takes his place in line. I think about the last time I had a good burger and realize it's only been a little over a month. Of course, that's how long I've been back in Chris's company. I could swear it's been longer than that.

I see a couple girls close to my age, sitting across the way at a table. They're ogling Chris as he stands in line. He doesn't notice, naturally. He seems to be oblivious to his own appearance. Kind of like Clara Winter, when I was in her company. I speak to his mind, *You know you're gorgeous, right?*

Do you?

Yes, I know you are.

He turns and glances at me. *That's not what I meant.*

I don't have Runner's genetics like you. You are the only Runner in, like, a mile. You kind of stick out like a sore thumb. I, on the other hand, blend in with the locals.

Just then, Beth and Brand join Chris in line.

Correction, you're the only male Runner in a mile.

I look over at the girls who now have sour, disappointed expressions. I read their minds just to confirm what I already suspect. They view Beth's beauty and body dimensions as a threat. What is it with girls? Why do we berate ourselves so quickly, I wonder?

Maybe it's because in the normal world I've grown up in, certain people seem to end up together: popular with popular, rich with rich, middle-class with middle-class, beauty with beauty. The girls at the table automatically figure Beth is Chris's girl based on her appearance. Why is that?

I get that her looks are on the same level as his, and that's why the girls quickly discount themselves. Perhaps this is part of the evolution of mankind and the primitive need to mate, as Maetha would put it. Maybe females are attracted to individuals who they feel are strong enough to protect them, and that this isn't about attractiveness at all. I know I've read something like this before in all my studies. It's one thing to read about. It's another to witness the behavior. The question is, why are girls so quick to discount themselves around a female who, in their opinion, outranks them? Those girls don't even know Beth and Brand are together. They assume Beth is with Chris because he's the taller, better-looking guy. Hmm, interesting. This makes me wonder as well. Why is Beth attracted to Brand? Well, aside from his dimples and superpower?

My eyes are still on the girls when Chris sits down next to me and kisses my cheek. The girls' expressions change to shock for a moment, then back to sour. I guess I'm glad to see they view me as a threat instead of a non-threat.

"What are you looking at?" Chris asks.

"Nothing. I like watching people and their behaviors." I look around for Brand and Beth. "Where did they go?"

"They're heading back to the hotel. It will be dark soon."

"Are they still afraid of the Demons even though they're not dangerous anymore?"

"I am, and I don't have any reason to be anymore. They have good reason, even though all the Demons have been transformed."

"I bet you're happy you don't have to worry anymore."

"Among other things."

The cashier calls out a number and Chris leaves to grab our food.

I remember how excited Chris was to be able to walk into the dark after our experiments with obsidian and the Demons. The Pulse Emitters I designed were useful for a little while, and I'm glad I researched and had them made, but now the Demons are no longer a threat and I'm kind of stuck with the credit card bill. I'm sure Maetha or Crimson would take care of it if I asked them to, but I can't bring myself to doing that.

Chris returns with our tray and sits across from me this time. He's ordered the same meal deal as mine, which astonishes me.

"Is your system going to be able to handle this?" I point to his food.

"Well, I am a Healer now." He grabs a couple fries with his fingers and slides them in his mouth.

I take a bundle of fries and bite into them. Mmm. Crunchy, salty goodness. My eyes are drawn to an older woman entering the store. She's hunched over a bit and walks as if she's in pain. I feel sorry for her and decide to use my Healing power to look inside her body for ailments. I find she has arthritis.

"Chris, see the woman in the red jacket over there." I nod my head instead of pointing.

He turns around and says, "Yes."

"Have you ever used your Healing power on strangers?"

"What?"

"Try to feel inside her body to see if anything is wrong."

"Her joints are stiff and painful," he surmises.

"Yeah, that's what I found too."

"Should we help her?"

"You gave me an important lesson about healing once. Now let me teach you what I know, what Maetha taught me about how Diamond Bearers should determine who to and who not to heal. That woman is a good candidate to practice your healing power on because her arthritis isn't a terminal disease."

"What if it was? What if it was cancer?"

"Healing someone with a deadly disease isn't wrong as long as you're not prolonging their natural lifespan. But first you need their permission . . . like with Jonas. You also have to consider that your strength will be exhausted, leaving you vulnerable. As a Bearer, you don't want to put yourself in a position that might lead to your death. In that weakened state, you won't be able to use the Healing power on yourself. Have you used the power on yourself yet?"

"Yeah."

"What was wrong?"

"Nothing."

"Then why did you use the power?"

"I wasn't injured. I just needed to use the power on some . . . um, inflammation."

"What was inflamed?"

He doesn't answer. Instead he looks embarrassed and takes a big bite of his burger.

"Oh . . . oh! Sorry." Now I'm the embarrassed one.

Chris sips on his soda, then takes the subject back to the woman in the red jacket. "She's not going to die anytime soon. Helping her with her pain would be a good thing to do. Can I try?" he says, wiping his mouth with the back of his hand.

"Yes, go ahead."

The woman stands in front of a large display of various sale items. She bends forward slightly, then stands upright. She looks around and opens and closes her hands. Confusion spreads across her wrinkled face. I read her mind and find she thinks she's about to pass out, even though she's not. She doesn't know why her pain is gone. She takes her purse out of her cart and leaves the store.

"Did I help or just confuse the woman?"

I laugh. "I think she'll be fine. Check out the man at checkstand two."

"The one with the headache?"

I realize there are two men standing there. "Yes."

"Should I heal him?"

"I'm going to leave this one up to you, Chris."

"Okay. Well, healing the arthritis was something the woman won't have to deal with again. This man will have more headaches in the future, so healing this one is kind of pointless. I'm not going to."

"That's your call."

We eat our food, pointing out different shoppers to each other, examining the minor issues within their bodies. Together we heal a twisted ankle, a wicked toothache, an inflamed spinal disc, and calm an irritated toddler to help the mother. I like the way Chris uses wisdom to make his decisions.

A man enters the store riding an electric scooter. He's severely overweight.

"What do you think, Calli?"

I read the man's mind and find he has a genetic condition which disqualifies him for gastric bypass surgery. His family has a history of not waking up from anesthesia. I say, "He's not a candidate for surgery. We can't do anything about the extra pounds on his body, but we can alter his hunger cravings."

"How would you do that? Is that mind-control?"

"No, I'm going to readjust his brain chemicals to tell him he's full a little sooner. I'm also going to help him with his depression, which is part of why he overeats."

"His future shows he'll shed many of those pounds," Chris confirms.

"Hopefully, he'll stay on that path and continue losing weight."

"You know, Calli, I could do this all day long. I feel fantastic helping people."

I smile. "I know what you mean. Unfortunately, sometimes it's not so great." The smile falls from my face. "For instance, like now." I motion to the cart about to go past the eatery. A child about three-years-old stands inside the cart. She has Down Syndrome. I look to her future and find she will contract pneumonia in a couple months and die due to her smaller than normal airways. I say to Chris, "I could heal her airways today. Let's look to the future to see if that would help."

Chris says, "She'll only live a little past that. Heart problems. We could heal her heart, too."

"No, she'll still die. Leukemia."

"So, no matter what we do, she's still going to die young? We have to do something at least," Chris pleads.

"Let's heal her airways so she doesn't have to die painfully with pneumonia. Her heart problem will result in a painless death and she'll never have to go through chemo or the other issues with Leukemia. I think we should strengthen her mother's patience, too."

Chris looks at me with high regard. "You are a wise Healer, Calli."

"You taught me to be so. Will you heal the child? I'll work on the mother, and then we'd better get back to the hotel."

"Okay."

When we return to the hotel, the five of us stay in the same room, going over files till bedtime. Crimson invites the guys to go to their room and then excuses herself. She speaks to my mind after she leaves, *I'll be able to hear you if you need me. I don't foresee any danger for you tonight, though.*

Okay.

About two minutes to the second after Crimson leaves, someone knocks on our door. Beth checks through the peephole. "It's Brand." She opens the door.

He saunters into the room. As he passes the television cabinet he lazily drags his finger along the edge. "So, I was thinkin', if Crimson's gone, there's no reason why we can't do a little mixin' things up."

"What do you mean?" I ask.

"Sheez Calli, you're so naïve." Brand rolls his eyes. "I mean, like, you and me trade rooms."

"No," I say. "Crimson assigned us these rooms."

"Okay, so we switch back after a couple hours."

"No, Brand. Does Chris know you're trying to finagle things around?"

"Who do you think sent me?"

"What?" I go to Chris's mind. *Did you send Brand to talk me into coming to your room for the night?*

No, he said he was going for ice.

I point to the door. "Get out, Brand. And don't forget the ice you told Chris you were getting."

He looks at Beth, who looks rather amused by his actions. "It was worth a try."

I clear my throat loudly, then shut and lock the door after he leaves. I grab my nightclothes and change into them as I ask Beth, "Did you know he was going to do that?"

"He talked about it while we were shopping. I told him it wasn't a good idea, but you know Brand. He had to try anyway."

"Doesn't he understand Crimson is aware of everything we do?"

"Well, it's not like we're kids, or this is some school outing." Beth straitens the files on the table.

"That's true. But Crimson set the room assignments. I, for one, am not going to go against her wishes."

She turns and faces me. "Don't worry, Calli. I wasn't going to either."

"What do you see in Brand anyway?"

"What do you mean?"

"What is it about Brand that you're attracted to?"

"He gets me. No one else ever has. Plus, he makes me laugh."

"Do you ever compare his physical appearance to other guys?"

"No. I don't need to. Believe it or not, Calli, I like charm over looks. Besides, Brand isn't lacking in either department." Beth puts an end to the subject as she says, "I'm going to jump in the shower."

"Okay."

I think I'll call my parents while she's showering. I haven't wanted to do so in front of her out of respect for her loss. She can't call her parents ever again. I don't want to rub that fact in, nor do I want to give her any other reason to point out how "lucky" I am. I walk over and sit on my bed and pick up the phone to dial my home number.

My mother answers and we talk for a little while. I just want to hear her voice and to also let her know I'm all right. We talk for the fifteen minutes Beth is in the shower. Once I hear the water turn off, I end my call with my mother.

When she comes out of the bathroom, Beth asks, "Are your parents doing okay?"

"How did you know I called?"

"The walls aren't that thick here."

"Yeah, my parents are doing well."

"They're probably really sweet and cater to your every need."

"Yes, they do." *Please don't say I'm lucky.*

Beth climbs under her covers and fluffs the pillows. "My parents were never like that. Dad loved his bottle more than life itself, and Mom preferred pills to taking care of the kids she'd squeezed out. Once my running power surfaced, I was able to get out of that hellhole. I just wish I could have taken Nate with me. But at least he's going to go work with Clara Winter. He'll finally have a good caregiver."

"I'm sorry, Beth."

"For what?" She reaches up and turns off the lamp by her bed, darkening the room.

"Sorry I ever lit into you when I arrived at the compound. I had no idea."

"Don't be. You helped me have the courage to stand up to them. Your example helped me more than you'll ever know. I think it's why I'm not all broken up about their deaths. I was able to say my peace while they were alive."

"You've been on your own most of your life, haven't you? Separated in your mind, I mean."

"Yes."

"When is their funeral?"

"I'm really tired, Calli."

"Oh, okay. Good night," I say, and pull my blanket up

around my neck. I feel guilty for having had a plush, protected life. Learning what Beth grew up with has opened my eyes a little more to how unlucky other kids are.

Chapter 4 – Powerful Prisms

The next morning, I awake to find Crimson sitting at the table with the files.

"Good morning, Calli. You'd better get moving. We need to leave in thirty minutes."

Beth is already in the bathroom, so I get up and organize my belongings while I wait for Beth. I'm excited, and a little nervous, to wear the green dress Chris had me buy. I go ahead and change in the room, slipping the dress over my head, hoping it fits. I still can't believe I bought a dress without trying it on first. I mean, the dress is the right size, but that doesn't always guarantee a good fit. I look at myself in the mirror and am amazed. This dress looks fantastic on me. Now, if only Chris would tell me more about his vision.

Someone knocks on the door. I let Brand and Chris into the room. Brand lets out a whistle to show he's impressed and walks over to Beth. She's wearing a black sleeveless dress and has either forgotten to apply her black eyeliner or she's not going to put any on. She looks different without the liner—good different.

Chris's voice fills my mind. *I told you that dress would suit you well. You look stunning. I kind of wish we weren't headed to a funeral just now.*

You're not too bad yourself, sir. Our eyes share a quick glance and I look away. He takes my hand.

He announces, "Time to go. Calli and I will go check out and meet you in the van."

❖ ❖ ❖

Crimson drives us to the old church with a cross on top where Anika's parents' funeral will take place. Crimson says, "I'll see to it that everything is loaded on the plane. You'll be leaving later this afternoon and heading to Denver. I'll meet you at Chris's father's home."

As I climb out of the car, my attention is drawn across the street to four adults walking back and forth, carrying picket signs.

"What's that all about?" Brand asks.

Beth says, "Didn't you guys know? Anika was raised by two dads."

"Two dads? Gay guys?" Brand blurts out.

"Shhh," she admonishes. "Those are protestors of their, um, preferences."

"I don't think there's anything lower than people like that," I hear Chris say.

I'm more than shocked by his statement. I wouldn't have pegged him as an anti-gay kind of guy. I'm bothered by this quite a bit. I glance over at Chris, trying to think of what to say, only to find a disgusted expression on his face as he glares across the street at the protestors. He says, "Why do they have to do that right now when all these people are in mourning?"

Relief, in epic proportions, warms my heart. I touch his arm and say. "They have the right to their opinion. Everyone does."

"Well, *my opinion* is they shouldn't be here ruining this funeral."

Once we enter the building, Anika rushes over to greet us. She has swollen red eyes, but seems pleased to see us.

"I want you to meet my grandparents. Come on." She leads us toward a large room. On the way, we pass an enormous arrangement of flowers with a large photograph of two men.

Inside the room, folding chairs are lined up to accommodate the guests. Flower arrangements on elevated stands are placed everywhere around the perimeter, and an organized receiving line of who I assume are family members of the deceased leads up to two caskets with the heads against each other.

An intense wave of despair hits my gut. Seeing the parents of Anika—dead—brings everything we've been through into sharp focus. They died because of General Harding and his revulsion of people with powers. They died because of intolerance and hate—ironically, not because of intolerance and hatred toward their sexual orientation. I look over at Chris, but he's no longer next to me. Brand hooks his thumb past his ear, motioning the direction Chris went. I can tell Brand is trying hard to keep his emotions in check.

I leave the room to look for Chris. He's outside the front door, standing on the step.

I push the door open and walk to his side. I thread my fingers with his and lay my head on his shoulder. He rests his head on mine. I say, "That just got very real in there, didn't it?"

He doesn't respond, just squeezes my hand.

The voices of the chanting protestors across the street catch my attention again. I read their signs and am dismayed. One of the signs chastises the church and pastor for allowing the funeral of two gay guys to take place inside. Another sign states gay people shouldn't raise kids. Then there's the typical sign letting everyone know how God feels about homosexuals. The last sign is a dry-erase board and the holder is currently changing the message. I hesitate for a moment, knowing what I'm considering doing is wrong, but then decide to go ahead and use Mind-control on the lady to help lighten Chris's emotional state.

"Watch this, Chris," I say.

He lifts his head. "What?"

"Watch the protestor who's writing on her board."

The lady is bent over for a minute, then stands up and holds her board up high while chanting her message. "God Hates Haters! God Hates Haters!"

The other protesters stop cold in their shoes and pretty much tackle the lady, taking the board from her grasp. One guy uses his elbow to smudge her message.

Chris laughs. "Thanks, Calli. I needed that. Let's go back in."

We turn and enter the building. I release my mind-control hold on the female protester.

Anika finds us again and introduces us to her grandparents. We shake hands and offer up our condolences. I'm amazed at their level of control over their emotions. They've lost their sons. Forever. How is it they are so calm?

I read the mind of the first grandmother Anika introduced. She feels she'll see her son again in the next life and that when she does, his gay-ness will be gone—healed. She's happier that he's in heaven now.

I look into the mind of the other grandmother and determine she's incredibly angry about the murder of her son. She had accepted him when he came out in public with his sexual orientation, supported him in bringing a child into the relationship, and has always been there for Anika. Her son's murder, and that of his partner, is something she's always feared.

I choose not to look inside the grandfathers' minds. The insight I've gained from three different perspectives is enough for one day.

Beth and Brand have already chosen their seats, reserving two more for us. We join them.

As the funeral services proceed, I ponder the great mysteries of life and death. Crimson was right when she said people are afraid of the unknown. I feel that no one really knows where we go when we die, if we go anywhere at all.

The preacher tells the crowd that just believing in Jesus will get you into heaven. It seems to me the bar is quite low when it comes to who will be alongside Jesus in heaven. Maybe there's more than one heaven. Maybe the Jesus-believing protestors across the street will be in a different location than the homosexual-accepting people in this room. Heaven better be a big place, that's all I can say.

I think about Beth and her deceased parents. According to the preacher, as long as they believed in Jesus, they are saved and are currently in heaven. I wonder how that makes Beth feel. I have no idea, and I'm not going to read her mind to find out.

What about Chris and his father's death? Religious beliefs aside, is he going to realize one day he's lost the chance to finally gain his father's respect and love? Or has he already mourned sufficiently, as he claims?

After sitting through the services, I conclude I need to live this one life I have in front of me to its fullest. Yes, my life will last longer than most, but that's why I need to make sure I make the most of it.

The four of us hitch a ride to the cemetery with other family members. The graveside services are short, and soon we are piling back inside the car, heading to a family member's home for a meal and further mingling.

After eating and talking some more with Anika's grandparents, Chris and I locate a comfortable porch swing where we spend most of the time cuddling.

Chris says, "Thanks for understanding me, Calli."

I push my head away from his chest and look into his eyes. "You're welcome."

Brand and Beth come outside and stand in front of us. Brand says, "What time did we need to be to the airport?"

"In two hours. We should figure out how we're going to get there," I say.

Chris stands. "I'll call for a taxi."

Anika joins us on the porch. "I'm really thankful you all came to support me."

Beth gives her a hug. "No problem at all, Anika. It's been an enlightening day."

I give her a hug. "Your dads must have been wonderful. I'm sorry for your loss."

"Thanks, Calli." We end our hug and she addresses everyone. "I'm going to stay with my family for a little while. Okay?"

"Take as much time as you need." I squeeze her hand.

"I'll catch up with you guys later," she promises.

After boarding the plane, heading for Denver, Chris pulls out his cell phone and inserts the battery. He checks his voicemail and finds he has three messages. I can hear the messages as if the phone is up to my own ear. The first message is from his mother, wondering how he's holding up and when he'll be able to come and visit. Once the message is finished, Chris deletes it when prompted. The voice on the second message sends a nervous chill through my body.

"Hello, Mr. Harding. This is Special Agent David Whitman. I would like to set up a time to ask you a few more questions. Please call as soon as possible. Thank you."

My eyes meet Chris's and I hear his thoughts. *This doesn't feel good,* he says.

No, it doesn't.

The automated voice prompts Chris to delete the message. He does so.

The last message is a female. "Hi Chris, it's Kikee. You told me to call when I got to New York. Well, I'm here. I talked with your mother the other day. She's so sweet. She told me you recently lost your father. I'm so sorry for you. I feel bad I can't be with you right now. Please call me as soon as you can. Kisses."

I feel every muscle in Chris's body tense. He hits the end button on his phone and then dials a number.

He says to me while he waits to be connected, "Nothing serious happened with Kikee, Calli."

I try to appear unaffected by the call. "What are you going to tell her?"

"I don't know exactly, but it will be the truth."

"Yeah, but you can't tell her about Diamond Bearers. Do you want me to use my power of persuasion to get her to forget about you?" I'm half kidding, half serious.

Chris speaks into the phone. "Agent Whitman, Chris Harding here. I'll be at my father's home in Denver tomorrow. You're welcome to drop by, if that's convenient. Goodbye."

Brand pops his head over the back of the seat in front of us. "Hey, is there food at the house?"

"Probably not anything you'd like."

"We'll need to get some then. I'm starved. These granola bars aren't doin' it for me. I need like a steak or something."

"We just ate all the food at the funeral dinner," I say, rather perplexed that he can be hungry already.

Chris says, "There's a good restaurant close to the house. We'll go there for dinner. I'd better make reservations, though." Chris gets up and walks to the front of the plane to speak with Capt. Rutherfield. His mind is blocked for the most part, but I can hear his voice. He says, "What time will we be arriving?"

"6:50 p.m., if the weather holds out," Rodger replies.

"Would you like to join us for dinner? I'm about to make reservations."

"Thank you, but no. I have other arrangements."

Chris enters numbers into his phone again. He connects with the restaurant and sets up dinner for four at 7:30. Then he takes the battery out of his phone and puts it away. I expect he will get up and come back to me. Instead, he asks a few flying-related questions of the captain.

I lay my head back and close my eyes, focusing on my blocking ability. The last thing I want right now is for Chris to know how much Kikee's call bothers me. I certainly don't want Maetha to know what I'm thinking. She lost her Blue shard over the whole fiasco with Kikee. I almost lost my life.

Kikee didn't leave a number. Does that mean Chris already has her number, or is she assuming he'll use the one automatically stored in the phone? I don't know if he was only nervous, or if it was on purpose, but he didn't delete her message. He ended the call, which saves the message.

I really need to think about something else.

◈ ◈ ◈

We land in Denver and climb into a taxi. Brand and

Beth sit in the back seat with me. They talk excitedly with each other, holding hands, and laughing. Chris sits in the front with the driver. He directs the driver to his father's home so we can drop our luggage and the boxes inside the door, then we continue on to the restaurant.

At the restaurant, Chris takes me by the hand and leads me inside. My instincts are on full alert. The interior reminds me of my birthday dinner and the server, Sven. It's unlikely anyone will be tampering with our food tonight, but as Crimson said, "Never let your guard down." I look to my future to see if danger lurks. I see myself tomorrow, sitting at the dining room table, so I stop searching. I'll live through dinner. Crimson would be proud, I think.

Our time at the restaurant is almost identical to the taxi ride here. Brand and Beth jabber on and on, Chris and I don't say much to them or to each other. Our food arrives and Brand chows down on his enormous gourmet burger and fries. I'm amazed how Brand can talk so much and also inhale so much food. Beth pokes around at the salad she ordered. Chris and I both chose the clam chowder. He isn't eating much, though, He's swirling his spoon in the soup, his mind a million miles away.

I send my thoughts to Chris. *Are you all right?*

Yeah. I don't like this town, that's all. I've got to settle my dad's estate and figure out what to do with the house.

I feel like a dummy for not considering what Chris might be stressing over. Here I thought it was the message from Kikee. I respond, *You've got a lot on your shoulders. I'll help any way I can.*

Thanks. How about you hurry these two up? I want to get out of here. He smiles at me.

Crimson connects with my mind. *I'm at Chris's father's home.*

"All right guys. Crimson has arrived. Let's go."

We pay for the meal and leave.

"Let's walk to the house. It's only a couple blocks," Chris says, once we're outside.

"Is it safe?" Beth asks no one in particular.

I double-check to make sure I'm not going to die in the next ten minutes. "Yeah, it's safe."

Following a non-eventful walk, we arrive at the house and Crimson lets us in.

I look around the room at the shelves full of interesting books and artifacts. One set of shelves by the dining room table is full of assorted rocks and crystals. A rather large selection of obsidian is part of the collection. *Uncle Don would love to see this,* I think. Some of the obsidian is in chunks as large as my fist and have dusty-white exteriors.

The dining room table is covered with the contents of the boxes, including many files and groups of crystals.

"Crimson," Chris says, "I've decided to follow your advice and open this house up to the Bearers."

"I'm pleased to hear your decision. And the vehicle too?"

"That too. I don't need it."

"I'll admit I already foresaw you choosing this move. I've arranged for my financial consultant to come over tomorrow to take care of the details," she announces, then smiles slyly. "Everyone come sit at the table. I have some things to go over with you."

We sit down at the table. Crimson has some additional documents from General Harding's compound and the many quartz crystals used to capture individual powers spread out on the table. She tells us the individually-powered crystals have been inventoried and cross-referenced with the files. The findings indicate that an almost exact number of each power was run through the machine.

Beth stands and says, "I'm going to get some water. Does anyone else want a glass?" No one takes her up on her offer. She shrugs her shoulders and goes to the kitchen. She brings her water back to the table.

"Be careful not to spill on these documents, Beth," Crimson points to Beth's glass. Beth repositions the water further to the side.

Crimson continues with her findings. "The vests that were being created, the ones with the green quartz and obsidian, were cataloged and numbered. Two are unaccounted for. We need to find these before they're used inappropriately."

Crimson picks up some other papers and says, "I've gone over more of the material taken from General Harding's compound. These documents reveal the power-removing machine was designed in Switzerland by a nameless company, under Freedom's direction. Calli, do you have the quartz prisms?"

"Yes." I get up and retrieve them from my bag. I set the small bundle on the table and undo the wrapping. Crimson picks up a crystal and examines it against the light.

Beth reaches toward the pile. "May I hold one?" she asks Crimson.

Crimson doesn't answer for a couple of seconds, as if lost in thought. Finally, she agrees.

Beth picks one up, then puts it down. "Uh, guys," she says, hesitating, "I think I just repeated."

Brand grabs a prism. He rotates it between his fingers, while chewing on his bottom lip. "What makes you think you repeated?" I can tell he's genuinely curious.

"I knocked over my glass of water right after I picked up the crystal."

I've witnessed Brand using the repeating power many

times, and I've repeated with him. Beth has as well. If she suspects she repeated, she probably did.

Brand picks up a crystal, then pulls the repeating quartz from his pocket and places it on the table. He tightens his grip on the prism in his hand. "It has ten seconds of repeating power. They all do." He sets the prism back in the pile and picks up his repeating quartz. "I couldn't detect the power while I had this on my body," he says as he returns the quartz to his pocket.

I ask, "If these hold the repeating power, why didn't I sense it while I carried all the prisms?"

"Dunno." Brand leans back in his chair. "You must not have had a moment you wished you could change. That's how the power is accessed at first. I mean, that's how I figured out I had the power. I walked into the dark and started being ripped apart by the Demons. My first instinct was to think I shouldn't have gone outside. Next thing I know, I'm back inside the house, not a scratch on my body."

Beth says, "Like me, just now. I spilled my water, and immediately wished I could undo my mistake. The room spun around and, ta-da, I hadn't spilled my water yet." Beth takes her glass of water back into the kitchen.

I think back to when I removed the crystals from my pocket, from my body. It was that night in the hotel room at Lake Patoka. Too bad they were on the bathroom floor while I was saying the wrong things to Chris.

Brand says to me, "I assume, while you carried the prisms, you never accidentally accessed the powers because you weren't in threatening or precarious situations. The question is: What else can these prisms do?" He picks up a prism again.

Crimson's thoughts sound in my head. *They can be used to unite the clans.*

Before I can ask Crimson what she means, Chris asks, "Did you try to repeat with someone, Brand?"

Brand pauses, then says, "They don't work that way."

"Did you just—?" Chris asks. His eyes wide with delight. Chris grabs a prism in one swift movement and turns in his seat to face me. I don't need to read his mind to know he's about to kiss me. Yet, he doesn't. He only smiles.

"Wait," I sputter. "Did you kiss me and then repeat?"

Chris's thoughts answer my question, along with a projected memory of our kiss that I don't remember.

Crimson speaks to the group. "The power to repeat is not natural and can take away basic rights and choices. We will need to exercise caution with who receives these crystals. Brand, you and Beth go test the prisms for other powers."

They each pick up a crystal and leave the room.

Jonas and Mary bi-locate to the room. Crimson says, "Thank you, Mary, for bringing Jonas." Mary bows her head, accepting the thanks. Crimson continues. "Jonas I wanted you present to hear the current topics. As you three are my newest Bearers, I want you to work as a team as much as possible." Crimson gives a quick rundown on what we know already concerning the twelve prisms and the repeating power. "These prisms are powerful bargaining chips. They will be used to gain alliances and to restore Calli and Chris's credibility with the clans. The clans, whose leaders were killed after their amulets were taken, will be satisfied to receive a replacement crystal containing all the powers plus Repeating. They'll be especially pleased to have a crystal that isn't deadly to the touch, unlike the floating diamond shard."

Crimson motions toward the containers of quartz that contain individual powers harvested from people who were run through General Harding's machine. "These will be returned to the appropriate clans. Each piece signifies a human being who either died, or no longer possesses a power. The living will be pleased to get their power back. The deceased clan members should be memorialized and the quartz used at the discretion of the leaders. These files give us names and photographs to help identify the deceased."

Brand and Beth enter the room.

"Hey, Jonas," Brand says. "How's it going?"

Crimson asks, "What did you two find out?"

Beth says, "The running power is equivalent to a slower Runner's speed. Brand wasn't able to keep up with me. The hunting abilities are pretty strong, but maybe that's how they are normally. The Seer and Mind-Reader powers seem to be on track with the regular abilities. I can sense Brand's body using the healing power, but I'm not familiar with it enough to determine its strength."

"Well then, we better remedy that," Brand teases.

Beth playfully punches his arm. "I didn't mean *your body*, I meant I'm not familiar with the healing power."

Crimson says, "Good. I'm assigning Beth and Brand to investigate the employees and guards from the compound to determine their level of threat to the clans. Hopefully Anika will be able to join them soon."

Brand interrupts. "Crimson, someone named Agent Whitman is coming to the door in two minutes."

"That's not good," Beth mutters.

Chris looks at me in panic. "I told him to come tomorrow."

Brand points in Crimson's direction. "You and Calli should leave, don't you think?"

Mary and Jonas vanish right away.

Crimson reassures Brand. "Not to worry. He won't

see a thing. He doesn't know you and Beth. Tell him you are here to help Chris clean out his father's home."

Brand's voice squeaks as he says, "How is he not going to see all those crystals? What about the files and papers?"

"Close your eyes, Brand," Crimson commands gently. His lids close over his eyes. Crimson tells me to use my invisibility power. "Now, open," she says to Brand.

His eyes open wide. "Whoa! Just like that" —he snaps his fingers— "they're gone in a blink."

"We're still here," I say to Brand, knowing how strange it is to hear a voice coming from what looks like empty space.

Beth chuckles and says, "My whole perception changed instantly. I was looking at crystals, then they became stacks of plates, bowls, and cups."

Crimson says, "When Agent Whitman arrives, let him in and act as normally as possible. Don't worry about him wandering around the room. I won't let him near the crystals. Calli, you need to hide in a bedroom."

"What should I do?" Beth asks.

Brand cuts in, "You need to hide, too. You make him nervous."

Beth throws him a nasty glare.

"Hey, I'm only telling you what I've just seen. Go!"

Brand turns to Chris. "All right, let's see if we can get it right *this* time."

Beth leaves the room without hesitation. I follow close behind her.

The doorbell rings as if on cue. Chris lets out a huff of frustration. I can only assume he didn't like the negative tone Brand just used. Chris opens the front door.

Chapter 5 – The Mission

Inside the room, I see a vent at the top of the wall that might allow me to see the front room. I stand on the nearby chair and peek through the grate. Bingo.

"Agent Whitman. This is a surprise." Chris says, opening the door.

"I know. I apologize for dropping in like this, but I have to head out of town tomorrow and I was passing by when I noticed the lights were on, so I took a chance you'd see me."

"Come in." Chris opens the door wide.

Brand walks straight to Agent Whitman. "Hi, I'm Chris's friend, Brand."

They shake hands. "Nice to meet you, Brand."

"Have a seat," Chris says, motioning toward the couch. Agent Whitman takes his overcoat off and lays it on the arm of the couch and pulls out a small notepad and pencil from a pocket, then sits across from Chris.

Brand sits adjacent to them.

"Chris, I would like to talk to you about a couple things." Agent Whitman flips through the pages of his notebook and says, "When I interviewed Max Corvus, he said you were alone when the hard drive, files, and the, um, magic crystals disappeared. Is this true?"

Chris replies, "The stuff disappeared when Max and I performed the perimeter search for the missing prisoners."

"Max can't confirm that, Chris." Agent Whitman says, openly expressing his distrust.

"Well, I don't know what to tell you."

Whitman clears his throat and shifts nervously in his

seat. "Several of the workers stated you are 'one of them.' That you can run unnaturally fast. Is this true?"

"Yes, I can run faster than most people. I guess that's why my father was interested in me and others like me. He had me spying on the other Olympic candidates in Montana."

"I see." He scribbles something in his notebook. "What about these other 'powers' like healing? Can you do that too?"

Chris calmly responds, "No. I think a lot of that is the placebo effect. The mind is a powerful thing, Agent Whitman. Mind-readers are well-trained in cold-reading techniques. Seers are intuitive and pay attention to details. They're good guessers. Face it, my father was a paranoid, delusional man, in a position of power. He crossed the wrong paths and got himself killed."

"You said Samantha Juarez, or Deus Ex as she called herself, killed him."

"Deus Ex was clearly trying to steal a crystal when she was electrocuted. It's entirely possible she was not working alone. Maybe she had helpers in the compound we didn't know about. That's the only explanation I can give."

Agent Whitman seems to buy it.

Chris adds, "Are you investigating the murders General Harding's soldiers carried out?"

"Inside the compound?"

"No. The murdering of citizens related to the prisoners my father held captive."

Agent Whitman narrows his eyes and leans forward. "What are you talking about, son?"

"I overheard my father discuss the murders of one of the prisoner's parents. I think they were from North Dakota. They were gay men."

"I'm going to need more information than that,

Chris." Agent Whitman writes furiously.

"How hard would it be to search the recent unsolved murder cases in North Dakota? Bismarck, I believe. Look for the murders of two gays. That should stick out, don't you think?"

"Do you have names?"

"No. Sorry. But, my dad spoke like they weren't the only murders. I would bet there are many open homicide investigations across the nation. I would also assume the murderers are soldiers who were working for my father."

"I'll look into it." Agent Whitman checks his watch and closes his notebook. He stands and reaches his hand out to shake Chris's.

Chris grasps his hand and nods his head. "Thank you." He then walks him to the door and shows him out.

After Chris closes the front door, Brand walks over and pats his back, and says, "Man, I wasn't sure we were going to get out of that one. You did great."

Chris plops down in a chair. "I feel like I'm going to be sick."

Brand freezes in place and says, "Hang on. He's coming back."

Crimson speaks to my mind, *Stay in the room, Calli.*

I motion to Beth to stay put.

Chris's thoughts merge with mine. *I can't stand all the spinning with repeating. I don't know how Brand deals with it.*

How many times did you repeat? I ask.

I lost count. Brand was getting mad at me for messing up.

What were you messing up?

I kept revealing too much, giving names, basically revealing I had powers. I don't know why I couldn't think straight.

The doorbell rings. Chris gets up and opens the door.

Agent Whitman smiles sheepishly. "I apologize, but I forgot my overcoat." He points past Chris's shoulder.

Brand picks the jacket up and flings it over his arm, causing something black to fall out of the pocket. The object hits the wood floor with a clunk.

My eyes focus on the black object that looks suspiciously like obsidian. Brand bends down and picks it up.

"Sorry about that. What's this?" he asks Agent Whitman, holding up the rock.

"Oh, it's nothing." Whitman's ears turn red.

Crimson says to my mind, *It's obsidian, but not the right kind.*

Chris says, "This looks like obsidian."

Whitman chuckles and reaches a shaky hand to take the coat and obsidian from Brand. "After hearing about it from almost everyone I interviewed, I thought it wouldn't hurt to have a piece of my own. Call me superstitious." He deposits the rock into his pocket.

"There's nothing wrong with being careful, Agent Whitman," Chris says. "Good night."

After his car leaves the driveway, Beth and I come into the room and Crimson becomes visible and I breathe a sigh of relief. I say, "That was a subtle reminder we all need charged topazes on our body at all times. We never know when we'll be in the presence of obsidian."

We settle in for the evening. Beth and I take two of the three bedrooms. Chris and Brand fight over the couch. I think neither one of them want to seem selfish for taking the remaining bed. Crimson finally settles the squabble by claiming the bedroom for herself, leaving the two guys to figure out their own sleeping arrangements.

I lie in my bed, pondering the events of the day. The funeral for Anika's dads was informative, in the sense that I learned much more about Anika. Her fathers were accomplished men with college degrees and good jobs. Yet, their sexual orientation seemed to discount their achievements in some people's eyes. Anika is a strong, confident girl, which is an indication she had a good childhood. She's obviously close to her grandparents. Perhaps her nurturing could be considered a group effort. I consider further how everyone is influenced by the many adults around them. The phrase, "It takes a village to raise a child," comes to mind. Not every child has a village of good people raising them, I know.

Take Deus Ex, for example. Hearing Chris and Agent Whitman talk about her tonight made me think about the little she'd shared about her neglectful, abusive childhood. She was resourceful and clever, just severely misguided. By the time she met up with adults who could be positive influences in her life, she'd already carved out her slot in the world—and that slot had no room for trust.

I think about Jonas. He also came from an abusive home. Yet, his personality is entirely different, as if he feels compelled to disprove the theories that he'll adopt the same behaviors. I know Chris worries about the same thing. He fears becoming like his father.

I roll over and hear Chris in my mind.

I love you, Calli.

I love you, too.

The next morning I'm drawn from my room by the smell of something good. I enter the kitchen to find Brand and Chris amidst a mess of vegetable peels, egg shells, and dirty dishes.

"Calli," Brand gasps upon seeing me.

Chris looks up from flipping eggs. "No girls allowed." He winks, sending my heart all a flutter. "Please wait in the dining room."

"Shoo!" Brand flicks his hand.

I leave the kitchen, feeling even more attracted to Chris. I'm excited to taste whatever he's cooking up in there and I'm sure it will be good. I sit at the table and let my thoughts wander. Before I know it, Beth and Crimson join me.

"What's going on in there?" Beth points toward the kitchen.

"It's a surprise. The guys are cooking for us."

"Oh, this will be interesting."

I scan the table littered with the papers, crystals, and files. "Do you think we should straighten up this mess so we have somewhere to eat?"

Crimson says, "No, I have things where I want them."

Brand's voice booms from the kitchen, "We're going to eat in here, just give us another second."

I take the opportunity to turn on my phone and try to call my parents. I get the answering machine. After leaving a brief message that I'm doing fine, I end the call and take the phone into my bedroom.

Chris calls from the other room, "Come and get it."

As Crimson, Beth, and I enter the messy kitchen, which seems to have become even more cluttered since I saw it five minutes ago, Beth exclaims, "Where did all this food come from?"

Brand sets the last setting on the small breakfast table. "Crimson went shopping."

"Yes, I did, but I didn't purchase a maid," she says, eying the condition of the kitchen. "Did a tornado touch down in here?"

Chris ignores her. "Grab your plate and come dish

up." He indicates the lined-up food choices on the stove.

Beth and I take our plates and fill them with eggs, hash browns, and sliced fruit. The unexpected whir of a blender frightens me a little. Chris is making what appears to be a green smoothie. *Yeah, that's my health nut.*

He smiles at me, muscles flexing in his arms as he holds firmly to the blender. Beth and I sit down at the table. The blender stops and Chris says, "Hey Brand, come here." I look over out of curiosity in time to see Chris lean his head near Brand and point his finger at me. "See that girl over there? I'm goin' with her."

Brand's confused glare shoots between me and Chris. "Well, duh!"

I smile brightly, feeling giddy and proud to be claimed. For the first time in my nineteen years, I feel what my middle-school classmates must have felt. My excitement quickly fades as I dwell a little too long on the reason— Crimson or Maetha probably interfered with any potential boyfriends, keeping me in the proper mindset for the diamond delivery. Before I can start feeling sorry for myself, Chris sets a tall green drink in front of me.

"Thank you," I say, bringing the smile back to my face. As he moves away, I reach out and grasp his arm. He turns around and I whisper, "And . . . thank you."

We enjoy our breakfast, laughing and sharing fun stories. Afterward, we clean the kitchen as a team. Then everyone joins Crimson in the dining room.

Crimson says, "Brand and Beth, when you investigate the employees of the compound to see what they know about people with powers, you need to be on the lookout for anyone who may be telling others about the facility.

Even though they'd get in trouble from Agent Whitman, I'd bet there will be at least one who can't contain the things they saw and participated in. You can stay here at the house while you investigate. I'll have Melvin Phillips get you a corporate card and an extra set of keys. He's the man I told you about yesterday who will be coming by today to take care of business."

Beth says, "I've gone through the files and have written up a list of individuals who live here in Denver. I was hoping Brand and I could get out today to start our investigation."

"The sooner the better," Crimson agrees.

Beth turns to Brand, "I'm ready when you are."

"Then let's go!" he says enthusiastically.

Brand and Beth leave the house within a few minutes.

Crimson says, "Calli will you put on a pot of tea?"

"Sure." I go into the kitchen and fill the kettle with water and turn on the burner. While the water heats up, I load a tray with assorted tea bags, cream, and sugar. The kettle begins to whistle. I reach for the handle in a careless manner and accidentally touch the burner with the side of my hand. I yank my hand back expecting to feel pain and burning, but feel nothing. I'm pretty sure I touched the electric coil, because I felt the heat, but I'm not burned. The only thing I can figure is my healing power is so intense I healed before the skin developed a blister.

Entering the front room with the tray, I set it down on the coffee table near Crimson.

"Sit down, Calli." Crimson pours herself a cup of water and adds a tea bag.

I sit across from her on the large sofa. Chris comes in from seeing Brand and Beth on their way. He sits beside me.

Crimson spreads her arms out wide and a blue mist

encircles us. Then, she says, "Do you recall when I said you were chosen for a larger task than what you've already accomplished, Calli?"

"Yes."

"When I chose you for the event, I had no idea your love interest would be Chris, or that he would also be a Diamond Bearer. The random, spontaneous choices of others can greatly affect the once perceived outcome. Future-sight isn't always dependable—remember that. However, one dependable aspect of being a Seer is knowing when natural cataclysmic events will happen and where. That said, I'm incredibly happy Chris will be by your side, Calli, to support you as you progress through your mission."

"What is my mission?" My heart rate picks up in anticipation.

"As you know, I can see the cosmic energy rays as they hit the earth. I can also foresee cosmic energy before it hits. This is how I've been able to make sure the children of Maetha's line have been Unaltered. I make sure the expecting mothers are safely out of range when a blast hits. For instance, when your mother was pregnant with you, I compelled her to go visit her parents where she wouldn't be affected."

"What power would I have had if you hadn't moved my mother?"

"The nearest energy ray held the Healer power. However, you wouldn't have developed superpowers. I imagine you would have still grown up with the desire to go into the medical field. Usually the people who are near a Healer-powered energy ray tend to gravitate toward professions of helping people."

She takes a sip of tea, then continues.

"Two thousand or so years ago, an amazingly strong

ray hit the earth in what is now northwest Oregon. I was perplexed with its rarity. Never to my knowledge had that particular power hit the earth, at least no one wielded the powers. I looked to the future to find out when that power would hit the earth again." She stops speaking momentarily and looks me in the eye. "In two years the cosmic energy blast will hit the same area, bringing the potential for a new power to arise unlike any modern-day clans have ever seen. This time over half a million individuals will be at risk in the Portland, Oregon region. This cosmic ray will be different than anything you've experienced. It will be deadly to those in the immediate contact zone. A large amount of radiation will accompany this blast. The people outside the blast zone will have the potential for developing illnesses and deformities, and as with all cosmic rays, any pregnancies in the proper development stage will be affected by the ray.

"The Bearers must be made stronger and join together to help reduce the number of casualties from the ray. The greater Portland region will need to be evacuated. The clans will need to unite and provide refuge for any affected individuals in the aftermath of the blast. Calli, this is your mission. You are the one to unite the Bearers and the clans in preparation for this blast. After the event takes place, you'll lead the operation to find and care for those affected by the ray."

"Whoa! What? Me?" I squeak out. I'd expected some kind of mission, but nothing on this scale. I'm utterly flabbergasted.

Chris's eyes widen and his alarmed expression tells me he's also blown away.

"Why me, Crimson? Why not one of the older, more experienced Bearers? Why not you?"

"Believe me, I've looked to the future with many

others in the leadership position, including myself. No one can accomplish what you can. Experience or age isn't a factor."

I laugh outright. "Are you kidding? The older Bearers aren't going to listen to me, let alone follow my orders."

"More Bearers will accept you as their leader than you realize."

Chris asks, "What kind of power will the blast contain?"

"This cosmic energy event will bring the power to control the elements of the world: water, fire, wind, etc. The future is difficult to read, but from what I can tell, some people will only develop one or two of the elemental powers, while others will hold the full range of destructive forces. Once the individuals who absorb this power die, the power will die with them."

I feel sick to my stomach. I take some deep breaths to try to calm down. "Not that I can even begin to wrap my mind around what you're saying, but what exactly do I have to do?"

"I don't have that answer. All I know is the future is optimistic with you in charge. Anyone else in your place will not make the same choices. I believe your strength comes from your fresh way of thinking, your problem-solving skills, and your willingness to try new things. Your brain works in a different way and it's this difference that will save humanity."

What? What did she just imply? My chest tightens. I say, barely able to speak, I'm so shocked, "Are you saying the world will end if I don't do this?"

"Humanity as you know it will die off in one-hundred-fifty years if you don't fulfill your mission."

I look away from her for a moment and take a second to gather my emotions, trying to still my anxious breathing.

In the back of my mind I can almost hear Brand saying, *"What's the big deal? It's not like it will be the end of the world . . . oh, wait."*

Chris says, "So Calli's job will be to help protect people from the blast and then round up any who display powers and watch them till they die?"

I can't help but notice he seems to accept I've apparently been born to do this task. A minute ago his jaw was on the floor with mine. Why isn't he almost hyperventilating like I am?

"Yes, you're correct, Chris."

I say, "You've known for a long time this was coming."

Crimson nods. "I've been preparing for this moment for many centuries. Maetha too."

She could have told me a little sooner. If Maetha had let me know what was in store for my future, I wouldn't have accepted the diamond. Maybe that's why she didn't say anything. I rub my sweaty hands across my pants to dry my palms. I can't seem to swallow fast enough and I'm certain I'm going to be sick. Focusing on my diamond, I try to ease my panic attack.

Chris asks, "Do you have any of the powers in the Primal Stone?"

"Yes."

"Can you show us what we're up against?"

"Melvin Phillips is coming over any minute now to get some paperwork signed. He doesn't know the extent of my powers and I'd like it to remain that way. After he leaves, we'll continue this discussion."

My head spins, but not like when Brand repeats. I wipe my hands again and swallow hard. Maybe a glass of water will help me feel better. I stand to walk toward the kitchen and feel faint. Before I can access my healing power, Chris is instantly by my side, putting an arm behind me and grabbing onto my elbow with the other hand.

"Sit down, Calli. I'll get you that glass of water."

My eyes follow him. I thought I had blocked my thoughts effectively. How did he know I was heading for water? If he was Brand, I'd know he'd repeated. Can Chris repeat? Maybe he has one of the quartz prisms.

Chris approaches with a glass of water in his hand. I try to read his mind but can't. I scan his body to see if I can detect a crystal or anything. Nope.

"Here you go. You look a lot better now. You were so pale, I thought you might pass out or something. Good thing I looked over when I did, right?"

"Yeah." I accept the water and down the whole glass. I probably over-analyzed the situation. I guess Chris was simply paying close attention to my needs.

Crimson must have opened the door while I was having my mini-crisis because a short, husky man now stands by her side. She extends her hand to me and says, "Calli, come with me."

I take her offered hand and stand, giving Chris my empty glass.

She's infusing my body with healing strength, I can tell. She guides me past the dining room table, picking up a box as she goes. Then she directs me to my room. Once inside she says, "Sit down on the bed and try to relax."

I do as she orders.

"I apologize for not being able to help you understand more about this task right now. The healing power isn't able to make you comprehend because lack of comprehension isn't an illness or injury, unfortunately." She reaches in the box and pulls out a flash drive, then sets the box down on the floor by the night stand. I'll bring in the laptop so you can look over the files on this."

She hands me the drive.

"Try to get your mind off what we just discussed. Put your focus elsewhere for now, please."

I nod my head. She leaves and returns shortly with the computer, then leaves the room, closing my door behind her. My eyes drop to the small stick that holds government secrets. Beyond it, I see the box on the floor. Inside are the prisms from the machine. I bend forward and grab the bundle and count them. Twelve. It was silly of me to think Chris had repeated, I conclude.

I take the laptop and reposition myself on the bed. After inserting the flash drive into the USB slot, I start opening files. Right away I realize how big of a job this will be. Some files have at least ten levels of files within files. Others are encrypted.

My mind wanders while I stare blankly at the screen. The thought of being the leader during the upcoming cosmic blast is so overwhelming. How am I going to get the other Diamond Bearers to listen to me? Will Crimson have to follow me around, thumping her fists on the table, ordering everyone to do as I say? She doesn't have time for that. Besides, she probably knows that's not going to work. The Bearers need to respect me before they'll decide to follow my orders. Based on at least four of their opinions, that's not going to be happening soon.

I return my focus to the screen. I open a file named "Power Generator" and find a few saved website pages of different kinds of rapid-speed generators. I remember that General Harding brought in one of these generators to be able to recharge the power-removing machine faster. I pause to think. This was probably one of the last files General Harding worked on before his death.

A file named "Vorherrschaft" within the power generator file catches my eye. I click on it and find a receipt for a generator. The date is recent. Vorherrschaft and an address are written in the top left corner. Switzerland.

I open the internet browser and search for Vorherrschaft. Several translation sites for German to English are listed and I click on one. Words like domination, supremacy, force majeure, and superiority show up. Well, I think to myself, anyone who would choose this word as their company title should probably be taken seriously.

I try to view the future of the upcoming blast by imagining myself in Portland. Nothing comes to mind. I look for strange powers emerging, but get nowhere. How do other Bearers search the future? I decide to look for my death. Again, nothing. Well, that's kind of cool, I suppose. I look for Chris's death and see myself slamming the diamond into his bare chest. Ironically, I'll have to kill him so he can live forever.

Using my intense hearing, I eavesdrop on the conversations in the front room. Of course, it's not like I'm spying. I could be in there, hearing everything along with them.

I hear Chris say, "I don't want any of it, except the money, and that's only so I can help my mother get out of debt and so I can provide for Calli and me."

"You don't want the house in your name?"

"No. Or the car, . . . or the ashes. You can take them with you."

Crimson says, "Chris, you should hold onto his ashes for when you're ready to deal with his death."

"I already have."

"No, you haven't.

"What do you know?" Chris's tone is full of anger and resentfulness.

"Chris," Crimson's voice drops a level, "have you

forgotten I was there the day your powers emerged, Chris? I was there for you when you voiced your sadness for being written off by your father. I've helped you all along the way and not once have I seen you properly cope with the destroyed relationship between you and your father. Not that you could—you didn't know how. Now that he's dead, you need to let go of the unfulfilled desire to earn back his love."

"That's easier said than done." Chris's tone has quieted, and he sounds calmer. "I wouldn't have made it all those years without you, Crimson. You were my rock. But I don't need to grieve like you think I do."

I hear some footsteps, then Chris's voice saying, "I'll keep this urn right here next to his rock collection."

"I think that's a good idea, Chris," Crimson compliments. "Melvin, have we finished with the details?"

"I'll draw up the papers and use the power of attorney form to process the death certificate for the life insurance policy. This will take a little time, but I'll let you know when everything is switched over in ownership or if I run into any snags."

"Thank you, Melvin," Crimson says. The sounds of the front door opening and closing tell me Melvin has left.

My thoughts turn to Chris. What must he be feeling right now? This must be difficult for him to be in his father's home, now complete with his ashes, having to deal with final arrangements. He's in need of comforting. Yet, so am I. My mind is still reeling from learning about my mission. How will I be able to help him when I need help too?

The bedroom door opens, and Crimson and Chris enter the room.

"How are you feeling, Calli?" she asks.

"Better," I say as Chris sits beside me and takes my

hand in his. "How are you?" I ask Chris.

"Fine." His one-word, brusque answer says otherwise.

Crimson takes a seat on the floor next to the box, sitting cross-legged. "Good. Let's talk a little more about the upcoming mission. Our quantum entanglement allows me access to your thoughts, Calli. However, I cannot tell you exactly what to do or how to do it. I won't be intervening with your life, except on occasion when it's called for. I know you worry about being taken seriously by both the Bearers and the clans." She points to the box beside her. "Those prisms and the quartz stones in the other room will be the key to pulling the clans together. I don't quite know how you'll do that, but I'm not too concerned. You'll figure it out. The Bearers, on the other hand, will take a bit more finessing. I will be having you and Chris meet with the Bearers where you will inform them of the upcoming blast. They need to choose to help you, not be strong-armed into it. As you already know, some of them may not choose wisely. We'll have to wait and see."

"You said while we were at Lake Patoka I should go back to college. How can I do that and pull this whole thing together? And, more importantly, does it even matter now that the world might end?"

"Yes, I want you to go back to college. You can get another year of classes completed and still meet with the different groups during your time off. Staying abreast of medical advancements is vital, Calli. As for the world ending, or possibly ending, I want you to consider something." She pauses and looks as though she's trying to formulate an explanation I'll understand. If I was in her position, that's what I'd be doing.

Chris sits up a little straighter, obviously curious.

"Consider the Cold War. For about forty-five years,

following the end of World War Two, the U.S. lived in fear of being bombed with nuclear warheads from the Russians. At any time, the world could have ended—and believe me, it almost did on more than one occasion. In fact, I began to wonder if I needed to be concerned with the coming Elemental blast at all. Many individuals simply gave up and stopped trying to better their lives with the attitude of 'what's the point?' " She reaches out and lays her hand on my hand. "Let me add that I think it's a normal human trait to feel this way from time to time, so don't feel like I'm scolding you for voicing the same words." She removes her hand from mine. "Even though some people were giving up, my spirits were buoyed by the tenacity of many people who were determined to survive a nuclear blast. They built bomb shelters and stocked them with food and supplies. Their desire to continue living beyond a cataclysmic event gave me hope for humanity. I assigned Maetha to the task of infiltrating the United Nations to find a way to put a halt to the Cold War. But that's a story for another day. My point is, if everyone had given up and given in to what seemed to be the looming end of the world, humanity wouldn't have continued to progress through the decades. Think about the advancements that occurred between the 1940s and 1980s. Those who pressed forward created the life you are now living.

"Calli, the future is difficult to discern at this point. There are too many variables that muddle what I see. The important thing to note is that I do see a future for humanity. Having you spearhead the organization of the clans and unification of the Bearers is the answer. Try not to let the enormity of it go to your head. Just tackle one obstacle at a time, one day at a time. Keep an open mind to possible solutions, staying in line with nature's will, and I guess more than anything, just be yourself. What I don't want you to do is feel like there's no point in moving forward in your life."

I'm feeling much better about the task at hand. I say, "That makes a lot of sense. I have a question though. Why can't I view the future concerning the blast?"

"What exactly are you looking for?"

"Um, the blast," I say, instantly feeling foolish for wording it that way. "I mean, I know I can't see the cosmic energy ray, but I'm looking for the moment when it hits."

"I think as you become more vested in this project, the future will begin to open up to you."

"What do you mean?"

"This mission has just been introduced to you. I don't think you have accepted it yet, therefore, you cannot envision yourself in Portland at the time of the blast. You have to accept your role before you'll be able to see the future."

"Okay."

My phone rings. I reach over to the table by the bed and pick up the phone. The caller ID shows my mother. "Hi, Mom."

"Hello, Calli. I got your message. I wanted to let you know a journalist called yesterday, asking about your diamond."

"Hang on, Mom, I want to put you on speaker so the others here with me can hear." I press the speaker button. "Go ahead Mom."

"Well, as I told Calli, a journalist called about Calli's diamond. I thought you'd want to know about the call."

"What did you tell them?" I ask.

"Nothing, of course," —her voice holds alarm— "not even when he asked detailed questions."

Chris and I exchange worried glances.

I ask, "What did the journalist want to know?"

"He asked if your diamond was a danger to your health or to others around you. I said I didn't know what he was talking about."

Crimson's concern melds with mine. *Ask her for more details, Calli.*

I nod. "Did he tell you his name, Mom?"

"No. After I hung up I realized he didn't even mention a newspaper or magazine."

"What else did he ask you?" I press.

"He asked the same questions a couple times, but in different ways. I think he thought I'd slip up, but he didn't know who he was dealing with. It's my profession to keep patient confidentiality, as you know. So, I pretended he was talking about a diamond engagement ring. I said, 'Wait, are you telling me my daughter is engaged? Why hasn't she told me yet? Why would a ring be a danger to anyone?' He hung up on me after that, which was a relief because my heart was racing, like it is right now just relaying the call."

"You handled it well, Mom."

"Who else knows about your diamond, Calli?"

"A relatively small amount of people, none of whom would call to ask questions."

"Are we going to have to go stay at the cabin again?" my mother worries aloud.

Crimson's voice enters my mind. *No. They will be safe where they are.*

I say, "No, I don't think so. I don't see anything negative in your futures."

"When will you be able to come home for a visit? We miss you, Calli."

"In a couple days. I'll let you know. I love you. Tell Dad I love him."

"We love you, too. Be safe and take care."

Chapter 6 – Created Quartz

After hanging up the phone with my mother, Crimson says, "This is what I was afraid of when we dismantled the compound. Too many individuals knew too much. Even though we stripped the building of evidence, we couldn't strip the minds of all involved. One or more people will need to be dealt with. That's what I have Brand and Beth working on."

"Did you already know this when you assigned them to the task?"

"No. I figured something like this would pop up, though, and we'd need to identify the troublesome individuals. But, I also knew that with the coming cosmic blast, the world of superpowers will be exposed like never before. We won't be able to hide forever. I only hope we can keep Diamond Bearers under the radar."

Chris points out the obvious. "Looks like from that phone call we're not going to be so lucky."

"This is an excellent example of taking issues as they present themselves and finding a way to deal with them. Whoever called your mother knows about the diamonds. That means they are probably from the compound. They are most likely aware of the machine and its capabilities. In addition to learning who called your mother, we need to figure out more of the details concerning the machine and the quartz prisms. While Brand and Beth investigate the employees, I want you and Chris to take the prisms to Don in Miami. Perhaps he'll know more about where these types of quartz are found. I want to learn about the technology used by the machine and why these quartz prisms are integral to how it works." She pauses, then speaks directly to Chris, "Your Uncle Don needs to be told about his brother's death."

The air in the room thickens with tension. Or maybe it's just my own uneasiness, knowing how Crimson feels about Chris's reluctance to grieve.

Chris responds in an upbeat tone. "It will be nice to talk to someone who shares the same feelings as I do toward my father."

"That too," Crimson agrees, and doesn't dwell on the topic. "I will be joining you at Uncle Don's." She turns to me. "I'll let you know when I arrive. Take the flash drive and continue to research the files. Oh, and I don't want you two playing around with those quartz prisms. Got it?"

"Okay," I say with a heavy sigh.

"Chris?" She prods for a response.

"Okay." He sounds like he's guilty of already planning on using one.

"I'll get in touch with Rodger and find out how soon a flight plan can be cleared." She stands. "Pack up, and Calli, turn off your phone."

We don't have to wait long before being able to start the four-hour flight to Miami. Once we're in our seats, Chris says, "What's on your mind?"

A satisfying smile spreads across my face. "I guess that means I've mastered mind-blocking."

"Yes, you have."

I take a deep breath and say, "Things feel surreal to me. Like I'm living a dream. So much new information keeps surfacing. I can't digest the first thing before the next is piled on my plate. Does that make sense?"

"More than you know."

"What's on your mind?" I lean toward him and lay my head on his shoulder.

"Everything. Like you said, before I can grasp a concept, another is added to the stack. The only thing I know for certain is I want to be by your side through it all."

"Good answer, sir!" I kid around, then become a bit more serious. "I feel the same. But, I also know that's not possible in the literal sense. At least when we're apart we can communicate telepathically with each other. Plus, once we learn to bi-locate, the distance between us won't feel so bad."

"Except I won't be able to touch you in your bi-located state . . . but maybe that's for the best."

I lift my head and turn in my seat to face him. "Why?"

"I already told you. I don't want to scare you away by moving too fast."

I rub the back of my neck, trying to squeeze the tension out, wishing I could read his mind to figure out the real reason. "You make it sound like you're a monster or something and you don't want me to find out. If you're so worried about my sexual maturity, why don't we just have sex and get it out of the way?"

"No, that would cause more problems." He clenches his jaw, rippling muscles along his jawbone I wasn't aware could ripple.

"Well, you love me, right? You said that was important to you and you wanted to wait till it felt right."

"I'm not ready and I know you aren't. Besides, with the new information about your mission, the last thing you need is more problems."

"How would you and I becoming closer create more problems?"

"Ask Beth."

The bottom drops out of my stomach and I exhale an exasperated, "What?"

"No, I didn't sleep with Beth. She could help you understand the problems that come from relationships moving to the next level, that's all."

"But I didn't even ask you about . . . are you using a prism? Are you repeating?"

"Why would you think that?"

I jump out of my seat and open the bag containing the prisms. All twelve are there. I turn around to face Chris, only to find him standing directly behind me.

"Don't you trust me, Calli? Would you immediately assume I'm lying instead of doubting your own mind-blocking abilities?"

"But I thought my block was solid. You just told me so. Were you lying about that?" My blood pressure seems to rise. "Is my mind not really blocked and you're using my inability to keep tabs on my thoughts? Who doesn't trust who, Chris?"

He runs his hand through his hair. "This is what I'm talking about, Calli. Neither one of us is ready to move this relationship forward."

"You didn't answer my question."

"I can't give you an answer. Lying or obscuring truth is part of everyday life, especially our lives. Overall, white lies make the world go around. Sometimes we're ordered to lie, like when you carried the diamond. Sometimes we choose to lie to prevent someone from getting their feelings hurt. But, before you go demanding to know what's going on in my mind, whether I'm lying, or can be trusted, think about the situations you've been in and what you know about the world of Diamond Bearers. And please remember that if I've been ordered to lie to you, for whatever reason, I can't disobey."

Why would he have been ordered to lie? "I don't know what to say."

"Don't say anything. Just know I wouldn't do anything to intentionally hurt you. I now know I will never be asked to betray you, like I had to do with Neema, or be put in a position where that would happen. You're far more important than me in this Diamond Bearer game." He takes my hands in his and says in a near-whisper, "And please go easy on me later when your question gets answered."

I exhale and feel a sense of relief, even though I realize I'm being left out of some "plan" involving me. Chris envelops me in a comforting embrace and I return the gesture. "I'm sorry I doubted you, Chris. It's just that your behavior reminded me so much of Brand."

"It's all right. I'd be worried about you if you ever lost your critical eye and attention to detail. That includes scrutinizing me, if it's called for."

We sit back down after grabbing a couple juices from the fridge. I take the laptop out of the bag and turn it on. "I'd better look over this information like Crimson asked. We only have a four-hour flight."

"I'll help you," Chris volunteers.

We arrive in Miami where Crimson is waiting near the hangar with a rental car.

"I'm really curious about her flying, Calli," Chris whispers.

"Ask her about it. You never know, she might give us more details."

"Calli," Crimson says, "Grab the bundle of prisms and put them in your pocket."

"Okay. What about the other documents in the boxes?"

"Leave them on the plane."

Once in the backseat of the car and on our way to Uncle Don's, Chris squeezes my hand and addresses Crimson. "Is the flying power within the Primal Stone, Crimson?"

"Yes." She doesn't take her eyes off the road.

"Is it an Elemental power?"

"Yes. It's rooted in gravity and atmospheric control.

"How fast can you go?" Chris leans forward with his hands on his knees.

"Pretty fast."

I become alarmed because I sense obsidian in my future. "Crimson, I sense trouble. Obsidian."

"I do too," Chris says, after concentrating for a moment. "Wait, Uncle Don wears obsidian on his necklace. Maybe that's what we're sensing."

Crimson pulls the car into Don's driveway and turns the engine off. "We must not ever assume anything," she says. "Always be cautious. Do you have your Runner topazes?" she asks both of us.

"Yes," Chris says, and I nod my head.

"All right. Let's go."

We walk up the perfectly-placed stone walkway and I press the purple gemstone doorbell.

The door opens. Don fills the doorway, wearing a ratty T-shirt that at one time was probably white. One hand holds garden shears and the other is cloaked in an old garden glove. In a flash, my keen eyesight spots a couple thorns dangling from the fabric. Coupled with the floral aroma hitting my nose, I conclude Don is in the middle of trimming roses.

"Hello, Chris. Good to see you again." Don reaches

out and wraps his arms around Chris. I move my head to narrowly miss the shears as they move past my face. Don squeezes Chris in a manly hug, then releases him. Don's eyes shift in my direction momentarily, then move to Crimson.

It's the necklace, Chris confirms in my mind. He says, "Uncle Don, you remember Calli Courtnae." Don nods, but his eyes are still on Crimson. Chris adds, "This is my good friend, Jo Jo."

"Any friend of Chris's is a friend of mine. Come in." Don steps back, opening the door to let us in.

Chris enters Don's house first and glances around the room. "Are you alone, Uncle Don?"

"Yes."

Chris motions for Crimson and me to enter.

As I walk past Uncle Don, he pats my shoulder twice in a kind gesture. My powers rush out, rush in, rush out, rush in. I've never experienced this kind of nauseating on-off sensation before. My healing power is necessary to calm my stomach. I speak to Crimson's mind, *You already knew we didn't have anything to worry about with the obsidian. Am I right?*

Yes. However, I won't always be by your side and you must take your safety seriously. Chris demonstrated proper precautions.

Don closes the front door and mumbles to Chris, "You didn't tell me you'd be bringing a guest."

"Sorry." Chris's bottom jaw moves sideways as he grimaces.

Don leads the way through the house and out onto the back porch where he shows us his rose bushes. His long-stemmed roses are worthy of a gardening magazine. Don sets his shears and gloves on his workbench and says, "I'll be right back. Please, make yourself comfortable." He enters his house.

I look at Chris who stands beside me and shrug my

shoulders. Chris speaks to my mind, *He's not comfortable with strangers.*

I return my focus to the deep red roses in front of me. I reach my hand to caress the velvet petals. A half-opened rose is behind another. I reach into the plant and free the struggling bud from the leaves that seem to be preventing the petals from opening. When I pull my hand out of the bush, thorns snag deep into my forearm, bending the roses in my direction.

Chris lets a pained hiss out of his teeth and reaches to free my arm from the thorns. He pulls my hand toward him to examine my injuries. "That's got to hurt, Calli."

"Actually, no, it doesn't."

He searches my skin for scratches or blood. My hand and arm are completely normal. Chris casts a confused glance at me.

"I guess I'm pretty good with my healing ability." I try to lighten the mood, but I'm just as puzzled.

Uncle Don reappears, wearing a different button-up shirt. He has misaligned the buttons. His hair is wet and freshly combed, indicating he's definitely flustered with Crimson's presence. I wish I could read his mind, but his obsidian piece prevents that from happening.

Don shows Crimson around the yard, giving her the tour of his small open shop where he works with gems and rocks. She asks him a few questions out of politeness, to which he stumbles over his answers and drops two different tools, then trips on a protruding stone slab.

"Oh, watch your step, Jo Jo," Don warns, reaching his arm in her direction.

He likes you, Crimson, I tell her mind.

She doesn't respond. She only throws a "don't encourage it" glance my direction.

Chris interrupts, "Uncle Don, we need your expertise

on something.

"Certainly, Chris. Let's sit down." He motions to the table and chairs on the patio. "Can I get drinks for anyone?"

Crimson says, "I would love a glass of water, Don."

Hearing his name seems to bother him further. He goes inside the house. Chris follows him.

Crimson and I sit down.

"Calli," she says, "pull out one of the quartz prisms."

I reach into my pocket, pull out the bundled prisms, and begin to unwrap the secured crystals. My mind connects with Chris. He's talking to Don in the kitchen.

"Who is she?" Don asks.

"She lives down the street from Mom. She's like me, Uncle Don."

"I figured as much. Chris. I'm sorry about your dad. Even though he was a sociopath, he still didn't deserve to be shot down."

"Oh, I didn't know you'd already heard about him."

"Yeah, I was contacted by an investigator."

"Agent Whitman?"

"Yes. He said you witnessed the shooting."

"I was there. Dad had mixed himself up with some pretty frightening people. He used to tell me, 'You can't scratch the devil's back from a distance.' " Chris mimics his father's voice rather eerily. "Dad got too close to the enemy, and he lost his life. Occupational hazard, I suppose."

Neither speak for a moment, then Don says, "How are you holding up, Chris?"

"I'm good. I've got Calli."

"I'm relieved to hear that. Well, if you ever find yourself in need of a listening ear, don't hesitate to give me a call."

"Thanks."

I can't help but feel guilty for eavesdropping on their conversation. I separate one prism from the rest, rewrap the others, and put them back in my pocket. I look up as they return to the patio with four glasses and a pitcher of ice water. Chris sits adjacent to me and across from Crimson. Uncle Don sits across from me.

I ask Don, "What can you tell us about quartz?" I scoot the prism across the table.

"What do you want to know?" he says, picking up the quartz.

"Everything." I smile after my single-word reply.

"This is a beautifully clear prism, one I'd give my left arm to find in nature. Double terminated." He runs his fingers over the six-sided points at each end. "Perfect faces . . . where did you get this?"

"We found it at General Harding's compound in Denver."

Don twists the crystal between his fingers. "Quartz is silicon dioxide and the most abundant mineral on earth."

Crimson interrupts. "Excuse me, but feldspar is the most abundant."

"Well, technically you're right. Feldspars as a group are more plentiful, but quartz as an individual mineral is the most common. I apologize, Jo Jo. I don't mean to split hairs."

"No apology needed, Don. Please continue," Crimson says, leaning forward in her chair.

"All right. Quartz is resistant to most corrosives and can withstand high temperatures. It outlasts other minerals and filters down through sedimentary layers, filling in gaps. Quartz is found in . . . " he pauses and sets the quartz on the table. "This would be easier if I knew what information you really want. I could go on and on about this subject, but I'm guessing you're here for a specific reason concerning *this* quartz."

Crimson doesn't waste a second. She points to the prism in front of Don and asks, "Where does one find a crystal like that?"

"In a laboratory." Don leans back in his chair, stretching his back.

"Excuse me?"

"That is a manmade quartz, grown in an autoclave—a pressure cooker."

Chris asks, "How can you tell?"

He leans forward and picks up the quartz again. He balances it on one end. "There are no obvious horizontal striations." He drags his fingertip across the short side of the prism several times. "It's too perfect. Plus, if you look closely at this end, you'll see it's chipped where it had to be broken free from the autoclave." Don carefully lays the crystal down on the table once again.

Crimson asks, "Are you certain this quartz is man-made?"

"I'm sure. I've seen rather smooth quartz from Brazil at gemstone conventions but nothing this perfect. From what I've learned, the controlled environment and sped-up growth process that occurs in an autoclave creates crystals like this. The manufacturer can pre-determine the length of the finished crystals by how long they are allowed to grow."

I ask, "Why is quartz grown in labs? It's not like they're valuable or anything. They're not diamonds."

Don says, "Don't be fooled by the inflated price tags on diamonds, Calli. Diamonds aren't as valuable as you might think—well, except for blue diamonds. Those are being grown in labs for their semi-conductor qualities. But I digress. Back to quartz."

I'm stunned to hear him talk about blue diamonds. Crimson says to my mind, *We'll ask him about that later. Let him finish about the quartz.*

He continues. "When sliced at the perfect angle to the crystalline axis, quartz can be used for its piezoelectric properties."

"What do you mean?" I ask.

"Quartz is one of a few minerals that produces a charge or voltage when compressed or bent. Additionally, when a voltage is applied to quartz, the quartz will bend. Not just any quartz can be used for piezoelectricity, though. Only high quality, clear specimens," he picks up the quartz, "like this one." Then he sets it down. "The demand for high-quality quartz in the manufacturing of watches, clocks, and other electronics created the need for lab-grown crystals."

Chris squeezes his eyes shut in frustration. "You've lost me with the pie-zee-oh-whatever stuff."

"Pie-eezo-electric, Chris."

"Whatever. How is it used?"

"Timepieces, for one. Watches, clocks, and timers usually have a quartz crystal inside which maintains a steady megahertz, keeping accurate time without one having to wind the watch. My question is: What's the deal with that particular quartz?" He points, but doesn't touch the quartz. "Why do I feel strange when I hold it?"

Crimson says, "This quartz has an electric charge."

"But it's not being hit with voltage."

"Not any longer. It was being used in a machine that removes cosmic powers from individuals."

"What kind of a machine?"

"We're not entirely sure," Crimson says. She pulls a couple papers out of her bag which have schematics about the machine. "This is what it looks like."

Don takes the papers and looks them over thoroughly. "Who is the manufacturer?"

"We don't know yet." Crimson pours more water into her glass.

"Did the machine work? Did it do its job?"

"Yes."

"I'm intrigued with this, Jo Jo. I'll do some research tonight and see what I can come up with."

Chris clears his throat. "Uncle Don, would we be able to spend the night here?"

"Sure, well, if you don't mind sleeping on the couch."

Crimson says, "You don't have to worry about me, Don."

Disappointment washes over his face. "Oh, do you need to leave?"

"I have other things I can work on through the night."

"All right, then. Calli, you can have my bed. Chris can take the couch." He looks at Chris and says, "Your mother would have my hide if she knew I put you two in the same room before you're married."

My eyes shoot to the floor, not wanting to look at Chris.

"Don't worry about it, Uncle Don," Chris says. "The last thing I want is for you to be in trouble with my mom."

When morning arrives, we're about to leave when Chris stops and turns around to Uncle Don. "Oh, I almost forgot." He digs deep into his pocket and pulls out what looks like a topaz. "When we were here before, you said you wanted an Imperial topaz. I have one for you. It's charged with healing."

Uncle Don's eyes mist over, making me feel like I'm

intruding on a personal bonding moment. He whispers, "Thank you, Chris."

"The topaz on the necklace you gave Calli saved her life. I figured it was the least I could do to thank you."

Don clears his throat. "Healing, huh? So, how do I use it?"

Chris eyes Don's hand and points to an obvious thorn scratch from yesterday's pruning. "In your mind, think about your scratch healing. Make it heal."

I am amazed with how easily Don is to be able to heal his minor injury, and how thrilled he becomes. I'd forgotten how excited I felt the first time I used the power.

Chapter 7 – They Are Among Us

We say goodbye to Don and leave. Crimson escorts us to the airport and to Maetha's waiting airplane. Before Chris and I climb out of the car, Crimson says, "Calli, give me the prisms. I'll keep them safe until you're ready to meet with the clans."

I obediently pull the small bundle from my pocket and hand them over the back of the seat. We say our goodbyes and get out of the car. Rodger Rutherfield waits next to the stairs to the plane. The light breeze brings the smell of Rodger's cologne to my nose. I identify the scent as the same one my father wears.

"Ms. Courtnae, Mr. Harding," Rodger greets us and shakes our hands.

"Captain Rutherfield, good to see you again," Chris says.

"Please, call me Rodger."

We board the plane and take our seats, fasten our belts, and wait for clearance to depart. Chris and I sit quietly. After a few minutes, Rodger's deep smooth voice sounds through the speakers. "We're cleared for takeoff. Seatbelts, please."

The plane accelerates down the runway.

In the short time of silence, I realize I miss Chris's identifying scent of wood and citrus. That's the downside of him being Unaltered. Maybe I'll send his jacket away to a perfumery and have them create a scent for me. But that would mean parting with the jacket. Not a chance!

I liked being around the other Diamond Bearers at the gathering and not having my senses assaulted by individual aromas. I wonder if this overload of smell bothers Hunters. Perhaps it's normal to them. I personally don't like the Hunters' powers. My vision is too erratic. It's like I have an uncontrollable digital-zoom feature on my eyeballs. For instance, I'm looking at Chris's profile and my eyes instantly zero in on his jaw line. I can see each individual hair of his two-day beard growth. My vision tightens and I see the ends of each bristle and the slight angle the razor left from the previous shave. I find it interesting how his beard hairs are not all the same color and how thick they look—like tree trunks with crooked cuts. I look away from his face, suppress the excitement that builds in my stomach, and turn my attention to the small window to my right. I close my eyes, afraid the view of the ground that's moving farther away may rush up at me. Why haven't I noticed the full extent of the hunting power before now? I wasn't aware they had such incredible vision.

Crimson's voice soothes my mind. *Calli, you're relaxed enough for the sensory powers to consume your mind. They aren't stronger today than yesterday, you're just more focused on them. The last few days were spent toiling and stressing, worrying about Chris, and so on. This peaceful moment will change soon enough.*

I don't know if that's a good thing or not, I respond.

As a Bearer, and my liaison, you'll find you don't have many boring moments in your life. In fact, you'll come to treasure moments like this one.

I guess I should appreciate the calm then.

Yes. On a different note, you can go ahead and heal the scar on your chest from where the diamond entered your heart. The only reason you had the scar was for your parents' sake, and now they know you have a diamond.

I focus my thoughts on my chest and will my scar to heal. A scratchy sensation causes my chest to itch. Without thinking, I reach up and scratch my sternum. I feel different now that my original shard is gone and I have a full diamond in my heart. However, I miss the connection to Jonas. I don't miss the excruciating pain of the movements of the shard. The Blue Diamond doesn't irritate my heart like the other shard did.

"What are you doing? Are you in pain?" Chris asks.

"No, Crimson told me to heal my scar. It kind of tickles and itches." I put my hand back down on my lap. I change the subject to get his attention off my chest. "So, when will you take me on a date?"

"Soon."

"Better be. We're going to be parting ways soon."

"But not forever."

"That's what you think, buddy," I tease.

He changes the subject. "Calli, I've been trying to view the future, using the diamond, but I can't seem to figure out how to do it. So far, all I'm getting is random snippets of other people's futures. I don't seem to have any control. I'm worried I won't be able to keep an eye out for danger."

"Well, that's not good. What I've learned is to look for a specific thing or person. If you try to view something too detailed, you'll just see a jumbled mess."

"How were you able to see the future when you first carried the diamond?"

I discuss with him the process I went through to try to figure out how to save his life. How I tried different scenarios and experiments. I'm about to say more when I hear Maetha's voice in my mind.

She says, *Something important has come up. We need to communicate as a group. If you and Chris focus on my diamond, you should be able to hear and participate in the discussion.*

What's going on? I ask.

Focus on my diamond, Calli.

I look at Chris to see if he got the message too.

Apparently, he did. He takes my hand in his and lays his head back on the seat and closes his eyes. I do the same and focus on Maetha's diamond.

Mary's voice takes charge. *Jonas has discovered an Internet blog revealing detailed information about the clans. The blog recommends everyone wear obsidian. I can't use my Seer ability to determine who's behind this. The blogger must be using obsidian.*

Chuang asks, *Has someone used a topaz powered with future sight to see who it is?*

Not even the Imperial topaz holds a strong enough charge to see the details, Mary says.

What is the blog called? asks Alena.

Jonas says, *They are among us—all one word—dot anonymousblog dot com.*

Who would be doing this? Duncan asks.

Mary says, *Based on the information, it has to be someone from General Harding's compound.*

I've assigned the Repeater to investigate the compound workers, Maetha says, even though it was Crimson who asked Brand.

Jonas says, *Whoever is writing this has incomplete information and comes across as being a paranoid alarmist. The comments are great. 'Got a tinfoil hat?' and 'My ex ran pretty fast after I caught him cheating.'*

Merlin says, *I found it. Looks pretty amateurish. Actually, the design choice looks female to me. The colors don't scream male-designed.*

Jonas responds, *That doesn't mean anything, just that maybe a female designed the blog for the author.*

Maybe there's more than one person operating it, Merlin suggests.

Jie Wen says, *The whole thing comes across as silly, in my opinion. No one will take this seriously. I don't think this is anything to worry about.*

I'll keep my eye on it for updates, Jonas says. *Right now the blog doesn't have a rank with the search engines.*

The what? Kookju scoffs. I can almost imagine his facial expression.

Search engines, you know, Google.

Merlin says, *The blog has comments. That means people are seeing it.*

I speak up. *Maetha, let Brand know to look for any connection to the blog when he investigates. Jonas, are you concerned with your IP address showing up on the blogger's stats? What will it reveal?*

Maetha jumps in. *It's set up in Miami, Calli. Besides, he's masking his identity.*

What's an IP address? Chuang asks.

Seriously? Jonas sounds frustrated. *Have you guys been living in a cave? It's the identifying address of the internet provider your computer connects with.*

Before anyone can comment on Jonas's insult, I quickly ask, *Are you able to look up who registered the blog?*

I already looked. It's not specific. A lot of these free blog sites are like that.

What's the name of the site again?

Actually, Jonas says, *I don't think it's a good idea for everyone to be looking at this site. This could be a calculated effort to locate people with powers. Keep that in mind.*

Do you think the government is behind this, Merlin? Amenemhet asks.

Highly unlikely. But if this site gains enough traction, the government will take notice.

Jonas adds, *If any of you want to see this site, bi-locate to me and I'll show it to you. The fewer IP addresses showing up on their reports, the better.*

All right. I believe we're done for now, Maetha states.

I open my eyes and glance over at Chris. My insides

are twisted when I see his self-deprecating expression. "That blog has information I've fed my father over the years."

"You don't know that." I try to calm his mind. "Your father was studying the clans before your power emerged. Stop beating yourself up." I sit forward in my seat. "Who do you think is behind the blog?"

"Whoever it is, they're divulging classified information. They'll be in big trouble when Agent Whitman catches them."

Crimson's voice enters my mind. *Calli, I want you to return to Brand and Beth and help them with this investigation. Chris, continue to the Pentagon. Merlin has found you a job.*

I look at Chris and motion to my ear to see if he's hearing Crimson too. He nods.

She continues. *Several of the compound employees are working at the Pentagon as well. You can investigate from inside the government.*

I ask, *Crimson, what do you see in the future concerning this blog?*

I'm keeping my focus on the long-range outlook. The future is still optimistic.

◈ ◈ ◈

We arrive outside my parents' home. I'm shocked to see my Mini Cooper parked in the driveway. Maetha must have had something to do with my car being returned.

"Nice Mini," Chris says and whistles appreciatively.

"Thanks. It's mine."

Chris walks all the way around the car, peering inside. "Is this the 228 model?"

I shrug my shoulders. "It's fast and fun to drive. That's all I know. I'm not a car enthusiast."

He finishes his inspection and joins me by my side. "Calli, do you think your parents will like me?"

"It doesn't matter, Chris. I like you and that's what counts." Truth be told, I'm not sure which of my parents will give Chris a harder time. I didn't want to alarm him, but I know my parents aren't going to go easy on him. His age will certainly be an issue with both of them. But they don't understand that in the scope of things, our age difference is nothing.

We enter through the front door. My mother's voice is on the air from the direction of the kitchen. "This is Dr. Charlotte Courtnae. Yes, he's a patient of mine." She's obviously on the phone.

I take Chris's hand in mine and escort him toward my mother's voice. His reluctant feet slow our progress. Without warning, he yanks on my hand, causing me to spin around and crash into his chest. He steals a kiss . . . well, as much as can be stolen, before I melt into his arms.

After a few moments, he pulls his lips away from mine and whispers, "Had to get one last kiss, just in case they ban me from seeing you."

"They're not going to do that."

My mother's voice startles me. "Calli? I didn't hear you come in."

Chris pushes me away from his embrace, as if we've been caught red-handed. I have to admit, I'm a little confused with his behavior. I walk forward and hug my mother. Right off, I see her iridescent aura, like mine.

"Hi, where's Dad?"

"He was on call last night. He'll be here shortly." She holds me out at arm's length and smiles. "You look healthy and happy."

"I am."

"Are you going to introduce me?" She glances beyond

me to Chris.

"Yeah. Mom, this is Chris Harding. Chris, my mom, Charlotte Courtnae."

They shake hands and resume their comfortable distance. My mother's mind is easy to read: *He's so old! Is this the boy Brand Safferson said would be our son-in-law?* She asks, "Where are you from, Chris?"

"Kansas."

"What do you do?"

I raise a hand and step between them. "Mom, come on, we just got here. Can we wait to do this drill till Dad gets here?"

"Of course, dear," she says, forcing a smile. "Come in and sit down. Have you had breakfast?"

"We've eaten, Mom."

"How about something to drink?"

Chris clears his throat. "I'll take a glass of water, please."

I nearly laugh out loud. *Poor guy.*

His thoughts enter mine: *Quit laughing at me.*

I wasn't.

You were going to.

"So, Chris," my mother says as she hands him a glass of water, "how did you and Calli meet?"

Do you think she'll take it well if I said I saw you in a vision? he teases.

Probably not.

"I met Calli when she came to the Montana facility."

"Oh, and have you kept in contact with her over the last three years?"

"No, we met up again a couple weeks ago."

He's only known her a few weeks? Oh dear. She turns her attention to me. "Have you had any troubles or problems from your appendicitis surgery?"

"I'm healed, Mom. I was healed before I left the cabin with Duncan."

"You sure had us worried, Calli. I still worry."

"I know. I'm glad you do."

The back door opens and my father walks in. He deposits his overcoat and briefcase on the bench by the door and heads directly to the sink to wash his hands. I've watched him do this same routine every night for years. With all the washings he does all day long, I wonder why he has any skin left on his hands. I read his mind as he walks toward Chris. *He looks strong, protective.*

Chris stands and reaches his hand out.

I stand as well. "Dad, this is Chris Harding. Chris, Allan Courtnae."

"Nice to meet you, sir," Chris says, clasping my father's hand firmly.

Good firm grip. Confident. Arrogant? Dad's mental assessment continues.

"Likewise." My father looks at me, gives me a hug, then searches my eyes with his pointed gaze. "How are you doing? And don't tell me you're fine."

"I'm doing well, Dad. I've healed completely and don't think I lost many brain cells."

"Good to hear." He tenderly pats my back and indicates for us to sit back down. "Tell me about yourself, Chris."

Oh boy, here we go, thinks Chris.

I feel his inward grimace.

"What would you like to know?"

My father gently coaxes him. "What do *you think* we'd want to know about the man who's dating our daughter?"

"Um, I grew up in Kansas. My father is a . . . was an Army general. He taught me how to work hard and with conviction." Chris pauses momentarily. "My mother taught me how to respect women, cook, and clean up after myself. I love your daughter, sir, and will do anything to protect and care for her."

My parents share an impressed look between each other.

Chris says, "I don't really know what else to say."

My dad asks, "How well do you know my daughter?"

"Sir?"

Dad looks at me. "Is Chris like you?"

"Yes. We met at the Montana compound." I withhold the fact Chris also has a diamond. "Chris knows everything about me." I place my hand over my heart.

Both my parents nod their heads in acknowledgment of my secret message. I feel it's good to practice not saying the word "diamond", even when around my parents, from here on out.

My mother asks, "Did you graduate from college, Chris?"

"No, ma'am. I never attended college."

"Well then, what do you do for a living?"

"I uh, I—" Chris pleads with his eyes for me to rescue him.

I take pity on him. "He's in-between jobs right now, Mom."

"Yes. I'm about to begin a new job at the Pentagon."

"The Pentagon." My father's eyebrows raise, and he nods his head respectfully.

My mother prods the college issue further. "Well, do you plan on attending college?"

"Yes, I would like to."

My father jokes, "Why don't you just have Calli look into the future to see if you will?"

"Dad," I beg, hoping he'll lay off Chris.

"Well, son, it sounds as though you've been taught

well, you've got good intentions, and my daughter obviously adores you."

"Yes, sir."

My dad settles back in his chair.

My mom jumps back in as he backs off. "Calli, how's Brand? Do you see him much?"

Really, Mom? "He's fine. I've been with him for the last several weeks."

"You mean, during the time when we thought you were with Janice Johnson?"

"Yes."

"He's such a sweet boy." *And he's your age, not an older man preying on young girls.*

"Mom, you know I can hear your thoughts, right?" If she only knew Brand used to be the one to avoid.

Her hand flies to her mouth as she gasps.

I try to calm my mind before I continue. "My powers are something you may never understand. I know that. But give me some credit here." I really hope Chris didn't hear her thoughts.

"I'm sorry, Calli. I worry. We've given you every opportunity to succeed in life. I just don't want you to miss out on securing your future." *I don't want you taken advantage of, either.*

"Mom!" I angle my head toward Chris and throw a stern glare at her. "Your thoughts are not private."

Her eyes widen, even though she doesn't fully understand what I mean.

My father asks, "Calli, you are still planning on attending college, aren't you?"

"Yes."

"Okay. I was worried with all the excitement you'd feel you didn't have time for it. Classes start soon."

"Yeah, I know.

"Calli," my father asks carefully, "as I understand it, you can see the future. Can I ask you a question" I nod my head. "When you view the future, how do you know you're really seeing the future, and not just coincidences? What I mean is, sometimes I can envision how something will turn out, but it's nothing more than a 50/50 guess."

"Reading the future is tricky, Dad. However, when a vision of the future comes to me, it's pretty clear I'm seeing the future. Like, for instance, your phone is about to ring. It's the hospital, calling about the last patient you admitted just before you ended your shift."

He chuckles. "My phone always rings, and it's always the hospital." Right on cue, his phone rings. He tries to hide his amazement. Glancing down at the screen and accepting the call, his mind says, *Huh, it's the hospital.* "This is Dr. Courtnae. Yes, increase dosage to seventy-five milligrams. Thank you." He ends the call and looks over at me. "All right Calli, that was almost believable, but not quite. As I drove home, I figured they would call for an increased dosage. Does that mean I can see the future, too?"

I see his point. "Okay, how about this. Tomorrow night at 6:42 it will start raining hard. You two will be on your way to the symphony and Mom will wish she'd brought a better coat. Make sure you look at the clock when the downpour hits. 6:42. Unless, of course, you think I might be on the roof of the car dumping buckets of water on you."

"We'll see, now won't we?" My father smiles. "Even though our plans for tomorrow are posted on the calendar on the fridge, and you could have checked the weather to see if it would rain tomorrow, guessing the exact time the downpour will hit our car is pretty specific."

"Well, I guess we'll just have to wait and see." I smile.

My father changes his line of questions. "How do you use your power of healing? What are you able to do?"

"It's not so much what I'm able to do, as much as it is what I should or shouldn't do."

"Well, in what ways have you used the power?"

Chris scoots forward in his seat, with a glimmer of excitement in his eyes. "The first time I witnessed her using the power was to extract two bullets from fellow Runners' bodies with her mind. That was the most incredible thing to see."

Both my parents' eyes widen with disbelief and the inability to comprehend. I know all too well their minds are deep-seated in scientific fact, and my healing ability doesn't fall in that range.

Chris takes my hand. His voice drops. "Another time, she healed my broken legs and infused me with strength."

I'm feeling quite uncomfortable. I don't like being bragged about, because I don't feel what I did was extraordinary. Anyone with a diamond could have done what I did. I ask, "Can we change the subject?"

"This is fascinating, Calli," my dad says. "I wish I could experience it or even have that power."

"You actually do, Dad. Only it's not as strong. How many times have you guessed correctly about a diagnosis before the results came back?"

"That's just learning and training."

"Next time you're examining a new patient, analyze what you're feeling. You may find your gut instinct is speaking more than your knowledge."

"I'll do that."

We go on to talk about my mother's patients over the years who were most likely people with powers. She hasn't wanted to believe in the possibility of supernatural powers. But now that I have the abilities, she says she'll be more aware.

She says, "I still can't believe Charles Rhondell is dead, and that you witnessed the shooting."

"Chris was there as well." I nod my head in his direction.

"Oh my. You two have been through a lot together." She continues in her thoughts, *I hope she doesn't think experiencing crisis and leaning on one another for support equals love. Those types of relationships don't last.*

I purse my lips together, biting my tongue, then change the subject. "The little girl, Sasha, was a Mind-Reader. She was afraid of the Shadow Demons in the dark. She had every right to be afraid."

"Oh dear. Good thing I didn't encourage her mother to take her outside."

Chris says, "The Demons are gone now. Calli figured out how to kill them."

"Not exactly, Chris. They're still there, I just took their power."

My parents glance at each other with confused expressions.

I glance at the clock on the wall. "Oh, wow, look at the time. I need to get a few things from my room and then we've got to go."

I run upstairs and grab the items I wanted to pick up, mostly clothing, then come down and meet everyone outside. After dumping my things in the backseat of my car, I give my mom a hug and say, "If the journalist calls back, asking about you-know-what, please let me know as soon as you can."

"I will."

I hug my dad. My parents give Chris a cordial goodbye with handshakes and partial hugs.

My father says, "It was nice to meet you, Chris. Please take care of our daughter."

"I will."

Chapter 8 – Working Out the Kinks

I drive away, my parents framed in the rear-view mirror, and let out an exhausted huff. "That went well."

"Your mom doesn't think very highly of me."

"You heard that, huh? Thanks for not saying anything."

"It wasn't my place. Besides, I probably won't go so easy on the first guy who comes knocking for our daughter."

His casual mention of "our daughter" brings the sensation of butterflies swarming in my stomach.

Jonas connects with my mind. *Calli, I need to talk to you. Give me a second to pull over.*

I slow the car down and turn into a large parking lot.

"What's going on," Chris asks.

"Jonas needs to talk," I say, as I stop the car and turn it off.

"Why didn't he speak to both of us? Why only you?"

The jealous tone in Chris's voice doesn't go unnoticed by me. "I don't know, Chris."

Before Chris can respond, Jonas bi-locates to the tiny space between us. At the same time, Mary appears in the backseat.

Jonas says, "Oh, good. I caught you before you rented the car, Chris. With my web searches and the help of Mary, I found out you two are still persons of interest in Tennessee. However, don't panic just yet. The authorities are looking for the wrong people. They've *conveniently* been given a tip pointing them in the wrong direction. So that's the good news. The not-so-good news is the future shows you will be outed as the two on the surveillance video from the truck stop/gas station."

Chris says, "I haven't been able to see anything about it."

"I know," Jonas says. "Me neither. But Mary said she's foreseen you being questioned."

Mary leans forward. "It's true, Chris. I don't know how far in the future the questioning takes place. Maetha says once you get to the Pentagon you should try to hold a few interrogations of former compound workers before everything escalates."

"Okay, thanks," Chris says.

Jonas holds his hands up in front of him. "Wait, there's more bad news. Calli, your name is on the TSA's no-fly list."

"What?"

"You boarded a flight bound for New York but disappeared before the plane landed. The Transportation Security Administration gets a little freaked out when something like this happens."

Chris looks over at me with parted lips.

I'll tell you about it later, Chris.

Jonas continues. "I don't know how you did it, but you and Janice Johnson are flagged."

"How can that be? I've been flying around on Maetha's jet since then and haven't been caught."

"All those flights were within U.S. airspace. Private planes don't have to submit a flight manifest for flights departing and arriving in U.S. airspace, so the TSA didn't know you were flying. Now, if you'd tried to fly to Bermuda that would have been another story."

"Well, I don't plan on taking any commercial flights anywhere, Jonas."

"At least not until I can get your name removed from

the list."

"You can do that?" I ask.

"I have high hopes."

Mary sighs. "Things were so much easier before technological advancements."

"I bet," I say. "Jonas, don't break your back over this. Crimson advised me to avoid public transportation."

"Yeah, but if you ever plan on flying to this island, your name will have to be put on the manifest."

"Work your magic, Jonas."

"Anything for you, Calli." Jonas and Mary vanish.

I stare into the space between Chris and me, then meet Chris's stormy eyes.

He repeats Jonas's last statement. "Anything for you, Calli?"

"What can I say? He's a fan." I try to downplay the comment to help dissipate the dark clouds of suspicion that have formed over Chris. I turn the car on and maneuver back into traffic.

We arrive at the car rental store. I accompany Chris inside and wait with him. An uneasy feeling settles in my gut as I realize we are about to head in different directions. I don't want the last thing on Chris's mind to be doubts about my feelings for him, so I say to his mind, *I don't want you to go. I've been dreading this moment, Chris.*

Me too.

I've gotten used to being with you over the last little while. I playfully bump him with my shoulder. *I think I might have developed a severe crush on you.*

"Next," the rental associate hollers.

Chris moves forward to the desk while saying to me, *A crush? Do crushes say 'love you?'* He looks at me and smiles, then sets his ID and credit card on the counter. "I'd like to rent a car."

❖ ❖ ❖

Chris drives away in his "grandma car" as he called it, heading back to the Pentagon. I feel like a huge piece of me is leaving. I keep his taillights in view, wishing he'd turn around and come back, knowing he can't. I miss him already.

Crimson addresses me. *Calli, you should run to Denver instead of driving. You'll get there faster.*

I'm not going to fly in the plane this time?

No. Maetha needs it.

Why didn't Chris run back to D.C.? Wouldn't that have been faster, too?

Chris is heading into denser population where it would be more difficult to stay out of sight. In the end, his trip would take twice as long if he ran. You on the other hand are heading toward less and less population.

Oh. Should I take my car back home?

Yes. There should be a running suit in your bag from Maetha.

I turn the car around and drive home, passing the mall where Suz and I used to go watch people. I wonder what Suz is up to. Discovering Suz's betrayal was the first time I learned something about my life was not as I'd thought. Boy, I sure have topped that experience many times over. Now, if I were to find out someone pretended to be my friend because of feeling guilty, I'd laugh it off.

My world has become so much larger and more complex.

When I arrive at home, I find my parents have left. I call my mother's cell phone and leave a message, letting her know I decided to take other transportation and have parked my car at home.

After changing into my Runner's suit, I begin my solo run to Brand and Beth. Having a full diamond in my heart allows me to run even faster than before. Exhilarating! At this speed, I'd have worn friction holes in my jeans in no time.

As I run, my mind thinks back to the day at General Harding's compound when Clara Winter was brought in with Beth's brother. The two guards from the truck were wearing vests with quartz and obsidian. *Of course,* I think, *they might be the guys responsible for the blog.* Who are they? Where are they? Are they also the murderers of Beth and Anika's parents?

As I run, I use my future sight to keep an eye out for situations where someone might see me pass by, like what Duncan did when we ran to Martha's Vineyard. Some of the time I slow down to a jogging pace to keep my disguise as a regular runner and to avoid raising alarms. After everything I've gone through in the last month, I don't want to bring the government's attention back to the Diamond Bearers or the clans.

I run for about three hours, then have an "ah-ha" moment and come to a halt in a farmer's field. *I can appear freakin' invisible!* Why am I wasting time running slowly? I look around to make sure no one is nearby, then activate my invisibility and take off running.

Sometimes I forget how many powers I have. I guess because I've been a regular human longer than I've had a diamond, my brain isn't used to utilizing my abilities. I'm still doing things the hard way.

I stop somewhere in eastern Nebraska after the sun goes down. I notice altered Shadow Demons following me. At first, I'm alarmed. They look like zombies. No longer the leathery demon-animals as before. They aren't dangerous, but they seem to be drawn to me when before they'd move out of the way.

Interesting.

I take off running again and a while later arrive at the Denver house, invisibly. I'm about to connect with Beth's mind when I notice the same Demons from Nebraska. At least some of them are the same. *Why are they following me?*

I send my thoughts to Brand. *Hey, can you let me in the back door? I need to keep invisible. Be careful, there's altered Shadow Demons out here.*

He opens the door and cautiously steps out on the lighted porch to allow me time to enter. Then he steps back inside.

I stop being invisible in their eyes and materialize in front of Brand, Beth, and Anika. Brand wraps his arms around my body and hugs me right off the floor.

"Calli—you can go invisible?" Beth exclaims.

Brand lets go and I face Beth and Anika, who both have open mouths. I put my finger to my mouth. "Crimson wants this to remain a secret. Can you keep my ability a secret?"

"Mmm hmm." Anika and Beth nod their heads together.

Brand asks, "Can you control minds, too?"

"A bit."

Beth clears her throat. "Did you run here?"

"Yeah, from Ohio."

"Calli told me there are Shadow Demons out there," Brand says, pointing to the door.

I nod. "They're altered from the obsidian, but they are here. They seem to be following me."

Anika says, "That's weird."

"I just checked. We're safe," Brand assures everyone.

Beth points out, "Yeah, but you're Unaltered now. They wouldn't want you anyway."

"I know. That's why I took you with me." He grins wide, exposing his teeth.

"Where's Chris?" Beth asks.

"He's back east." I turn to Anika. "How are you doing?"

"Good. I got here earlier today."

She seems to be emotionally solid. "How are your grandparents doing since the funeral?"

"I helped them heal as much as I could. The rest is up to God."

I nod my head, not really knowing how to respond to her. Turning to Beth, I ask, "What do you guys have so far?"

"We've kind of hit a brick wall. We've interviewed everyone on the list living in Colorado, but several are gone or moved."

"Chris is going to interview some who transferred to work at the Pentagon. I thought about something on my way here. There were two guards—" I explain what I saw when the prisoners were delivered to the compound.

Anika puts a few papers in front of me. "Here's the list of people on the payroll we couldn't find. I should point out that Agent Alpha, or Freedom, *wasn't* on the payroll."

Brand and Beth stare at me with question in their eyes. I quickly surmise these three have been speculating about the seemingly endless stream of money the Bearers apparently have. I ask Anika, "What's your point?"

The three of them share glances with each other. Then Brand says, "Where do the Diamond Bearers get their money? I mean, flying that jet is several tens of thousands of dollars each trip. The jet itself is probably worth many millions of dollars."

"I can't believe you guys are worried about where the money comes from," I chastise them. Although, I can't say I haven't wondered, too. "These people have been around for centuries—some for thousands of years. They've amassed gold, silver, jewels, antiques, you name it. If you three choose to be Bearers, you can start collecting stuff too. I bet your Hot Wheels collection will be worth a pretty penny someday, Brand. Same goes for you two," I point to Beth and Anika. "Hang onto your treasures and someday they'll fund *your* flights across the nation."

Anika says, "I noticed on the Internet that some items from the times of Alexander the Great were 'found' recently." She uses air quotes. "Do you think maybe one of the Bearers staged a significant find to be able to cash in?"

"Anything's possible, Anika."

Anika takes a different stance. Her body straightens, and her chin rises a little. "If they have that much money collectively, they should be using it to help the hungry children in other countries. Not flying everywhere when they can drive or just run."

I'm floored by Anika's statement. Is she implying I've caused many children to starve to death because of all my recent flying in Maetha's plane? I don't quite know how to respond. I say, "Someday, when you're a Bearer, you can run everywhere you go and use your money how you see fit."

Beth scratches her neck in an uncomfortable way. I read her mind.

I'm so glad you're here, Calli. Since she arrived, Anika has been on her soapbox trying to straighten out the world. I don't think I can keep my tongue under control much longer.

I smile at Beth and address everyone. "Are you guys aware of the blog about powers?"

"No," Brand and Beth say together.

I tell them what I know and that Jonas is monitoring the activity.

Remembering what Crimson told me about uniting the clans, I ask Beth, "Do you know how the clans feel about me and the amulets?"

"They still believe you stole the amulets and killed their leaders. I've tried to explain as much as I can without giving too much away . . . you know, Diamond Bearers, Crimson, and everything else."

"I appreciate your attempts, Beth. Don't be sorry."

Beth adds, "Clara believes me. She told me she knew you ended up with a diamond shard in your heart, so it made sense to her that you'd end up with the rest of the shards. I think she's the sole reason the clans aren't hunting you."

Brand interrupts with a rather abrupt change in his tone of voice. "Okay, I just gotta ask, Calli. Why doesn't Crimson step in and straighten everything out?"

"Because that's not how she works."

"But she could do it."

"In order for her to straighten everything out, she'd have to reveal how she knows I didn't steal the amulets. She'd have to reveal herself."

"Yeah, but you're going to have to do the same thing."

"I'm not Crimson. If I'm hunted down after exposing myself, it won't be as big of a deal as if she was sought after. Remember, the clans know the powers within the diamond are similar to the known powers that already exist. Crimson's powers are so much more."

Anika says, rather confidently, "The reason Crimson can't intervene is she can't outdo God. Her limitations are set, and she knows it."

"Perhaps, perhaps not." I decide not to confirm or deny Anika's beliefs as I don't know myself. She has the right to believe what she wants.

"There's no perhaps about it, Calli. God's ways are higher."

Brand jumps forward to confront her. I have a hunch

this isn't their first conversation on this topic. "We're not talking about God right now. We're talking about Crimson, Anika."

I raise my hands in front of my body to try to calm the escalating situation. "Look, the better answer here is Crimson has foreseen that I will straighten out the quarreling amongst the clans and unite them for a bigger purpose."

Brand responds, "You should have led with that statement, Calli. What's the bigger purpose?"

"A cosmic energy blast is going to hit in a couple years and potentially cause a lot of damage. The clans need to be united to help out."

"See," Anika beams. "Crimson bends to God's will."

Brand practically explodes. "How can you still believe in a god when you have all this evidence there can't be one?"

"This evidence proves to me there *is* a god." Anika folds her arms across her chest.

"If there is, why does he let all those kids starve to death every day? Why did he let your parents get killed? And don't tell me it was His will!"

I glare at Brand, shaking my head as Anika bursts into tears.

He turns to me and says, "Sorry, I have a short fuse today."

The room spins wildly around me and I find myself at the point in the conversation where Brand says, "Okay, I just gotta ask . . ." he changes directions with his question, "who else is starving?"

"We just ate a couple hours ago, Brand," Beth exclaims.

I'm still hungry. I say, "I could go for some food."

"There's some leftovers in the fridge," Anika says.

"Come on, Calli." Brand motions for me to follow. Once we're in the kitchen, he whispers, "I'm so glad you're here." Then, rather unexpectedly, he wraps his arms around me and hugs me tight. I hug him back.

"Thanks. You know there's no other place I'd rather be." I'm kidding, of course.

"Whatever." Brand lets go, obviously picking up on my disingenuous tone, and opens the fridge. "The only good thing with this arrangement is Anika's an excellent cook. She made a killer dinner."

I touch his arm and ask, "How's Beth doing?"

He lowers his voice. "She's not talking about her parents. She didn't go to the funeral or wake or whatever service was held."

"Well, just keep giving her your support. She'll get through it, eventually."

As Brand and I dish up potatoes and chicken gravy, I realize I miss hanging out with him. He's really fun and witty. Never a dull moment. As he plops some cold gravy that jiggles more like Jell-O on my plate, I say, "I really am glad I'm here, Brand."

"You might want to reserve judgment for a couple more days."

"How are you doing?"

"Fine," he says. "Why do you ask?"

"Well, you know, after being a part of Freedom's death, and Suz not working out, I just wondered how you're doing."

"That was so long ago, Calli. I'm over it."

I have to remind myself what it's like inside his head. Even though the events took place only a couple weeks ago, in Brand's mind it might as well have been years ago.

I change the subject. "How is your quartz working?"

"Exactly the same as before. My repeats are spot-on

and I can still take people with me, obviously."

"I hope the power lasts forever."

"Me too. I'm thinking of having the quartz inserted under my skin."

"Really?"

"Yeah, I'm afraid of losing it."

"But you were so willing to part with your power at General Harding's," I say.

"I know. I didn't want the ability any more. But then I realized if the power was going to be stored in the quartz, I'd better be the one to guard it so the wrong hands don't get hold of it." He pauses for a moment, then says, "I'm immune to obsidian, Calli."

I contemplate his words for a moment while my food warms up in the microwave. Brand is right. If someone with the wrong intentions stole his quartz, the results could be catastrophic, especially if obsidian cannot cancel the power. Not many people know his repeating power is contained in the crystal. I think it's a good idea to keep it that way.

"I think you made a good choice, Brand." I pause, then say, "What's going on with Anika? She's changed."

"I don't know. She's been like that since she got here."

"Well, try to be patient with her. She's been through a lot."

"We all have, Calli."

After we eat our food and clean up after ourselves, Brand says, "Before I repeated a little while ago, you said something about a cosmic energy blast coming soon."

"Yeah."

He points to the other room. "They don't know what you said. You know, because we repeated. Do you want to tell them again?"

"Well, yeah. It's kind of the reason I came out here.

That, and to help you guys."

We walk into the room and sit with Beth and Anika.

Brand says, "Calli has something to tell us."

"Uh, yes, so in two years there's going to be a big cosmic energy blast that affects a lot of people."

Anika is the first to speak. "How do you know?"

"Crimson told me. She can foresee the blasts."

Beth asks, "What kind of power will it bring?"

"A new one. People affected will be able to harness fire, water, and wind. There's some other powers too, but I'm not sure exactly what they are."

"So, it's more than one power?" Brand leans forward, intrigued.

"No, it's just one, but think of it like the Hunters. They can smell, see, and hear long distances. Some have stronger smellers than others. Some have stronger vision than others. With this new power, some will be more powerful than others, but the overall cosmic energy has to do with the elements. Those who gain that power will be called Elementals."

"What are we supposed to do about it?" Anika asks with genuine concern.

"The clans need to be united to be able to help those with the new power learn about the will of nature," I say.

Brands smirks. "Well, that sounds a whole lot easier said than done. If I had control over the elements of nature I wouldn't think anyone could teach me anything."

I think about what he just said. "That kind of gives me an idea of what Elementals might possibly think."

"You said two years?" Beth says.

"Two years to the blast in Portland, Oregon. The power will manifest depending on how the DNA evolves. Some of the powers we have now manifest as soon as a child is able to vocalize what they're seeing in the future or reading in others' minds. So, I guess it's safe to say we could be dealing with affected kids in, say, five years."

Beth says, "What does the future show? What do you see?"

"I can't see clearly enough to determine details. I can tell you I imagine the possibility of big trouble. I've been assigned with uniting the clans and Diamond Bearers for the event."

"Oh, no stress there." Brand chuckles. "But why you? You're like the youngest. Well, besides Jonas."

"Believe me, I asked the same question. Crimson chose me for this task. That's all I know."

Anika says, "I don't think this power will be as bad as you think, Calli."

"Why do you say that?"

"Because it's not like the world is going to end."

"Go on." Brand encourages, as he moves his hand in a circular motion.

"God is at the helm. He won't allow the world to be destroyed by a cosmic ray."

"Maybe he's the one sending it," Brand says, feigning over-the-top excitement.

"I know you're teasing me, Brand, but I think you're more right than you realize. God is in control of His ship. He's not going to let anything destroy this planet."

"Except for Him, right?"

"Well, we are His creation. He has that right."

Brand looks at me and puts his thoughts on the edge of his mind. *Do you want me to repeat?*

"No," I say aloud.

Anika throws a questioning glance at me.

I ask, "Where is this coming from, Anika? I haven't known you for very long, but I've never heard you speak about your beliefs before. Why now?"

"I guess my perspective has changed with the deaths of my parents, and earlier, the murder of Brand's father, and Neema and everyone else. There's been so much death. I'm just trying to process it all, and the easiest way—the only way that makes sense in my head—is by going back to what I've been taught."

"That's understandable," I say. "I want to clarify something. The coming cosmic blast isn't going to destroy the planet. It will irradiate the region where it hits and many lives will be lost unless we help. I'd like to think that if it's God's will that we shouldn't interfere, then every effort we make will be thwarted and we may feel like it's not meant to be, but we will have at least tried."

"I agree, Calli," Anika says.

"I think I'll charge you a topaz with the Seer power so you can understand what I'm talking about. You can best honor your parents by helping other people. I hope you'll help."

"I want to help, Calli."

"Great. I think it would be good for all of us to agree not to discuss religion, neither for nor against. We all have a very long time to spend together if you three choose to become Bearers. Let's not spend it quarrelling over beliefs. Let's focus on the task at hand and figure out what needs to be done."

They nod their heads in agreement to my suggestion.

It's bedtime. I take the couch because I don't want to oust any of them from their beds. Anika had already established the house rules of propriety before I arrived—according to her beliefs—meaning Brand and Beth have to stay separated. I can see how this is weighing heavily on

Beth and Brand. I muse to myself that Anika wouldn't last a day in my college dormitory. Brand surprises me, though, with his acceptance of Anika's chastity rules. I was able to read his mind for a second to see that he's trying to get along with Anika out of respect for her recent loss. That's why he keeps repeating conversations back, to preserve the unity of the group.

One thing I noticed throughout the entire evening was that Beth didn't join in on the conversations. She was rather quiet. I'm left wondering what she was thinking.

As I lay on the couch, I feel for Chris's diamond, then stop. I check the clock on the wall and add two hours. It's 1:00 a.m. his time. I figure if I'm able to bi-locate to him, he'll be asleep—there shouldn't be any harm in that. I focus on his diamond, imagining our two diamonds as one, but I can't seem to make a connection. I try to speak to his mind. Nothing.

I roll over and press my head into my pillow.

I send my thoughts to Crimson, figuring with our quantum entanglement she'll know I'm struggling to use my powers. I wait for a response. Nothing.

I try to connect with Maetha's diamond. Right away, she says, *What is it, Calli? Are you all right?*

Yes, I'm fine. I just wanted to make sure I can connect mentally with Diamond Bearers. I can't seem to connect with Chris.

Let me try.

I wait for her response.

Hmm, I can't connect with him either. I'm sure everything's fine, Calli. Ask Crimson if she's with him.

I can't get her to respond.

Oh, okay. That makes sense. She must be with him and has protected the conversation. She can hear your thoughts, though. Don't worry.

Okay, thanks. I remember Brand's conversation about

the quartz. *Wait, Maetha, one more question. Do you think the quartz crystals could be inserted into a person's body? Would the body accept them?*

Do you mean under the skin? Or in the heart?

Probably under the skin.

I'll look into it.

We end our mental connection. I lie on the couch thinking about how I inherited the Blue Diamond from Maetha because she went over Crimson's head and gave Freedom a diamond. Neema had fallen in love with him and persuaded Maetha to bend the rules. Both women made bad decisions because of emotions, because of love.

A couple days ago, Chris said he couldn't believe I'd never had a boyfriend before age nineteen and that scares him. I've gone over his words in my head, thinking through the reasons. Why wasn't I attracted to any particular boy, or a boy attracted to me? I know I was quite nerdy and never really put myself out there, and my expectations were set quite high, but was there another reason why I was that way?

I think about my earlier hug with Brand in the kitchen. Would I have fallen for Brand's charms back in high school if I hadn't had Chris in the back of my mind? Would I have felt attracted to Jonas if Chris and I were not an item? What about Travis at the college mixer? Sure, Travis was only following his duties working with Freedom, but what if?

Pondering my past social awkwardness and my apparently abnormal hormones brings new questions to mind. Crimson told me I've been protected all my life. Does this mean I've been protected from myself? I wonder exactly how much involvement Crimson or Maetha have actually had in my life.

I call out to Crimson in my mind. *Please talk to me.*

Crimson replies, *I'm here. But I'm not sure you're ready to hear the answer.*

So, you have meddled with my hormones, haven't you?

Crimson bi-locates to my position. I sit up and face her. "Secure our conversation, Calli."

I stand and walk around her projected image, whispering, "No one will be able to hear." The blue shimmering mist develops and connects in a glittering circle. I sit back down.

"Yes, Calli, situations around you were controlled. For you to be in the proper state of mind to carry the diamond, you needed to be free of attachment."

"You controlled my mind?"

"Maetha did, somewhat, under my direction."

"Are you telling me I haven't been in control of, or in charge of, my life at all?" My blood is beginning to boil.

"No, I'm not saying that," she says. "I know what you're feeling right now, Calli."

"No! No, you don't."

"You're feeling betrayed. You put your trust, your happiness, and your life in my hands and now you've learned things weren't what you thought they were."

Now I know how Freedom felt. "Yeah, I do feel betrayed. I feel cheated out of a normal life. Chris is completely afraid to touch me for fear I'll break or something, or maybe I'll run in the other direction. If I'd had any relationships or simple dates even, I wouldn't be so scary to Chris. Finding out I've been lied to and manipulated has messed with my mind. Was any of my life real?"

"You're not a robot, or a computer-game creature being told what, when, and how to act. You are a human girl. I manipulated your life only when possible detractions were about to interfere—like making you walk a little slower to narrowly miss getting hit by a speeding driver who was running a red light, or preventing a boy from interacting with you prior to your track meet so you would be unattached when you went with Chris on the delivery."

"Oh, so I'd be attracted to Chris?" I reply angrily.

"No, Calli, I didn't have anything to do with your attraction to Chris. That was you, one-hundred percent. The mind-control power can't force someone to fall in love. However, what if you had a boyfriend back in Ohio when you went to the Runner's compound? You would still have been attracted to Chris, but you wouldn't have betrayed your boyfriend. You also wouldn't have felt the intense need to figure out why Chris was about to die. The delivery would have played out completely different. In fact, it wouldn't have played out at all."

"What are you talking about?"

"Many people and situations were manipulated at the last minute to make everything come together properly. If something fell out of alignment, I would have scrapped the attempt."

"You know, you're always going on about choices, Crimson. Did I get to make my own choices anywhere in all this?" My voice squeaks, on the verge of tears.

"Yes. You could have said no to going to Montana. You could have called your parents to go home."

My tears overflow and my throat constricts, making my voice change. "I felt pressured to go with Clara. Everyone expected me to go."

"You still made a choice. You chose to alter the future to save Chris. No one pressured you to do that, and not everyone put in your position would have made the choice. I want you to know it's all right to feel anger right now. Frankly, I'd worry about you if you weren't. What I ask of you is that you remember the Blue Diamond cannot control other's hearts or emotions. For instance, I cannot force you to accept this. You've made choices all your life. Yes, some of your life's happenings were manipulated, but you were never not in control of your life or your happiness."

Her words don't really make me feel any better. "What about Chris? Would he have been attracted to me if he hadn't seen me in a vision? If he had walked past me on the street, would he have done a double take?"

"Don't dwell on this line of thinking, Calli."

Oh no! I didn't want her to answer *that* way. Tears roll down my face. "Why not?"

"The world is full of 'what if's' and chance occurrences. I couldn't tell who you would sacrifice yourself for until Maetha ran the scenarios. I didn't know it would be Chris or I would have prepared him better."

"Don't you mean you would have controlled his life more?" I immediately regret the snide remark.

Crimson pauses and studies my face.

I wipe my eyes and try to stop my involuntary hiccups. I wish I could tell what she's thinking. Here I am, her only option for saving the world, and I'm having a meltdown.

"I'll tell you what's going through my head, Calli," she says in a calming tone. "I think the enormity of your situation, your past, present, and future just crashed down on you. You've been so concerned about everyone else and the tragedies in their lives, you haven't taken the time to look at what you've had to deal with. Everyone's burdens and struggles are real. Yours are no less significant than those of the next person. The difference between you and everyone else around you is you're actually allowing yourself to feel the pain of your burden. I know you've been thinking you've had a perfect life and feeling like it's been unfair so far. I protected you to this point because I wanted you to become the strongest Bearer. You need to be the strongest."

I wipe my eyes again, gaining better control of my emotions. "I'm sorry."

"Don't apologize for expressing discontent toward me, Calli. I allow all my Bearers to be vocal. It's healthy for you to do so. I worry when people bottle up their emotions, like with Chris. He needs to address his issues with his father to be able to perform his duties up to my expectations. I'll be working with him more on that."

Her words bring the topic back around to Chris. I say, "Was Chris's mind manipulated the first time he saw me? Did Maetha show him the vision to make him fall for me?"

"What exactly are you asking, Calli?"

"The first time. You know, when Maetha ran scenarios to see who would stand out as someone I'd sacrifice myself for. Can you tell me if Chris was attracted to me the first time around, or was he only attracted to my power? No, wait, don't answer that. I think I already know. You altered his vision, so he'd be attracted to my aura."

"Yes, I altered his vision, but remember the heart cannot be manipulated, Calli. The simple answer you're searching for is, he's not shallow. Being able to see your aura the first time around is what drew his attention to you. From there, he watched you with a scrutinizing eye. You were the slowest Runner, as planned. You read his mind at the waterfalls, but only discovered his insecurities. He knew you had done so, which escalated his interest in you. He saw you as a glowing perplexity. Then each power began to surface, along with detecting Jonas's cancer. Chris became jealous that you were so fixated on Jonas. Chris fought for your attention, Calli. You were unlike any other girl he'd ever encountered—intelligent, unselfish, strong-willed, determined, and beautiful. Yes, he thought you were beautiful, and yes, your glowing aura was the first thing to draw his attention, but his developing love came from his own heart. Think back on the vision of you healing his legs at Justin's compound. Compare that to when you found him and healed him. Was your experience the same as the vision?"

"For the most part. But I felt like the vision held more significance, if that makes any sense."

"What do you mean?"

"Well, like his sense of surprise and excitement was greater in the vision."

"You're doubting his feelings for you, but you shouldn't. Remember the analogy of snooping at Christmas presents? He was quite excited to see you enter the room to fix his broken legs the first time. To see it play out in real time, as expected, the overall excitement was not as strong. But, the meaning was stronger, even if you couldn't sense it. Calli, you've already claimed his heart. Not much can change that now. I know for certain from the first moment you saw him, you melted into a puddle at his feet."

"Yeah, but that was just lust," I openly admit.

"Now stop and consider this. He doesn't know how everything played out for him to recognize you at Justin's place in the vision. He doesn't know how he developed such strong feelings for you. He only knows he has them."

"Is that why he wants to go slow with our relationship?"

"You'll have to ask him. But, I'd give him a day or two. Earlier tonight, he bi-located for the first time to you and found you hugging Brand and telling him you didn't want to be any place else."

"Oh no! I was being sarcastic."

"Give him some time to calm down. Also, don't try bi-locating to his position without his permission first."

"So I don't catch him indecent?"

"Well, that too. The more important reason being he must keep up the pretense that he's removed from you and the Diamond Bearers. If you suddenly materialized at his side, at the wrong moment, you could blow his cover."

Chapter 9 – To Catch a Blogger

This morning I decide to read through the files again to see if I can find anything I might have missed. More than anything, I'm just trying to keep my mind busy, so I don't dwell on last night's conversation with Crimson.

I sit at the table with Dr. Condi's file, examining his education, known addresses, and accomplishments.

"Calli." Chris's low voice sends chills up my back.

I turn in my chair and nearly fall off. Chris stands beside me . . . well, bi-located Chris.

"Chris, you scared me. I mean, I'm really glad to see you." My heart is still racing a mile a minute.

"How's everything going there?" he asks.

I pick up on his strained tone and know what I need to say. "Chris, last night, I didn't know you were there, but I was being sarcastic with Brand."

"What are you talking about?" He acts innocent.

"I know you bi-located last night."

"Oh."

"I'm sorry I upset you." I pause, waiting for him to say something. He doesn't, so I ask, "How is it you figured out how to bi-locate before me?"

"I'm a natural traveler, I guess."

"How's everything going on your end at the Pentagon?"

His mood changes and he says, "I met with one of the guards from my father's compound. I want to share my memory with you so you can let the others know how the meeting went."

"Okay."

"I'm putting the memory forward. Close your eyes and open your thoughts." His voice relaxes my mind. I close my eyelids and begin to see his memory. Observing through Chris's eyes, he stands facing a mirror, wearing only a pair of boxer briefs. *Oh boy.* He attaches a topaz to his stomach with a piece of flesh-colored medical tape just below his waistline. I hear him think: *Hopefully this mind-reading-powered topaz will work in the off chance there's obsidian and I can't use my diamond's power.* He pulls up his jeans and fastens the button. The waistband fits perfectly over the topaz and will help hold it in place. Then he pushes his arms into a button-up shirt and fastens each button, concealing his bare upper-half. He leaves the shirt un-tucked and rolls up the long sleeves.

I'm left with his shirtless image in my head, and a growing desire to go get his jacket and inhale his unique scent.

Chris's memory jumps to a scene where he's sitting at a table in a sports bar type restaurant. Across the table sits a familiar looking guy. I know I've seen him before but can't remember his name. The body language of the guy seems at ease and comfortable—not what one would expect from a guilty person.

Chris says, "Yeah, I just got into town. I have a job that starts tomorrow. How have you been, Max?"

Of course! He's Max Corvus. The guy Justin leaked info to, the guy who shot Freedom, and who ushered me to the other prisoners after General Harding and Deus Ex died. And the guy Agent Whitman talked about at the Denver house.

"Since being at your father's facility, you mean?" Max asks.

"Yes."

"You have to admit, Chris, some pretty crazy crap

went down there."

"I know."

"At least the freaks escaped and didn't kill us all. Of course, they wouldn't have killed you. You're one of them."

"Not anymore. Dad sent me through the machine."

"No big deal. I went through it too. I've never felt better."

Chris straightens in his chair and leans toward Max. "I've had so much more energy since that day. I thought it was just me."

"No, man. I've talked with a couple of the other guys. They say the same thing. I've got a big question, though, Chris. How did Calli get into the machine room? The door was locked."

"I've wondered the same thing. I think she was already there before we entered." Chris takes a couple gulps of his drink and leans back in his chair. He puts his elbow on the windowsill and crosses an ankle over his knee. He takes another gulp.

"Yeah, but how did she get in there? She would have had to get past me."

"I dunno. She does have a diamond in her. We don't know the full extent of those powers."

Max nods his head. "Were you bummed that Deus died? I could tell she liked you."

Chris laughs. "No, she didn't. She would have killed me if I hadn't given the diamond to my dad."

"You *gave* the diamond?"

"You missed that?"

"Holy sh—eeze!" Max exclaims in a high-pitched whisper, his eyes darting around the room.

"Yeah. After Dad and I both went through the machine, he had me pick up the diamond and give it to him."

"He made you . . . you held it . . . and you *gave* it to him?" Max looks as if he might choke on his own spit. "What was it like? To hold it, I mean."

"Incredible, man. I can't explain how amazing I felt for those couple of seconds."

Max leans forward. "If you could get your hands on one again, would you do it?"

"In a heartbeat! Why, do you know where one is?"

"If I did, I'd have it already."

Chris says, "Well, maybe the superpower blogger will find one." I like how Chris eases into the topic.

"The what?"

"The 'They Are Among Us' blogger. Someone has a site on the Internet, exposing tons of top secret info. I would have thought you'd heard about it already."

Max pulls out his phone and begins searching his browser. "Tell me what it's called again."

Chris relays the web address and drinks some more from his bottle.

"Whoa!" Max sits forward and puts his elbows on the table, phone in his hands. "Look at this. It says to wear obsidian." Max pulls a necklace with a small black stone out from under his shirt collar. "Done!" He scrolls down the page and continues reading.

Chris thinks, *I was afraid of that*. He tries to read Max's mind, using the diamond's power to see if it's Yellowstone obsidian. He's unable to get into Max's mind. Chris accesses the power in the topaz and can get right in. Max's mind shows he's intrigued with the blog, reading as if it's the first time he's seen it. Max reaches up to itch his head and wonders if his mind is being read.

Chris jumps forward, extending his hand to the space above Max's head. "Dude, look out! There's a bee in your hair." He fans his hand at the imaginary insect and then says, "Okay, it's gone."

"Thanks, man." Max runs his hand over his head and scratches the top of his scalp. "A little late for bees. You sure it's gone?" Max looks all around the diner. "Maybe my mind is being read."

"Maybe. It looked like a bee to me." Chris looks around the diner too.

"Who do you think is running this site?" Max brings the attention back to his phone.

"I don't know. It's not my problem, that's all I care about."

"Two teens are running around with diamonds in their hearts, with unimaginable powers, and you're not worried? What about the diamond you gave to your dad? Where did it go? This blog's information shows whoever's running it knows their stuff. Does it talk about the diamonds?"

"I don't think so, but they put new stuff up every day, so there might be something on it."

"You know more about these freaks than anyone else, Chris. You'd be a wealth of knowledge, wouldn't you? Not that you need the money or anything."

"I'm not the blogger, Max, and I know better than to blab about what was going on in that facility."

"I believe you. I'm going to look into this. I'll let you know if I find anything."

Chris's memory ends.

I open my eyes and find Chris looking intently at me. "Well, what do you think?"

"He doesn't seem guilty."

"Yeah, that's kind of what I thought. I have a few more people to meet with tomorrow."

"You might want to look into the two guards who were driving the truck that brought in Clara, Beth's brother, and the rest of the prisoners."

"Good idea. I'm pretty sure that was Trevor and Bob."

I have a sudden realization about something I'd completely forgotten. I lurch toward Chris. "Max saw Crimson."

"He did? When?"

"Yes. When he came in the room after Deus died, I read it in his mind. He was confused because Crimson disappeared."

"Odd that he didn't say anything to me about that."

"Yeah, it is. Maybe he'll bring it up with you." I change the subject. "What is your new job?"

"I'm a delivery man," he says. "How ironic is that? I'll be transporting top secret type info, so I guess it's not so bad. At least it's not delivering pizzas."

"Can I try to bi-locate to you?"

"Right now?"

"Is this a bad time?"

"Well, yeah. I have to leave."

"Okay. Maybe later, then."

"Calli, um, . . . I'm sorry I kept you at arm's length for so long. I thought I was doing the right thing."

"What are you talking about?"

"I don't know . . . nothing. It's just . . . ever since Maetha showed me the vision of you healing my legs I've had you built up in my mind as someone I didn't deserve. I wanted to become a better person before I met you. But that didn't happen. So, I thought it would be best to hold off on getting close to you until I thought you were ready."

"What about what I wanted, Chris? Do you think I want a perfect guy? And what about all that 'when we both feel ready' talk?"

"Uh, I'm trying to apologize for assuming control."

"It feels like you're still trying to be perfect in my eyes. Chris, I love you just the way you are."

He dips his chin to his chest then gazes with sincerity into my eyes. "I love you, too. I really have to go, sorry."

"Bye." I smile and blow him a kiss before he vanishes.

I continue to stare at the space where he stood, replaying his words through my mind. Now I think I know why he showed me his half-naked body before the meeting with Max. He probably thought I needed an image of him burned into my brain so I wouldn't be tempted by another guy. If he only knew what kind of images I've already conjured up in my mind about him, he wouldn't worry.

Brand yells from the bedroom, "Hey Calli, come take a look at this."

I peek my head in the doorway of the bedroom. He's sitting on his bed with the laptop. He motions for me to come over. I sit beside him on the bed and look at the screen which displays the blog. "The headline for the day is, 'If your head itches, someone might be reading your mind.'"

"Or you might have lice," I joke. Yet, I'm alarmed at how closely related the topic is to Chris's memory with Max.

"This isn't funny, Calli. Whoever this is needs to be stopped."

"I know. We're doing everything we can. Hold on, are you on the actual website?"

"No, Jonas sent screenshots through email." Brand scrolls down the page. "Oh, great! Listen to this comment: 'I saw something unexplainable once. Three people wearing green suits ran by so fast they were a blur. I blinked, and they were gone. For years I thought I was nuts. I probably still am but now I know I'm not alone. Got my obsidian now.'"

Brand reads further on in the comments. I can see that more and more people are gravitating to this blog. It's evident in the increased activity. At the bottom of the paragraph is a link to purchase obsidian for the "low, low price of only $49.99."

I point to the screen, "Click on that. Let's see where it takes us."

"I can't, Calli. It's a screenshot."

"Oh, right. Okay, let's go to the website."

Brand opens a browser page and enters the web address. Once there, he clicks on the obsidian advertisement. A new page opens with an order form for personal obsidian that includes payment requirements and an address of where to send a money order. "Look, it's a Denver address." He looks up at me, seemingly shocked. "We got em', Calli."

"Got who?" Anika asks as she comes into the room.

Brand proudly announces, "The blogger is accepting payments for obsidian to a Denver mailbox. Let's go find it."

"Just search it on the Internet," Beth says, entering behind Anika.

I get off the bed and put some distance between Brand and me. The last thing I want is to upset Beth or give Brand the wrong idea. Nor do I want Chris bi-locating and seeing me in another questionable situation. I move closer to Anika.

Brand types on the keys of the laptop, searching the address. He says, "That was easy. It's a shipping store that rents mailboxes. Come on."

"Wait," I say. "What do you plan on doing? Do you actually think the person at the counter is going to just tell you who owns the mailbox?"

"Brand can get information out of anyone. I would

have thought you knew that by now, Calli." Beth smiles confidently.

I shake my head. "Okay, let me say this in a different way. Do you really think the blogger would use their real name to set up an account?"

Brand's tone changes and softens. "Nooo. That's why youuu are coming with us. You can read minds and make people do things."

"I don't know if I can use those powers while appearing invisible. I can't blow my cover."

Anika says, "Experiment right now, then. Go invisible and try to read my mind and control my actions."

I don't waste a second. I control the others' perception of me, making myself invisible in their eyes.

"Oooh, that's sooo cool!" Brand says. "I wish I had a topaz with that power?"

I look into Anika's mind and find she's handling her parents' deaths quite well, all things considered. Her faith and belief that she'll see them again have made it possible for her to skip several important grieving steps. That can't be entirely good.

I say aloud, "I'm able to read Anika's mind."

"Great," Brand shouts, pumping his fist in the air.

I focus on Anika and try to make her walk to the other side of the room. She doesn't move. I say aloud, "Walk to the window." She does, but not without freaking out about having her body controlled.

"This is wrong! I can't stop! Make me stop!"

Brand and Beth are literally laughing on the floor.

I release my hold on Anika and become visible again. "I couldn't make you move without speaking. I've noticed Maetha spoke out loud whenever she used the power too. At least to my recollection, anyway."

"Don't ever do that again," Anika shrieks.

"You told her to," Brand reminds her as he reigns in his laughter and gets up off the floor.

"That was before I knew what it would feel like."

Beth stands and says, "Let's go find out who owns the mailbox."

I say, "Hang on a second. Are there any extra topazes here? I need a couple."

"There's a couple more in the other room."

Beth helps me attach two topaz to my chest. I plan on charging one with thought-projection and the other with mind-reading. Hopefully, I won't need to use either right away.

I use my Blue shard to appear invisible before leaving the house, just in case Agent Whitman is watching the premises. We get into the car Chris turned over to the Diamond Bearers for this very use. Beth volunteers to drive, Anika sits up front with her, and Brand sits in the back with me. I ponder as we drive through the city of Denver what life would be like if General Harding hadn't been shot by Deus—if he'd been able to become a Diamond Bearer.

Crimson's voice enters my mind. *I wouldn't have let it happen. However, I'm relieved I didn't need to act, and that Deus took care of the situation.*

Anika asks. "What's the plan?"

Brand clears his throat and says, "I'm going to ask to set up a mailbox and see what happens from there. Calli can use her bag of tricks to help. Together, we'll walk out of there with a name."

"Confident much?" Beth teases as she turns the car into the parking lot of the shipping store.

Brand gets out of the back seat and holds the door open for me to climb out. Anika and Beth remain in the car. I use my telepathy to speak to Brand's mind instead of verbally communicating as people are nearby.

A customer exits the building and Brand grabs the door and holds it open for me to go inside.

I'm in, I tell him. Together we wait in line. I notice a sign on the wall stating the requirements of setting up a mailbox account. Applicants need to provide photo ID and proof of address. This gives me hope we'll be successful.

"Can I help you?" a young female employee named Janette asks.

Brand dives right in. "How do I find out who owns mailbox number thirty-seven?"

"I can't give that information."

The ground spins wildly and we come back to Janette asking how she can help Brand.

"How do I set up a mailbox?" Brand asks.

Janette runs down a list of items needed to begin the application. Brand doesn't have everything needed to set one up.

Brand repeats back with me and says to Janette, "Can I pick up an application for setting up a mailbox? I don't have time to fill it out here."

"Sure." She turns around and opens a stuffed file cabinet drawer. I notice the files are in numerical order, making me think those numbers might correspond with the mailbox numbers. She pushes hard against the mass of files to get into one of the forward files. "Oh, sorry, looks like I need to print off more applications. It will only take a minute or so." Janette pushes the drawer almost closed, but not quite. She hurries away.

I'm going to try to see who is in file thirty-seven, I tell Brand. I'm about to hurry around the counter when the ground whirls around once again.

"Could I get an application to set up a mailbox, please?"

"Sure."

"Go now, Calli," Brand whispers.

I move quickly and get positioned by the drawer. Janette realizes she'll need to print more applications and leaves. I slide the drawer open slowly, trying not to draw attention from the other employees. The file I need is visible. I slide my hand into the file to try to get a look at a name and address. The first paper doesn't have the information I'm after, so I thumb over the edges of the other papers until I find the right one. Before I can get a look, the room zooms in a sickening circle and I'm back to where I started from.

"Go now, Calli," Brand whispers.

How does Brand do this? I'm going crazy trying to keep up. At least I know exactly what I'm going after this time. I don't waste a moment thumbing through the papers. Instead, I go right for the goal. The registered name reads: Dorothy Ruby. I don't recognize the name. I memorize the address and move out of the way just as Janette comes back with the papers. She bumps into the drawer and realizes it's opened more than when she left it. I read her mind and find she dismisses the issue, figuring one of her co-workers opened the drawer. She scratches the top of her head.

"Here you go. I included a list of the required documents you need to provide when you return."

"Thanks Janette." Brand dishes out a big dose of charm and leaves the building.

Piling into the car, I give Beth the address I retrieved from the file.

Beth says, "Is it okay to use my phone to look up the address?"

"No, probably not. Are there any maps in the glove box?"

Brand opens the center console and pulls out a GPS device and cord. "Use this, Beth."

"Does that even work?"

Brand nods his head.

While Beth plugs in and turns on the GPS, Brand says, "Wasn't that fun, Calli? I told you we'd leave with a name. Oh, and look," he points to the GPS screen. "The address isn't far away. We're gonna catch a blogger today, folks."

Enthusiasm is high in the car, until we arrive at the address and find a large, sprawling, single-level building with well-manicured lawns and flower beds. The large framed sign over the front doors says East Side Assisted Living.

"What do you make of this, Brand?" I ask.

"Must be a resident who set up the mailbox."

"Or a dead end," Beth states. She parks the car and turns it off.

Brand says in a rather defeated tone, "We're not getting anywhere. There's no one by that name here. No employee, either."

"You repeated?" Anika asks.

"Yeah."

Anika grunts at his response, which draws my attention. She says, "They're not going to just tell you information like that, Brand." She unhooks her seatbelt and turns to Brand. "I want to try something. Come in with me, Brand."

I speak up. "I'm coming too."

Anika, Brand, and I get out of the car and walk inside the foyer. Anika says to Brand, "Wait here."

The front door opens and a lady hurries inside the building, almost running right into me. I jump out of the way, barely missing having my invisible-self exposed.

Anika says, "I'm from Denver Radiology here to pick

up Dorothy Ruby's records."

The receptionist reaches for the stack of files. "What was the patient's name again?"

"Last name Ruby, first Dorothy."

"We don't have any residents by that name. Are you sure you have the name right?"

"Yes."

"Let me make a call. Perhaps she's a new resident." The receptionist picks up the phone. I take the opportunity to read her mind. She doesn't know anyone by that name. "Denver Radiology is here to pick up a chart for Dorothy Ruby . . . okay, I thought I better double-check." She hangs up the phone and says to Anika, "Sorry, we don't have a patient here by that name."

"Okay. I'll call my office and figure out what to do. Thank you."

Anika walks to Brand and they push open the door. I keep my eyes on the receptionist and notice a man comes to the desk asking for details about Anika's request. His eyes follow Brand and Anika. I hurry out the door before it closes.

We all sit quietly in the car for a moment. Dead end is right.

Beth is the first to speak up. "Well, what do we know? Someone set up a mailbox with a fake name and address. That someone has to show up to the shipping store eventually to get their mail, right?"

"Are you going to perform a stake-out, Beth?" I ask.

"Yes. Why not? We have pictures of everyone from the compound. Besides, this is the only solid lead we have."

"There's got to be a better way."

Beth starts the car and backs up. "I'm returning to the mailbox store. Maybe there's some other information in the file like a phone number or other address."

"That's a good idea," I say. "What do you think, Brand?"

"It's too far out to tell. Keep driving."

We're about five minutes away from the mailbox store. I realize Brand must be bothered by only being able to repeat two minutes. At this moment, he seems agitated and restless. I think he doesn't like time to play out naturally. I choose not to read his mind, even though I could.

I say, "When we get there, I'll go inside and check to see if there's any mail in box thirty-seven."

"How? You don't have a key," says Anika.

"The boxes are accessible from the backside."

Beth adds, "While we're waiting, we can go over the compound's files in search of Dorothy Ruby."

We arrive back where we started from. As we pull into the parking lot, Brand says, "There's mail. Calli just checked." Then he turns to Beth. "Park over by that light pole. We'll be out of the main traffic area, but still in position to see inside the building."

"Okay," Beth says, and moves the car.

I ask, "Brand, did I look in the file cabinet when I was in there?" It's so weird asking him about what I just did when I can't remember myself.

"No, we're waiting here till someone opens . . . okay, in two minutes the drawer will be opened. Go inside and get in position. I'll repeat if you get caught."

"Aren't you coming?"

"No, Janette will recognize me and ask questions."

"Who's Janette?" Beth asks, her expression pinched.

Brand doesn't answer, instead opens the car door to let me out. We have to keep up appearances. If the car door opened on its own, someone might take notice. If this was a van with an automatic opening door, that would be a different thing. I'm able to get inside the building without a fuss. The frequency of customers entering and exiting is convenient for what I need. Moving around the people within the small building is another story.

Janette opens the drawer again and pulls out a file for a customer.

Now's my chance, I think. I hurry around the counter and carefully slide my hand into file thirty-seven. I try to imagine what it must look like to anyone paying attention to the files. They'd look like they were parting by themselves.

A loud commotion comes from the direction of the front door. I look, along with everyone else in the store, to see Brand half-buried under the toppled stack of display boxes by the door. He catches my eye and says, "Yank the whole file when I knock the boxes over." Then the room whips around me in nauseating fashion to where I haven't gone around the counter yet. Janette opens the drawer and I move around the counter. I slip my fingers on either side of the correct file and wait to remove it until the signal.

A thought comes to my mind. Will this file become invisible to everyone like I am? How will I know if other people can see it? I figure Brand will repeat if we run into a problem. Wait, Brand has *already* repeated. This must mean I need some extra cover.

The tumbling boxes by the door pulls everyone's attention away from the file that's seemingly rising out of the drawer. I wrap my arms around it.

"Hide!" Brand shouts.

Hide? I act quickly, slipping around the corner into the back room, figuring the file didn't turn invisible and Brand is trying to help out.

Brand continues talking loud, "Hide-ee-oh, so sorry about that. I'm so clumsy. Here let me pick these up."

I stand with my back against a bulletin board. In front

of me, to the left, is the back side of the mailboxes. Beyond them is the rear exit. The room hasn't spun around yet, so I make the decision to run out the back door. But before I can take a step, the unmistakable rushing sensation of my powers fleeing my body causes me to reappear. I instantly access my charged topaz and reinstate my invisibility. Someone has a large piece of obsidian, but who? Luckily, no one is in the back room with me. I move into position and pause. I send my thoughts to Brand. *I'm going out the back door.*

Pushing the door open, I'm shocked to find Beth. She has moved the car to the rear parking area, with the back door open. I jump in the car without hesitation. She drives away faster than normal.

"What's happening?" I ask.

"I don't know. As soon as you went in the building, he jumped out and told me to go wait for you in the back, and then to drive back to the house right away."

"What about him?"

Anika says, "He can take care of himself."

"What, and I can't?"

Beth adds, "I'm sorry Calli, I'm just doing as he says."

I mentally stop using the topaz and focus on refilling it.

Chapter 10 – Trevor and Bob

We arrive at the house without Brand. I can't help but feel he's in danger and needs my help. But like Crimson said, I must be careful. I maintain my invisibility and the three of us go inside the house.

Beth paces in front of the living room window with her arms folded tightly across her chest. Anika is in the kitchen, chopping and dicing something, who knows what.

I open the folder I've just stolen and spread the papers out on the table.

"Beth, where's the list of names of people you haven't been able to find?"

She brings the paper to me and returns to her pacing. I compare the names listed on the mailbox registration form under "people with permission to pick up mail" to the names on Beth's paper.

"I found a match!"

Beth is by my side in an instant. I guess I forgot she *is* a Runner. I point to the two names and say, "Robert McKinney, Trevor Floyd."

"They put their real names on the form? Absolutely, positively stupid!"

I chuckle at Beth's reaction, then say, "Well, look at these applications. Setting up a box isn't an easy thing to do. Dorothy Ruby is probably a real person they know. She was probably with them when the mailbox was set up. Looking at this photocopy of the license, I think Robert and Trevor might have faked Dorothy's driver's license to reflect the nursing home's address. The font type looks different." I study the paper intently, then hand it to Beth.

"When we were at the nursing home, I read the mind of the woman at the front desk. She was telling the truth when she said they didn't have any residents there by that name. I think either Robert or Trevor works there, and they used that address for the required forms instead of their home address. Adding their names to the authorized list takes Dorothy out of the picture."

Beth says, "So, Dorothy is the face, the nursing home is the identifying address, and Robert and Trevor are authorized to pick up the mail and take it wherever they want."

"Looks that way to me."

I search through the personnel files from General Harding's compound for Robert's and Trevor's files. Once I find them, I remove the photographs paper-clipped inside. Their names are listed on the backside. Robert's photo also includes his nickname: Bob. Trevor and Bob. Those were the names of the guards with the vests, according to Chris.

The front door opens and Beth leaves my side so fast the papers in front of me fly up from her air displacement. Brand has returned.

"Don't ever do that again!" She points a finger in his face and then assaults him with kisses.

I give them a second, then approach him and ask, "What happened?"

"Well, a man walked in wearing one of the military vests that have obsidian and green crystals. So, I repeated to warn you."

I show Brand two pictures from General Harding's files and he identifies Trevor Floyd. "Yep, that's him," he says. "The obsidian on his vest caused you to reappear. I still had the power to repeat, because of the quartz, but I didn't, because I wanted to follow the guy. Trevor collected his mail, then went outside and made a phone call. He told whoever was on the other end that he raced to the mailbox store to grab the mail after someone came to the nursing home asking for Dorothy." Brand looks at me with a big grin. "See, we did find the guy and his name after all."

"Why would he wear a vest out in public?" Beth asks.

"Probably for protection," I say. "Think about it. How would anyone find out who the mailbox was registered to? And who would take the time to investigate? Someone with powers. He didn't want to take a chance."

"Well, this is quite exciting. Now we know who's working the blog and where the missing vests are. We'll have this wrapped up quickly." Brand sits on the couch and stretches his arms over his head.

Beth holds up a paper. "Except that these two are on the list of unknowns. We couldn't find them because we didn't have an address. We still don't know where they live."

"At least we know Trevor is in the area. Robert probably is too," I say.

"Time for another stake out?" Brand asks.

"Tomorrow."

I try to communicate with Chris. He speaks to my mind, letting me know he can't talk right now. I can't help but feel a little let down, but I know his work is important. I decide to try bi-locating to Jonas.

I communicate with Jonas's mind. *Hey, Jonas.*

I hear you, Calli.

Can I try bi-locating to you?

Sure.

I close my eyes and think about Jonas. When I open them, I'm still in Denver. I try again and again, then grunt. *I don't know how this works.*

Jonas says, *Mary told me you have to think about the*

diamond you're connecting to. Sounds easy enough, but I haven't been able to figure out how to bi-locate either.

His words remind me of Duncan's when he told me to think of other diamonds and let my diamond connect with theirs. I close my eyes and imagine in my mind what Jonas's diamond felt like while I carried it. The icy smell, the heat signature whenever it warmed in my pocket. Behind my eyelids, a view begins to swirl and shapes form, seemingly materializing inside my head. I see Jonas sitting in a chair next to several computers and monitors. He's looking right at me.

"You're doing it," he shouts.

I open my eyes and find myself in Denver. *Okay,* I think, *I've got to keep my eyes closed.* I try again and am amazed at how quickly Jonas comes into view.

"Wow, you're really good at this."

"Not exactly. I keep opening my eyes back in Denver." I look around the room he's in. "You've got a pretty nice setup here."

"I like it. Hey, how's Anika holding up?"

"She's doing well. Do you want to try bi-locating to me?"

"Not right now. I'm busy trying to get your name removed from the TSA's naughty list."

"Oh, well, good luck with that. We've had a busy day here." I go on to tell him about our mailbox escapades and the information we've gathered so far. Then I wave bye to him, disconnect my mind from his diamond, and open my eyes. I have to sit for a second and readjust my thinking. I'm in Denver, not in Jonas's office in Bermuda. My body sits in Colorado, yet my mind can travel so far away. Incredible.

❖ ❖ ❖

This morning we're going to camp out in the mailbox store's parking lot. I'll have a lot of time to sit and wonder why Chris didn't or couldn't communicate last night. I'll try not to let my over-active imagination get the best of me.

Anika chose to stay at the house today. She said four bodies warming up the car wasn't her idea of a fun time.

When we arrive, I do a quick recon inside the building to determine box thirty-seven does indeed have mail to pick up. I'm totally surprised by the amount of letters stuffed inside the small box. If each envelope has $49.99, these two are making a haul.

I stand by the door, waiting for someone to open it so I can leave. The door has stood motionless for several minutes. Maybe Brand or Beth will come rescue me. Of course, it's not like I'm stuck. I could push the door and sneak out, but I don't need to. So, I'll wait.

The sound of the employees and customers conducting business has a nice flow. Like a beehive. The phone rings and Janette answers it. I glance out the door and see a man coming toward the building. I'll be able to leave once he enters. My increased hearing hears Janette say, "Box thirty-seven? What's the name? Okay, let me look. Hold please." I turn around and watch Janette as she checks the contents of box thirty-seven and then returns to the phone. "Sir, Dorothy has mail." She pauses and listens, then says, "Yes, we can forward the contents of the box as long as it's to someone on the approved list. We do charge a fee for the service, though . . . okay, let me write the address down. Go ahead."

I hustle over to the desk to see what she's writing down, then panic. The file with the approved names isn't in Janette's file cabinet.

"What's the name? . . . Oh, hi Trevor. I remember you from the other day, so we're good."

I read Janette's mind and find she's violating protocol by not double-checking the name but wants to be accommodating in the hopes Trevor might ask her out. Lucky break that she didn't discover the missing file. I memorize the street and house number that she writes down and zip out the door as another customer exits.

I speak to Brand's mind as I approach the car. *I'm coming. I need into the car.* He opens the door and slides over so I can get in.

"What took so long, Calli? I lost my two-minute window."

"While I was inside, a call came in from Trevor requesting they forward his mail to a new address." I beam a proud smile. "I got the address!"

"What is it?" Beth asks, as she turns on the GPS. Once the device is ready, I tell her the address. The destination is only ten minutes away.

"It's not the old folks home again is it?" Brand asks.

Beth shakes her head. "Should we wait for more help? I mean, is it a good idea for the three of us to take these guys on? Should we ask Crimson?"

I try looking for the future but run into the black fog of obsidian. Normally this would cause alarm, but knowing Trevor is shipping obsidian eases my concern. Plus, I have my topazes. And I have Brand.

Brand responds to Beth's question, "I can repeat in the presence of obsidian. They don't stand a chance. The only setback is I can't repeat with both of you for you both to know what happened."

Beth says, "Then you should repeat with Calli, Brand. She is the leader of this operation and is the obvious choice, in my opinion. Besides, If we don't shut down this blog soon, many lives will be on the line. People with powers will be outed. Diamond Bearers will be in danger."

I nod, happy that she understands the severity of the situation.

I can tell Brand is relieved that Beth approves. At a time like this, the task in front of us is far more important than treading on relationship eggshells.

Beth follows the prompts of the GPS device and drives to the destination. She points to the left. "There it is."

I examine the small, rundown, matchbox-sized house. An intimidating, large dog runs free in the fenced yard, guarding the front door.

"Does your mind-control power work on Rottweilers?" Brand asks.

"I don't know."

"It doesn't," Brand answers his own question. "Great. Well, I can avoid the dog, but I can't prevent you both from being bitten when you stop at the front door."

Beth shudders. "Yeah, no."

I'm happy to not have a memory of that. "Have you made it in the door yet?"

"No. I worry the barking dog will alert them and the guys will take off and run."

"Or pull a gun," Beth adds.

Brand places his hand on her shoulder. "I can repeat, Beth. Even if they do, we can fix this."

"Well, only so many times, Brand," I say, then am hit with an extraordinary idea. "Brand, if you can get someone to open the front door, I think I can use my mind-control power to make them secure the dog on his leash."

"Awesome! I can totally do that. Oh, and watch out, they have a ton of obsidian in there. Beth, you have your running topaz, right?"

Beth pats her chest. "I'm ready to run if I need to."

"I'm set," I say.

Beth and I get out of the car and wait for Brand to make it to the door. His zigzag movements and quick footing reminds me of his fighting techniques, only I highly doubt he's going to hurt the dog like he would an assailant. From our perspective, it takes Brand about six seconds of dancing around the salivating mouthful of sharp teeth before the front door opens and a man steps out.

Got him! I use my power to make him call off the dog.

"Fang! Come!"

Fang trots obediently to his owner, making a slight whimpering sound. I make the owner attach his short leash which is attached to a metal pole far enough away, so we won't get attacked.

"Come on, Beth."

We run and catch up with Brand. I continue to use my control on the man I now recognize as Robert from the photo. "Take us in the house, Robert," I say.

With a vacant expression across his face, Robert turns and holds the door open for us. Using Mind-control in this way is new to me. I could make this guy do just about anything I want. He's lucky I'm basically a nice person. But in the wrong hands, this power could be extremely dangerous.

I say to Brand's mind, *Once we're inside, I won't be able to maintain the hold on Robert with my topaz. I'll use it to remain invisible.*

Brand puts his thoughts forward for me to read. *I know already.*

Of course, he does.

We enter the front room and immediately my powers flee from my body. The rickety table holds several large pieces of obsidian. Good thing I'm ready for it. I've already accessed my topaz.

Robert shakes his head as the control wears off. He

looks at Brand and Beth. "Who the hell are you?"

Beth takes charge. "We're from the department working on the investigation into the strange happenings at the government compound west of town. We need to ask you a couple questions."

Trevor enters the room from an adjoining door. "We weren't even there when everything went down. We already gave our statements."

I walk to the doorway where Trevor exited and peer in. Crates of obsidian are stacked floor to ceiling. The two vests we are after hang on rusty nails pounded into the wall. I tell Beth's mind I found the vests.

She replies with her thoughts, *Find the computer.*

I'm alarmed as I realize the Mind-reading topaz on my body isn't very strong. In fact, there's not much power stored in it. I'll have to be careful how I use it.

Beth continues talking to Trevor. "The file said you both have vests with crystals in them."

"No. We don't."

"Idiot," Brand mutters.

"What did you call me?" Trevor takes a defensive stance.

"I saw you wearing one, man. That's government property and you need to hand it over."

Robert moves forward toward Brand. "You were with that girl who came looking for Dorothy at the home. How did you get her name?"

"Homeland Security can access anything, didn't you know?" Beth says.

Brand adds, "Like the information you're leaking onto the Internet."

Trevor jumps forward. "Whoa, whoa, that's not us."

Brand picks up a chunk of obsidian. "How am I supposed to believe you when you've got the $49.99 obsidian right here? The same that's advertised on the blog. This is enough evidence to have you arrested."

I check the other room. I tell Brand's mind I can't find a computer.

Trevor says, in a whiny voice, "But we're not doing anything illegal. We're selling rocks. That's all."

"Let me see your computer." Brand folds his arms and taps his foot.

"We don't have one."

"Yeah, we do everything through the mail," Robert adds.

"Who runs the blog if it's not you two?" Brand asks, as he walks the short distance to the room with the vests.

They look at each other with terrified expressions. Neither speak.

Brand asks again, "Who runs the blog?"

Robert says in defiance, "Show me your badge, first."

"I don't have to show you anything. You two are in big trouble with the authorities." Brand grabs the vests off the wall and shakes them while mocking their words in a high-pitched voice, "We don't have any vests."

"Hey," Robert crosses the room quickly and tries to grab the vests from Brand. "You don't have the right to come in here and take whatever you want."

Brand moves out of the way flawlessly. He's repeating, I can tell.

"You're not with the authorities, are you?" Robert points his finger at Brand. "You're one of *them*."

"Why don't the stones work on you?" Trevor has a slack expression on his face.

"What's the matter? Haven't you ever met someone like me?"

"Get out of here before I call the cops," Robert threatens.

Beth folds her arms. "Tell us who's running the blog."

"No way!"

"Is it someone from the compound?"

"Who else would it be?"

I decide to go in a different direction. I say to Beth's mind, *Ask them where they got all the obsidian.*

"Who gave you the obsidian?" Beth asks.

"Nobody." Trevor goes on to make a derogatory remark about Beth. Brand moves in front of him in one fluid motion and knees him in the groin, making him double over in agony.

Robert puts his hands in front of him and backs up a couple steps. "Really! Nobody gave us anything. We chipped the rocks off the outside of the compound walls."

Beth laughs. "They let you do that?"

"Yeah."

I pass another message to Beth and she repeats my words. "So, you two are out with crowbars flicking obsidian off the walls, thinking you might be able to sell the stuff, if Max will let you?"

"No, we were selling it on our own site, then . . . the blogger approached us to sell our stuff on their site."

"On Max's site," Beth leads.

"Max is a good guy. I don't know why you're trying to paint him out as a bad guy. And anyway, Max isn't the one who approached us. You're not going to trick an answer out of us, either. Now, get out of here!"

"Fine. But we're taking the vests."

I tell Brand, *Take Beth back to the house. I'm going to stay here a little longer and see what they talk about after you leave. Maybe they'll drop a name.*

Okay, but don't let yourself run out of topaz power.

Too late. The mind-reading topaz is officially empty with that last read.

"Those are ours!" Robert points to the vests.

"Whatcha gonna do?" Beth taunts. "Call the cops and report the government's vests that you weren't supposed to have were stolen?"

Brand and Beth throw a couple nasty glares at the guys and then leave the house. The dog barks loudly when they walk past him.

Trevor watches out the window. He asks Robert, "Did you leash up Fang?"

"No. I don't think so."

Trevor opens the door and unhooks the clasp, letting Fang run free. Fang runs right to the fence on the heels of Brand and Beth, barking his heart out.

"We better call and report this." Trevor pulls out a phone and scrolls through his contacts. I try to get a look at the name, but don't want to risk exposing my presence. Trevor waits for a response. I wish I could use my Hunter's hearing to try to identify the person on the other end, but I can't.

I'm regretting not testing the strength of the mind-reading topaz. It sure would be useful right now.

"Hey, just thought you should know we were just visited by a guy and a girl who took the vests. I think they had powers, but the obsidian didn't affect them." He listens to the person on the other end for a moment, then says, "Because the guy could move really fast." . . . "No, they didn't show anything else." . . . "They wanted to trick us into saying who runs the blog, but we're smarter than that." He listens for a moment, then says, "Okay, bye."

I can tell I'm not going to get any more information out of them, so I decide to leave. Only, I remember Fang is loose, plus I'll have to open the door myself, which will alert them to my presence. My topaz will eventually run out of charge and I'll be disabled by the obsidian. I have my running topaz. However, the door is still closed.

I should have thought this through a little better. I wonder to myself what the harm would be in them witnessing the unexplainable occurrence of the door opening and the dog chasing something. At this point, I don't have any other options. My ability to remain invisible in their eyes is about to run out. *All right,* I think to myself. H*ere goes nothing.*

I move next to the door, keeping my breathing as quiet as possible. I slowly twist the knob and then yank the door open with gusto. Fang is laying on the step. His head perks up and his eyes meet mine. I use the Runner power and jump over him. I land awkwardly and feel my ankle twist beneath my weight, causing me to stumble and stop. Pain rips through my leg, but no longer from my ankle. Fang has sunk his teeth into my thigh. I look back to the doorway. Trevor and Robert are staring with dazed looks on their faces. I know it must look absolutely crazy to them to first see their door fly open, then to see their dog in an awkward position, front feet off the ground, growling with his mouth full, being dragged down the sidewalk.

I've moved beyond the reach of the obsidian and my powers rush into my body. Fang's teeth are pushed out of my flesh by my intense healing ability. Just before I launch forward with super-speed I notice the fur around his mouth is covered with my blood.

The houses and buildings fly by in a blur. I only run about a mile before I stop to examine my leg. Have I had a burst of adrenaline? Is that why I'm not in pain from either my twisted ankle or dog bite? My pants are torn and bloody, but my skin is healed. My ankle is perfect.

Perfect. Huh. I'm not going to over analyze this, so I continue running back to the house.

When I arrive, I find Brand and Beth aren't there yet.

It takes me a few seconds to realize they're still driving back. My intense running speed is quite a rush. I let my invisibility go and take a deep breath.

Anika comes in from the bedroom. "You're back. How did it—" Her eyes fall to my leg. "You're bleeding!"

"Not anymore. I'm fine." I peel off the mind-reading topaz and set it on the table. "This one doesn't hold a charge." I remove the thought-projection one as well, leaving myself with only the topaz for running, and the one for mind-control. Those two I know work well.

Outside, Beth pulls the car into the driveway. I open the front door to talk to them.

"Calli," Brand stammers. "How did . . . how?"

Beth races past him and pulls me back into the house. "Aren't you trying to stay out of sight? Wait, what happened to you?"

Brand comes inside, toting the vests. Our powers are canceled until the vests are locked inside a large metal footlocker. Then, I tell Brand and Beth about my extra minutes at Trevor's and Robert's house, and my fight with the dog. Anika sits nearby, trying to pick through the conversation.

Beth asks, "Why didn't you extract one of their minds?"

"I couldn't in the presence of obsidian. Plus, I don't think it would be a good idea. Imagine him running to the blogger and telling him about *that* power. We'd be reading about it in the morning."

"Yeah, but who would believe him?"

I sit down on the couch. "It doesn't matter if people believe him or not. Look at how much traction this silly blog has gotten. Trevor and Robert are flooded with orders for obsidian because of it. We don't want to give any reason to encourage more posts. I've already raised their suspicion because Fang could see me. I can only imagine what that must have looked like to see Fang being dragged down the sidewalk."

Later, I open the footlocker and examine the vests. The green quartz is eerie. For each quartz sewn onto the vest, some person with powers died. I study the green stones and realize they aren't quartz at all. The striations are wrong. They're vertical, not horizontal, to the axis. I remove my topaz from my chest and compare stones. My topaz also has vertical striations. I conclude the green ones are topaz. *Thanks, Uncle Don,* I think, grateful for his tutelage.

I can't wait to tell Chris about everything. I try to communicate with his mind, but don't get a response. I check the time and figure, being almost noon, he must be working. An idea comes to mind. What about using my invisibility while bi-locating? I haven't tried that yet. But I don't dare experiment with this power on Chris. What if I failed and Chris was exposed as a double agent? I decide to try bi-locating to Jonas. How much trouble could I possibly get into?

I close my eyes and imagine I'm invisible. Then I feel for Jonas's diamond like I did last night. The office materializes in my mind and I feel as though I'm there. I find Jonas, relaxed in a reclining desk chair with a keyboard on his lap, typing away. His bare feet are up on the desk. I'm in clear view. If I was visible, he'd see me, but he doesn't. I make a slight squeak sound, startling him. He brings his feet down to the floor, sits upright, and swivels his chair. He looks right past me.

Excellent.

I open my eyes and end my connection. My invisibility is still activated . . . so, without pausing to consider the consequences, I try to connect with Chris's diamond.

I hear voices and the clinking of silverware against plates before I see the setting where Chris is located. He's at a restaurant. From the looks of it, a very nice one. He looks good. No, better than good, he looks spectacular. I didn't know he owned clothes this nice. He's slouched in his chair, elbows on the arm rests, with a distressed expression. Another place setting is across from him with food that looks to have been partially eaten. Chris's plate is finished.

Without warning, he straightens his posture and sits forward in his seat. I follow his gaze to an approaching female who's dabbing her red, swollen eyes with a napkin.

I'm devastated. I look back to Chris and want to strangle him. Kikee? Really?

Chapter 11—
Crimson's Preferred Method of Travel

Chris hasn't even taken *me* out to a fancy restaurant yet. Is this his first date with Kikee? Or has he been with her already? Is this why he couldn't visit me last night? I need to calm down. I'm breathing too rapidly and am afraid he'll hear me. I move a couple steps away. The Blue shard within my heart would allow me to hear what he's actively thinking about or what he wants to say next, however his mind is blank and well controlled. I have to suppose this kind of control comes from years of training as a spy.

Kikee sits down. "Why couldn't you tell me over the phone so I could cry in the privacy of my room?"

Chris says with a level voice, "I wanted to let you know in person."

"Well, you could have warned me. You could have told me sooner before I packed up and came to New York."

The more she gripes, the more my mood lightens.

"You were already planning your trip before you ever met me."

"Toying with the idea, not planning. I really felt like we had something special. You told me so. Your own words, Chris." She throws him a pleading look, as if maybe she can get him to change his mind. I anxiously observe Chris to see how he responds to her persuasive words and behavior. When his facial expressions remain unchanged, she changes direction with her attempts. "You can't tell me someone could have that kind of power over your thinking. I mean, if what you said is true, and you'd forgotten you had a girlfriend, does that mean you were tricked into thinking you liked me?"

Chris leans forward, pushes his plate aside, and puts his elbows on the table with his arms folded. "I remember thinking you're attractive and that you obviously liked me. At that time, I liked everything about you. But once my mind cleared, I realized what I'd done. I'm so sorry, Kikee."

She lets out a breath in defeat. "Yeah, well, I guess I should have known when you didn't return my calls." She picks up her water glass and drinks several swallows, then sets the glass down. "You know, I think your breakup line will go down in the books as the most creative."

"What do you mean?"

"No guy has ever used the excuse of having their mind controlled as a reason for breaking up with me."

"You make it sound like you get dumped all the time."

I snicker and quickly slap a hand over my mouth. Chris's spine straightens, and he looks right at me, and then his eyes move side to side, up and down. I drop my connection to his diamond as fast as I can, hoping he can't see me. I open my eyes—back in Denver—and see Brand walking toward me. He freaks out when I appear out of thin air.

"Holy crap-o-rama. Calli! You can't do that to me. I'm too young to die of a heart attack."

"Sorry."

"What were you doing, anyway?"

"Just boosting my mood."

❧ ❧ ❧

172

I wait till the evening to send Chris a mental message to come to me when he can. I don't want to be too obvious or he might figure I was at the restaurant. Nor do I want to come across as being too clingy.

I'm sitting on my bed when Chris appears in front of me. "Hi Chris," I say, trying not to express my emotions.

"Hi. I'm really sorry I never got back to you last night. I had something come up with work."

"That's okay. How was your day?"

"Busy. Oh, by the way, I told Kikee I don't have feelings for her."

"You did? How'd she take it?"

"She was mad. And disappointed."

"I bet. Well, let me tell you about my day."

After laying out the events of the day, locating Trevor and Robert, retrieving the vests, and wrestling with a Rottweiler, Chris compliments me on my natural investigative instinct. I wish we could talk all night long, but he has work in the morning. We say our goodnights and goodbyes.

I lay in bed, contemplating my conversation with Chris when I hear Jonas in my mind. *Calli, come visit me again. I have news.*

I close my eyes and connect with his diamond. He stands in his office, waiting for me, with a big smile plastered across his face. "I did it, Calli! I got you off the no-fly list."

"That's great, Jonas," I reply. "How did you accomplish that?"

"Trade secrets, sweetheart, trade secrets." He uses his best Humphrey Bogart impression.

"Really? You're not going to tell me?"

"It's kinda boring stuff to non-nerds, but if you really want to know—"

"Never mind, Jonas. I just wanted to know whether you would tell me. What's the latest on the blog?"

"I have a program tracking the activity on each page of the blog, so I know everything that gets added, even comments. Something new shows up every day, but nothing noteworthy has been added lately."

"That's good, at least. Well, Jonas, it's late my time which means it's even later your time."

"No worries, Calli. With the diamond, I've found I don't really need much sleep. Besides, I've got to keep my eye on the blog."

"Thanks again for your help, Jonas."

"It's the least I can do to show my gratitude for you, Calli. Once upon a time, you tried to save my life. Remember?"

"Yes, but you don't have to repay a debt or anything."

"I'm not, I'm showing my thanks. Goodnight, Calli." He waves.

I open my eyes and stare at the ceiling for a while before drifting off to sleep.

◇ ◇ ◇

"Calli."

I'm awakened by Jonas's voice. Sunlight streams through the window, causing me to squint. Then I realize he's bi-located and stands next to my bed.

"Is Mary helping you bi-locate?"

"No, this is all me."

I'm about to congratulate him, but he cuts me off.

"Calli," I note his serious tone. "The blogger posted video news reports of the Tennessee convenience store robbery as evidence 'these people' are among us."

"Uh-oh."

"Uh-oh is right. You and Chris are clearly identifiable to anyone who knows you."

"I better talk to Crimson about this. I'll get back with you, Jonas."

"Can I meet with Anika before we break connection?"

"Sure, go ahead."

"Well, I can't really . . . er, exactly . . . without you."

I realize he needs to be in the same room with Anika to see and hear her.

"Give me a second, Jonas. I'll call for you when I'm ready."

He vanishes. I get up and change my clothes and run a brush through my hair. Then I go out in the front room where Brand and Beth are already responding to the news of the blogger. Jonas evidently emailed Brand.

Brand throws a troubled frown my way as I enter the room. "You're not going to like this."

"I already know. Jonas visited me."

Anika's ears perk up. "Jonas came here?"

"Sort of. He bi-located."

"But he didn't even say hi to me."

"He will," I reassure her and then realize she's jealous of Jonas's and my connection. Funny. I hadn't even thought how she must feel about that. "I'm calling him right now."

Jonas appears and Anika runs over to him, and then right through him, forgetting she can't hug his form. They laugh and talk animatedly for a few minutes, catching up on the last few days.

I walk a few paces away, over to Brand and Beth.

Beth watches Anika and Jonas and she comments, "Bi-locating is cool. It's like watching a hologram in real life."

Brand says, "All those sci-fi movies with teleportation

and projected images, right here in the living room."

I turn to Brand. "Show me the bad news, Brand."

He plays the uploaded video segments showing the surveillance footage.

Beth's hand flies to her mouth as she watches Chris get hit by one of the robbers. "That must have been terrifying, Calli."

The video moves forward in jerking motion showing the gist of what happened that day, with one shot for every four seconds. *A lot can happen in three seconds*, I muse. Maetha and Freedom appear instantly and I point to the screen. "Stop, go back."

"How far?" Brand asks.

"Just before the diamond kills the girl."

Beth's mouth hangs open in shock. "Is that how she died?"

"Yeah, and the guy, too."

Brand starts the video again, but this time advances the screen slowly. I watch closely for the diamond. Frame after frame pass by.

"What a relief," I say. "The diamond wasn't captured in the footage." I take a deep breath and send my thoughts to Chris about the blog.

He doesn't answer.

I sit down on the couch and think about the current situation. Anika and Jonas continue to talk to each other. Anika has moved onto religious topics with Jonas. I take my focus off them and return my thoughts to the blog situation. Even though the video cameras never caught a glimpse of the diamond, the cashier still saw it. Maetha and Freedom were captured as well.

Crimson's voice enters my mind. *It's a good thing Jonas removed you from the TSA's database. However, 'Janice Johnson' is doubly flagged. They cross-referenced her face with their facial recognition software with the FBI. Now she's known for disappearing from two locations.*

Is Maetha going to have to change her appearance?

Yes.

How does that power work? I haven't tried it yet, well, on purpose, I mean.

The power from the Sanguine Diamond that's used to dramatically change physical appearances is draining on energy levels. It's best used in short spurts, not for long durations. I'd recommend you don't try it out until you're in a safe location. The Grecian Blue's power to alter other's perceptions would be the better option for Maetha, but—

I interrupt. *She doesn't have a Blue shard anymore.*

Correct.

I could give it back to her, Crimson.

No, dear. Maetha will have to reduce her visibility through the use of Imperial topaz and by simply staying out of sight.

I ask, *What happens next? Do Chris and I have to go into hiding too?*

You two need to go to the Tennessee State Police and submit to questioning to get this cleared. I'll go with you.

Mary saw something like this in a vision, I think.

Yes. Pack a few things. I'm arranging immediate transportation for you.

Okay.

I bring my attention back to the room and find Jonas and Anika are butting heads over beliefs. Brand and Beth are observing, rather rudely in my opinion.

I call out, "Jonas, time to go."

He makes eye contact with me and nods his head. "Anika, we'll have to talk about this later. Think about what I said, okay?" I like the gentle tone he's using.

Anika says, "You think about what I said, too."

"I'll try. I've got a lot to do here."

"If I mean anything to you, you'll make it a priority." Anika's insistence puts the hair on my neck on end.

Jonas takes a breath and says, "Well, you know, I'm trying to help save the world and all that jazz, so . . ."

Yeah, Jonas isn't liking where this is going.

Brand and Beth look at each other with wide eyes and silently mouth the word "oh."

"I can't be with a guy who doesn't share my beliefs," Anika states firmly, issuing what might be the relationship death-kill.

I speak to Jonas's mind. *Maetha needs your magic fingers to erase her from the system, otherwise she has to go into hiding from the FBI, TSA, CIA, HLS, IRS, well, maybe not the IRS. Say goodbye, Jonas.*

"Goodbye, Anika." He waves and vanishes, having not properly answered her ultimatum.

Anika walks to her bedroom with her head hanging low.

I glare at Brand and Beth, who are way too entertained with the drama. I say, "Knock it off, you two. I'm leaving."

"Where are you going?" Beth hurries to follow me.

"Chris and I have to turn ourselves in for questioning because of that video. I need to pack."

Crimson arrives at the house before I finish gathering up my things. She points to my bag. "No, Calli, you can't take all of that."

"It's not much."

She grabs my bag and starts tossing things out onto the couch. *A change of clothing and basic necessities is all you'll need. We're flying,* she adds.

Flying? Like, flying-flying?

I throw a worried glance at the others as I pick up my mostly empty bag and walk out the front door.

Beth waves goodbye as the door closes.

Outside, Crimson says, *Are your topazes charged?*

Yes, with running power and mind-control.

Activate your invisibility and focus on your healing power. You might get a little nauseous.

I focus on invisibility and Crimson wraps her arms around me like she's hugging me. I can tell we're both invisible. *Hold tight, Calli. This might hurt a little.*

What? We begin to rise off the ground slowly. I tighten my hug, with my head just below her chin. She also strengthens her hold on me. *Why couldn't we use the plane?* I ask.

Rodger couldn't get a flight plan that would get us there soon enough. We don't have time to waste. The future depends on it.

We are now well above the rooftops. A brisk wind blows past us. I don't feel like I might fall, or that gravity is so strong I can't hold on. I feel like I'm hugging Crimson tightly while standing in the living room. If I close my eyes I might be able to convince myself otherwise. I can see for miles in all directions as we continue to rise like a gentle hot air balloon. I twist my head a little to get a better look, relaxing my grasp on Crimson.

I wouldn't do that, Calli. Hold tight. Here we go.

I follow her directions and strengthen my hold. In a blink, my brain gets crammed into my toes as we launch head first to the east. I scream in agony from the excruciating pain, but I don't hear any sound. It's as if the sound leaving my mouth isn't able to reach my eardrums, like maybe we're flying faster than the sound can travel. Then I realize I can't hear myself because of the deafening roar within my head. The pain is almost unbearable. I think every cell in my body has exploded. At least it feels that way. I use my healing ability to try to ease the severe discomfort, but I don't know what to heal or even how to do it.

I don't know how long we maintain the painful position before slowing down. The loud roar lessens, then stops altogether. Our feet lower so that we're upright. I open my eyes and look around. We're so incredibly high in the air, flying forward in a standing position.

Crimson says, *How are you doing?*

Are you kidding? I'm just peachy.

Well, if you need to vomit, please turn your head to the left, not the right.

Huh?

We're about to reenter the gravitational field. The first time can be a little jarring.

What do you—

My body feels like a burning meteor just slammed into it. I don't know how else to explain the abrupt burning pain consuming the entire right side of my body. It feels like I'm on fire, or maybe a huge invisible branding iron is being pressed against my right side. Then the nausea hits. I turn my head to the left, just in time to hurl my stomach over the lattice of farmers' fields below. The pain stops and my tummy feels better. Finally.

The calm moment is short-lived and replaced with the sensation of falling. My hair flies upward, strands whipping my face. We are definitely falling.

I scream, "Crimson! What's happening?"

We're landing. Don't worry, I have you. Just stay invisible. We're coming down in the middle of Nashville.

I'm freaked out to be falling without a parachute, but at least I'm not in pain . . . yet.

As we near the ground, I feel Crimson slow us down. By the time the ground connects with the bottom of my feet, we're barely moving. Never before have I wanted to sprawl flat on the ground and kiss it all over. If this experience is what flying is all about, then that's a big, fat, no-thanks in my book!

Are you good? Crimson asks.

I'm not going to puke again, if that's what you mean.

Come on. She leads me around a corner to a couple dumpsters. *You can become visible again. I will remain unseen. We are going into the police station where they will ask you questions about the robbery. I'll guide you through the proper answers. Remember, clearing your name is imperative.*

Where's Chris? I ask.

He won't be joining us. He'll come down tomorrow.

I let go of my invisibility and walk around the corner. The police station is another two blocks away. I was really looking forward to seeing Chris. After observing him dump Kikee, I've wanted to be near him.

We come to the civilian entrance of the station. I open the door and watch Crimson walk in, knowing I'm the only one who can see her.

"Can I help you?" says a portly man with dark-rimmed glasses at the information desk. The nameplate says, "Officer Rodriguez."

"Yes, um, I need to talk to the detective overseeing last month's convenience store robbery."

Officer Rodriguez stares blankly at me. "Which one?"

I lean a little closer to the desk and lower my voice. "The unexplainable one. I was there."

"Oh, you were, were you?" I sense he doesn't believe me. "Have a seat." He points to the folding chairs behind me, then walks away to the desks and cubicles in the back. I use my intensive hearing, along with my connection to his mind, to listen. After a few seconds, he says "I have a young lady saying she was at the truck stop robbery. She's out front in the chairs."

A female wearing a navy pants suit, white shirt, and feminine tie walks toward me with Rodriguez. I read her lips, "Yes, that's her. Get Dixon in here. Hurry," she orders. She pushes open the swinging, counter-level door and approaches me.

"Hi, I'm Detective Judy Webb." She extends her hand.

What name should I give, Crimson?

Your name.

"Calli Courtnae." I shake her hand.

"Officer Rodriguez said you were at the robbery."

"Yes."

"I'd like to ask you some questions. Would you come with me?"

"Am I under arrest?"

"No, no, I just need to ask you some questions about what you witnessed."

I stand and follow her into the back area. She takes me into an interrogation room, which I'd figured she would. Crimson slips into the room before I do.

Detective Webb says, "I've been looking for you for a while now. How come you haven't come forward till now?"

I put on my best act of scared, college-age girl. "Sorry, I was afraid. Then today, somebody put a video online and my friend pointed it out to me."

"Yes, I'm aware of that as well. What can you tell me about what happened in the gas station?"

"Well, I was traveling with my companion and we stopped for a bathroom break. We didn't know we were walking into a robbery."

The door to the interrogation room opens and a tall, lean, handsome man walks in. He has wrinkles around his eyes and a few gray hairs.

"Calli, this is Detective Dixon. He's my partner on this case."

I extend my hand to shake his before he does so. I

also read his mind. He's a Runner. It hadn't dawned on me to look into Judy's mind to see if she has powers. I do so and find she does not, however she was close to a cosmic blast containing the Hunter power which explains her interest in finding people.

"Pleased to meet you, Detective Dixon."

I read his mind again.

She doesn't look like a Runner, like the male, he thinks. "Ms. Courtnae, what can you tell me about this young man?" He slides a paper across the table—a still shot of Chris and me at the front doors of the gas station.

Oh, why didn't I listen to Maetha and stay off camera? I could have peed behind a bush, or tree, or mile marker. "He's someone I know from when I attended an Olympic training facility about three years ago. Sometimes it helps to be a fast runner." I point to the picture. "That was one of those times."

Judy protests, "You did more than just fast. You disappeared, according to the officers on the scene."

"I can't explain why they missed us running away. We are pretty fast sprinters and our outfits were dark, so I imagine we blended into the shadows fairly quickly. Perhaps something from the other direction distracted everyone momentarily while we fled."

Dixon thinks, *What about the Shadow Demons? Two Runners fleeing into the shadows, I think not.*

Judy points to Chris in the picture. "What is his name?"

"Chris Harding."

"Do you have an address or phone number for him?"

"I don't. We parted ways soon after that. I don't know exactly where he lives." *That's actually true.*

"How did you manage to hide from the police and roadblocks? We had the area locked down pretty tight."

"A group of motorcycle riders gave us a lift. When we

got to the roadblock, we were waved through."

Dixon asks, "Who are these individuals?" He slides another paper to me with Maetha and Freedom and the four robbers. Three of whom are lying on the floor.

"I'm not sure." I point to Maetha. "I saw her before when I was at the training facility with Chris." I put my fingertip on Freedom's chest. "This one knew her. I didn't know they were following us, I mean, they must have been following us to end up inside the same store at the same time."

"Where did they go?" Dixon asks.

"I don't know. They were still inside when Chris and I left."

Det. Web thinks, *Her story matches the cashier's story.*

I add, "If you'd like verification, you can call Clara Winter at High Altitude Sports in southwest Montana. She probably has a website or something. She can confirm some of what I told you."

Judy asks about the dead robbers. "How did these two die?"

"Heart attack maybe? I'm not sure. I'm not a doctor." I point to the other female. "This one was pushed down by that robber. She hit her head pretty hard."

Detective Dixon says, "One more question, Ms. Courtnae. Why did you two run? Why didn't you stay put and let the police sort everything out?"

"I was scared. Two people had just died right in front of me. The creepy guy was waving a gun everywhere and knocking out his own companions. I was afraid for my life. I ran." I shrug my shoulders, hoping my explanation is good enough.

"Okay," Dixon says and stands. He reaches his hand out to me. I shake it. "In the future, Ms. Courtnae, when you are involved directly or indirectly in a crime, you should stay put. It looks bad when you run—in more ways than one. Judy will take down your personal information in case we need to get in touch with you again. Good day." He leaves the room.

After signing my life away and giving up way too much private info, like my address, phone, parents' info, and a copy of my driver's license, I'm allowed to leave.

Once outside, Crimson directs me to hail a taxi. I do.

I'll follow you, Calli. Tell him to take you to the nearest hotel.

Chapter 12 - Twelve Thousand Years Ago

Today has been one seriously stressful day! First the pictures of me and Chris show up on the Internet. Then I go flying—literally flying—across several states so I can tell most of the truth to the Tennessee state police. Now, Crimson and I wait in an upscale hotel in the middle of Nashville for Chris to bi-locate to us.

Jonas just left after bi-locating to tell us he's working on getting the host server to dump the blog. He thinks he's found a way to make that happen. We'll see how that turns out.

The memory of flying creeps back into my head. I don't ever want to do that again. Now I know how Crimson gets around so quickly. Brand will love hearing about Crimson's ability.

"Just so you know, Calli," Crimson says, having read my thoughts, "I traveled slower with you today than I normally travel. I knew you'd be in too much pain as it was."

"So, how fast can you go?"

"After I leave the pull of the gravitational field and am above 50,000 feet, I can go pretty fast. I don't really know how fast, though. It's all relative."

"Do you break the sound barrier?"

"I can, but I try not to. Even though I can separate myself from Earth's gravity, the atmosphere is still moving. I use the Primal Stone's atmospheric control ability to divide a path through the air. If I travel at lower altitudes, I don't split the atmosphere because of the effect that would have on aircraft, which means I have to keep my speed just below the sound barrier. I prefer to travel in the high altitudes, above aircraft traffic lanes, where the air is thinner. By the way, this is all information you'll need one day, Calli. Atmospheric control and gravity manipulation will be present in the upcoming cosmic blast. If we succeed at capturing the power, you'll need to learn how to use it."

"What? I'm going to have to fly?"

"Yes." Crimson walks to the window and peers out at the city ten stories below us. "You know, the first time I realized I could control gravity was shortly after I found the Primal Stone twelve-thousand years ago."

Twelve-thousand?

She continues in a soft-toned recollection, "I couldn't control the many powers within the stone. I was a Healer, which is why I survived the insertion of the stone into my body. I healed myself with the added powers. But I'd developed many powers and my tribe was threatened by me. They tried to force me off a cliff about as high as we are now. I was heartbroken at the time. My love, Kirkuk, had turned against me and led the pack to end my life. I remember not really caring if I died. I was destitute. They'd taken my spears and blades. My skins and leather straps. My fire-making tools. Without these simple possessions I would surely die in the harsh elements, against the beasts and other exiles. I allowed Kirkuk to run me off the cliff because I didn't want to live without him. All because I listened to the intoxicating hum of the Primal Stone and picked it up."

Chris bi-locates beside me. I put my finger to my lips and speak to his mind, *She's talking about her past.* He nods his head.

Crimson doesn't seem to realize Chris has joined us. She continues, as she stares blankly out the window. "As I fell from the cliff, the Primal Stone burned within my chest. I wanted to rip it out and be done with it. The ground rushed up to me and I put my forearms in front of my face . . . I'm not sure why. I guess I wasn't ready to die. My body stopped inches above the rocky earth. The smell of the dirt just below my nose is still engrained in my mind as if it were yesterday. The amazement of realizing I stopped myself from hitting the ground took a little longer to sink in. That was the first time I faked my death. The connection I still had with Kirkuk's mind revealed he thought I hit the ground, and because I wasn't moving, he figured I was dead. I decided to let him think that.

"Learning I could control gravity meant I could defend against beasts and enemies by simply rising higher than they could. Of course, harnessing invisibility came soon after and that saved my life many times over." Crimson turns to look at me and seems shocked that Chris is in the room. "I didn't know you'd arrived, Chris. Let's get to work."

I'm let down a little. I want to hear more about her life. Learning how old she is and what kinds of advancements she's seen over her life makes me feel unworthy to be in her presence. I had no idea.

"Chris," she says, "You met with Max?"

"Yes."

"Project your memory so we can see what happened," Crimson orders. She's back in business mode. "Sentimental Crimson" is locked up tight. I'm really glad she told me a little about her life, although I wish I could have viewed it the way I'm about to view Chris's memory.

I close my eyes and feel for his projected memory. I see through Chris's eyes he's in an elevator with Max.

"Chris, this is you, isn't it?" Max points to his cell phone which has a frozen frame of the convenience store robbery.

"Where did you get this?" Chris grabs the phone, feeling horrified.

"It's on that blog you told me about."

"What?"

Max snatches the phone away and holds it up near Chris's face. "That's you and Calli. What's the deal, Chris? I thought I could trust you."

Chris lets out a huff of air. "Yes, that's me and Calli. I was doin' my job and we stumbled on to a robbery in progress. We ran."

"Was that before or after you told your father you were against them?"

"Before. Actually, right before."

"Why didn't you turn yourself in?"

"Why didn't Agent Alpha turn me in? He's the mystery guy in the next frame. Did you know that?"

"What?" Max forwards the video to the limited shot of Freedom and Maetha. "No it's not."

"Anyway," Chris tries to downplay the whole thing, "why does this even matter? The clerk vouched for our innocence."

"Yeah, but he thought he'd lost his mind because you disappeared in a flash and the other two vaporized. This is the perfect type of video to be on a blog like this. Un-explainable."

"Everyone with a logical brain knows videos and pictures can be altered. This would be easy to dismiss."

"Except you just admitted to me this is you."

"Did you record me just now or something?"

"No, but I wish I had. The bloggers are offering rewards for useable material."

"Really? Too bad it all disappeared from the com-pound. We could have been rich."

The memory ends and I open my eyes, meeting Chris's.

"He's headed your way, Calli. I overheard him buy a plane ticket for Nashville," Chris says.

"I've already met with the detectives," I tell him.

"You have? How? Didn't you just get there?"

"No, we've been here for a few hours. I got to fly with Crimson, Chris."

He turns to Crimson and says, "You can carry people?"

"Yes."

"Can't you come and get me instead of having me get on Maetha's plane?"

"No. It's faster the way I've arranged it. You'll be here soon enough."

I ask, "When will he get here?"

"Tomorrow morning."

What a letdown. I ache to wrap my arms around him and be held in his arms.

Crimson says, "Chris, tomorrow you and Calli will interview Bearers here in Nashville. I want you to meditate in the meantime. You need to be as much at peace as possible. Calli will be doing the same." She throws a knowing glance my way.

I wave bye to Chris. "Hug you tomorrow."

"Yeah." His one-word answer is laced with anticipation. His form vanishes before me.

Chris visits Detectives Dixon and Webb before coming to the hotel. He and Crimson enter the hotel room. She walks to the other side of the room, but Chris stays by the door. His presence changes the energy in the air dramatically. I don't feel I can breathe until I touch him. My heart leaps as I rush over and practically throw myself into his arms, wrapping my arms around his body, pulling him completely against me. He holds me tight, as if he's been waiting anxiously as well. His body feels so good. Not even a whole week has gone by since I saw him last, but I feel like our understanding of each other has skyrocketed. I tilt my chin upward and meet his lips with mine. He's ready for my kiss and takes control.

Crimson clears her throat, interrupting our private moment. "Come here, you two. You'll have time for that later. We need to stay focused so we don't lose the upper hand."

Chris cups the back of my head as he slides his lips over mine one more time before breaking apart. "I missed you," he says against my cheek. Then he takes me by the hand and walks to Crimson. We sit on the end of the bed.

She says, "I had to use Mind-control on Detective Webb during Chris's interrogation."

Chris turns to me. "I know Detective Dixon. He was the 'big shot' at the Runner's compound when my powers came out. He slipped up and admitted he knew me and, well, Webb kinda freaked out. Especially when he admitted Max arrived yesterday evening and tried to get information out of them about you."

Crimson says, "I calmed her mind and helped her to dismiss you two as people of interest. I don't normally like to interfere, but we were too close to failing. Dixon was none the wiser."

Chris chuckles. "He shook my hand and told me Olympic athletes have to watch each other's backs. I have to admit, I'm really glad he's a Runner."

"Okay," Crimson says. "On to the next situation. I had Maetha arrange for a few Bearers to meet with you two today. You'll discuss the upcoming blast and get their commitment to helping you on the project."

"Piece of cake," I say. Sarcasm exposes my concern.

"I'll be with you invisibly. But don't rely on me to solve any verbal battles. I'll be watching the behaviors of all involved."

I repeat, "Piece of cake."

"Thank you for meeting with us," I say to Jie Wen.

When Crimson said Chris and I would be meeting with some Bearers, my mind immediately listed off my least favorite, who I hoped would be last on the list. I should have known better.

"We didn't have a choice." Jie Wen motions to Chuang, Marketa, Kookju, and Ruth.

I say, "Of course you had a choice. Thank you for *choosing* to meet with us. I've been given an assignment that I will need the help of all the Bearers to accomplish."

Jie Wen snarls. "You come to us with your so-called assignment, wanting us to abandon our work to help you? We perform acts that will help humanity, young lady."

"You don't even know what I've been asked to do."

"I don't need to know. Nothing is more important than what I'm charged to do."

Yeah, this is going like I thought it would. "Your assignment is no less important than mine. However, all of the Bearers need to work together to save the most lives."

"The only lives we're concerned with are those who will advance humanity forward. Saving men, women, and children who don't serve that purpose isn't our concern."

I scoot to the edge of my seat. "Men, women, and children *are* the human race! We need to save as many as we can, or the world's population might end up being just a handful of really smart people. Humanity consists of all levels of intelligence, ideas, and age groups. If only one group of people are saved, humanity will struggle to survive."

"You have no idea what it feels like to struggle. To not know where your next meal will come from. No cans or boxes to open. No drive-thrus, no twenty-four-hour stores. Only a blade and the wild, and only if you were able to feed yourself would you consider breeding and becoming responsible for someone else."

"What's your point, Jie Wen?" I ask. "All you're saying is you've come from a time before progress and inventions created an easier way of doing things. You've personally saved people who then went on to invent machines and devices and medical techniques that have made the world into what it is today. You're right. We wouldn't have survived a day in the life you were born into. But we weren't born then. We were born now. We get to enjoy the fruits of your efforts, but don't think for a second we're not aware or grateful of just how far Diamond Bearers, such as yourself, have brought us."

"And you should be." He sits back in his chair and raises his chin and looks down his nose at us.

"We are. Your experience is needed to help formulate the best solution for the assignment I've been given."

Kookju joins the conversation. "What is your assignment?"

I turn slightly to face him. "Crimson told me a cosmic energy blast is coming that will bring a new power, one that is strong enough to wipe out humanity as we know it."

"Why would she put *you* in charge of this if it's so important?" Kookju asks.

"I don't know, maybe because I didn't already have an assignment."

"What if I refuse to help?" Kookju folds his arms across his chest.

"That's your choice. But I'm really hoping you choose to help."

I hear Kookju's thoughts, *She's too weak.*

Jie Wen says, "If this was truly important, Crimson would have asked the Bearers personally."

I tilt my head to the side. "How do you know she's not doing that right now?"

Jie Wen tenses his lips and hisses, "How dare you suggest you speak for Crimson!"

"I didn't say that. She gave me the assignment and asked me to tell the other Bearers and get them to help."

I can see Chris out of the corner of my eye. He's breathing quickly and his jaw is set.

Ruth enters the conversation. "Where is the blast going to hit?"

"Portland, Oregon."

Because of the Blue Diamond, I hear anonymous thoughts. *Cut her some slack. She's just doing her job.*

Yes, lighten up, Jie Wen.

Ruth says, "I'll look to the future to see if any lives in Portland are more important than the rest."

"Thank you, Ruth. I'll get back to the rest of you with other ways you can help."

Jie Wen stands. "No. I won't allow myself to be taken off task because Crimson wants her new pet to look important."

Chris stands as well. I sense his irritation level has maxed out. "What don't you understand? You won't have anyone else to preserve unless you help Calli. This new power could destroy humanity."

"If the world's population was really at the precipice heading to extinction, saving it would not be placed in the hands of a child."

"Don't insult Calli!" Chris warns.

Jie Wen laughs. "Or what? Then there's you, Chris. A Diamond Bearer by accident. You shouldn't even be here. You certainly haven't earned the right to bear a diamond."

That's it, I'm going to use my Mind-control on him.

Crimson orders, *Leave now!*

"We're done here." I grab Chris's arm, expecting I'll have to drag him away. He follows without incident. Then I realize Crimson must be forcing Chris to leave.

I hear thoughts as we leave the room. *They can't handle the heat. They're too volatile. What was Crimson thinking?*

Once we're outside the building, we head straight to our rental car we secured earlier today. Crimson says, *Get in the car. Chris, you drive. I'll follow beside the car.*

Where do you want me to go?

Just drive, Chris.

With Chris behind the wheel, we drive away from the building without a destination in mind. We drive in silence for a few minutes. I don't know what Crimson's going to say. I hope she discusses ways of getting through to Jie Wen and the others, because I don't know what else to do.

Chris pulls over at a park. He turns the car off and gets out and opens the back door. I sometimes forget he can't see Crimson in her invisible state. I assume she must be communicating privately with his mind, telling him what to do. I wish my Blue shard would allow me to read her mind, but no. He closes the door after she's inside the car, then he gets back in and shuts his door.

"Hold my hand," Crimson says. She reaches over the back of our seats for our hands. I place Chris's hand on Crimson's as he can't see her. As soon as we take hold, I notice the blue mist of secrecy surround us. She drops our hands and says, "Chris you cannot lose your temper like that. Calli needs you to be strong and calm in those types of situations."

"I'm sorry. I get angry when they insult Calli."

Crimson doesn't respond to his words. Instead, she says to me, "If you use your Blue Diamond on another Bearer, they will figure out you have it and not Maetha. Keeping the secret is imperative. Maetha was able to keep the Blue shard a secret for many centuries. Once she began to disclose the existence, she was careful with whom she told about the quantum entanglement. Only Mary and Duncan know about the mental connection between myself and the Bearer of the Blue shard, and up until Jonas received the diamond while you still had the shard inside you, no other instance of quantum entanglement existed."

"Is that why you assigned Duncan to me and Mary to Jonas? They were the only ones who understood?"

"Yes. However, Duncan does not know Maetha surrendered her Blue Diamond and I want it to remain that way."

"Don't you trust Duncan?"

"Loose lips sink ships, Calli. Have you ever heard that phrase?"

"No."

"Calli, at this point, I don't know who will choose to support my desire to bring in younger Bearers. I don't want them knowing you have the shard. As for Jie Wen and company, they already don't like you. If they knew I gave *you* the Blue Diamond instead of one of them, they'd hate you all the more. They'd have to respect you, but they would hate you. You need to earn their respect before they find out you have the shard."

"How am I supposed to do that? You heard Jie Wen."

"Your actions will speak louder than words." She turns to Chris. "You on the other hand, need to understand this clearly: if you lose your cool like that again, I won't allow you to accompany Calli on this task. She has more patience than you, but once you became enraged, she almost cracked and used the Blue shard. Your life has held many disappointments and anger-inducing events. You *must* control your anger. It's impossible to forget what's happened to you, but you *can* control your actions."

"I understand." Chris bows his head.

"Maetha and I have worked for far too long to have this upended at the last second."

We sit in silence for a few moments. After being reprimanded by the world's oldest human, I'm feeling pretty humbled. I think back on the tense moments in the Bearer meeting. Perhaps I could have approached the topic differently.

Crimson changes tone and speaks to my mind. *Marketa is trying to bi-locate to you. Listen to what she has to say.*

The blue mist evaporates and Marketa materializes in the back seat near Crimson who is still invisible.

"Calli, Chris, I want to offer my assistance and show my willingness to embrace the new direction the Bearers are moving. This situation with the blogger has opened my eyes to the need for more vigilant Bearers. I want to learn what you know about the world today. What would you have me do?" She bows her head and waits for a reply.

Crimson tells me what to say.

"Will you accompany me to college and be my protector?" *I can't believe Crimson wants me babysat at college.* "I don't want to take a chance with the blogger trying to locate me. Will you do that?"

"Yes. I'll work hard to keep the blogger away so you can focus on your studies. I've been slow to accept the new advancements of the modern day. What better way to learn than to be around you, and in a learning environment?"

Marketa seems nice enough, but her response feels a

little forced. I say, "Meet me on campus on the first day of semester.

"The University of Toledo, right?"

"Yes."

"I'll be there."

Marketa disappears and Crimson reinstates our private discussion. "With the Tennessee law enforcement off your backs before the blogger could get a crazed manhunt started, and with Marketa offering to help out, I believe we've accomplished what we needed to do here. I'll have Rodger fly you two to Ohio where Calli can get ready for school. Chris, you'll continue on to the east coast. I want you watching Max closely. Brand, Beth, and Anika are handling things nicely in Colorado. I've got some issues to tackle concerning Maetha and her new identity."

I ask, "Do we need to meet with more Bearers to discuss the blast?"

"Yes, but not yet. I'll let you know. For now, return to the airplane. Leave the keys in the ignition of the car when you get to the plane and I'll have someone take care of it."

She opens the back door and gets out, maintaining her invisibility. She closes the door. I watch as her body slowly lifts from the ground until she's obscured with trees. I lose track of her.

"She's gone." My head is cranked all the way back as I press my face against the window trying to see her. "I'm really glad I'm not with her right now. Flying is not my cup of tea."

Chris stares blankly out the windshield. He says, "I think she does this on purpose."

"What?"

"Limit our time together."

"Well, it sounds like we'll have a little time together on the flight to Ohio," I say, trying to cheer him up. But I'm just as let down.

Chapter 13 – Digital Warfare

Marketa is less than social. She doesn't talk much. For a roommate, she's rather boring. As a Diamond Bearer, she's all business. I know she can't read my mind because I had Chris test my walls on the way back to Ohio. Marketa's thoughts are normal and nothing to note. Dull. And that's okay.

I find her behaviors and habits unusual, though. I think she might be OCD because she's constantly straightening everything. She does strange things like readjust the bedspread, align the drapes and blinds, and rearrange books on my bookshelf. One day she'll arrange them in alphabetical order, the next day she puts the books in order according to colors of the covers, or topics, or smallest to largest. I've found myself straightening everything around me just so she won't.

One thing she told me is she likes the modern flat irons for hair. "They are so much easier than warming an iron over the fire or using an electric clothes iron." She describes how she'd have to lay her hair out on an ironing board and straighten it manually. I guess there isn't a cosmic power that straightens hair.

When I try to ask her about her history, she changes the subject. The only thing I know for sure is she's from the Czech Republic, even though she speaks like an American. I figure that's a good thing because it helps her blend in better with the students. If she had an exotic accent, she'd bring attention to herself.

I saw two female students in the dorm wearing what looked like obsidian on leather cords around their necks. I tried to read their minds but found what I feared. The girls were wearing Yellowstone Obsidian. I talked to one of them, asking where she got the necklace, pretending I liked it. She said she ordered it online. I didn't press for information.

My class schedule is back to normal, but not having Brand around to keep me company really stinks. Day in and day out I do the same thing. Attend class, eat lunch, attend class, eat dinner, do homework, study, and research the city of Portland.

I need to learn the layout of the Portland area, the major roads, highways, interstate routes, etc. If I'm going to be able to get the city's government to listen to me, I'd like to be able to suggest evacuation routes. I've concluded there are some obvious bottlenecks in the roadways.

The Columbia River hems the city in on the north and it's crossed by only two bridges: the 205 and I-5. Heading east, I-84 follows the river through the Columbia River Gorge. On the Washington side of the river, a two-lane, narrow and winding Highway 14 heads east. But for Portlanders to get to the 14, they have to cross the river on one of the two only bridges. A smaller road, Highway 26, heads east from Portland toward the inactive volcano, Mt. Hood. The road eventually connects with I-84. So that's an evacuation option.

Heading south, the 205 curves around and connects with I-5 about ten miles south of Portland. This could be a major bottleneck, backing traffic up into the hot zone. The highways that head west might help alleviate the southbound traffic. Highway 26 heads west directly from the city center and ends at Seaside, OR. Highway 30 follows the Willamette River out of Portland in a northwestern direction and eventually meets up with the Columbia River at the town St. Helens. The Pacific Highway heads southwest out of Portland along with a couple other minor highways.

The question is: how far away from the blast is far enough? Maybe an exit to the west won't even exist.

I try to view the future once again. I look for specific elements of the blast, such as where it will hit. Nothing comes to mind, but I'm not surprised. I can't see actual cosmic energy. I look for traffic jams associated with evacuation. I begin to envision several bridges in a row in the downtown area, all loaded bumper to bumper with vehicles. I see the dual-decked I-5 bridge curving up and over the Willamette River. All lanes are being used for southbound traffic.

I pull out of the vision and write down what I've just seen. A central point will need to be established from which everyone should move away in the opposite direction. The central point will be the location of the blast, wherever that's going to be.

I try to envision the blast. I see nothing. I look for my participation in helping capture the cosmic power in a diamond. Nothing.

I switch my thinking to the organization of evacuation plans. What kind of management and planning will need to be implemented to make this happen? Halting inbound traffic into Portland from the north, south, east, and west won't be a small task. I figure at some point I'll need to learn more about the city of Portland's evacuation pro-tocols.

I look back to my map. Vancouver, Washington, is only a few miles away from downtown Portland. Will it be far enough away, or will Vancouver need to evacuate too? If so, traffic flow on I-5 is essential for mass evacuation.

I scrunch my eyes closed and rub my temples to ease the tension. This type of study and contemplation occupies most of my days and nights, eliminating my social interaction. Several girls from the dorm have asked if I would perform my matchmaking services for them, but I've declined. I'm just not in the mood. I guess I'm a little frustrated not being able to do what I want when Marketa is around. I'd love to have Chris bi-locate to my dorm and talk, but talk about what? We have to be careful what's discussed around her. I can't use my invisibility or mind-control. At. All. That's the hardest, I think.

I've bi-located to Chris a couple times and we've had some heart-to-heart conversations, which is great. That preserves my sanity, plus I'm feeling like I know him so much better.

In a few minutes, the Bearers are having a gathering. We are to bi-locate to Jonas. Marketa prepares for it by closing and locking the door. Then she sits cross-legged on her bed and closes her eyes. I do the same on mine.

Connecting with Jonas's diamond is easy. The first thing I see and hear is the ocean and rolling surf as it slides up the gentle beach. Jonas sits on a log just out of reach of the waves. I look around and see several more Bearers materialize. Marketa is slow to connect with Jonas, which I find interesting. Chris appears across the circle and winks at me, sending my heart into palpitations.

Quit it, Chris, I tease.

Just wanted to see you get worked up, that's all.

Maetha says, "Jonas, go ahead."

Jonas looks around the circle and takes a breath. "I've been working on locating the origination point of the blog. I already tried to get the host server to shut it down, but that's how I discovered the host is an anonymous server. Freedom of speech is a big thing worldwide. These types of servers cater to individuals like our blogger to help them broadcast their views unchecked and unstoppable. This type of setup is a good thing when it's used to reveal corruption or scammers, but in our case and the world of the clans, this is terrible. The servers bounce around from Japan, to Malaysia, to off the coast of western Africa, so they're impossible to track down. But I have a plan. We're going to flood the Internet with similar websites that, with everyone's help, will outrank our nasty blogger and bury his site several pages deep." Jonas finishes and waits for questions.

I understand him perfectly. Chris probably does too. Everyone else has blank expressions as though Jonas has just spoken an unknown language which, to them, he did.

Kookju is the first to question. "What in the world does any of that mean? How do you flood a computer?"

Jie Wen joins in, "We have much more important things to be attending to, young man. Gatherings should only be called by Maetha or Crimson."

Jonas defends himself. "If this blog is not stopped, every last one of you will be hunted down and killed. You don't have to know much about technology to help me out here, but you *do* need to help. I can't orchestrate a website burial by myself."

Chuang asks, "Why can't we just put a stop to the Internet?"

Jonas makes a few grunts, pffts, and ughs. "Stop the Internet?"

I meet Chris's eyes across the circle. *I think Jonas is going to blow a gasket.*

Jonas's hands raise, palms up. "How can you be as old as you are and not know anything about the Internet?"

Jie Wen takes his typical condescending stance and says, "We have our own Internet, young man. We can connect and communicate with other Bearers in a much more advanced way than clunky boxes with flashing little lights."

Jonas makes eye contact with me, his lips pursed, before turning back to Jie Wen, saying slowly, "That's called an in-*tra*-net, not In-*ter*-net." Jonas's patronizing correction is well deserved, in my opinion. He continues. "If your way of communicating is so much better than the Internet, then why don't you go locate the server and shut it down?"

Chuang's eyes widen with an obvious idea. "Why don't we just shut down all the servers?"

Chris speaks up. "The Internet isn't contained in one place, like in one building. You can't just lock the front doors and make this problem go away. Servers are basically really large computers with access to the fiber optic lines that form a spider's web around the globe. They're everywhere and there's thousands of them."

"Then cut the webs," Chuang says, as if it's the simplest way to get control of this situation.

Chris shakes his head. "That would be next to impossible. Besides, they'd just reroute to an uncut line."

Jonas dumbs-it-down even further. "You'd have to take the world back to the days before computers to shut this down. Or kill electricity worldwide. Even with a global electricity shutdown, which would shut down major servers, others would use their back-up generators and stay online for however long their fuel holds out. This is a different world than what any of you have experienced. If you bury your head over this issue, it will get lopped off while your eyes are shut."

Jie Wen inhales as if he's about to speak. I jump in first. "Jonas is right. The blogger must be stopped. He's already taught the general population about obsidian. If the blogger starts posting about Diamond Bearers, you can bet more than the villagers will be after you with their torches and pitchforks." I turn to Jonas. "What do you need us to do, Jonas?"

"Thanks, Calli and Chris. I need everyone to have access to a computer and the Internet. I'll send you files that you'll upload to specific sites. I'll do all the work. You'll only have to learn a little bit about computers."

Maetha steps forward. "I'll see to it everyone is set up, Jonas."

Mary says, "I don't see why we shouldn't just take Max Corvus into custody. We basically know he's behind this."

Marketa responds to Mary. "He hasn't shown evidence yet, so we don't know for sure he's the blogger."

"Take him out and see if the blogging continues," Amenemhet says.

Marketa nods. "That's one way, but what if there's more than one behind this? Take one out and the others will fight with a vengeance."

Maetha says, "Marketa's right. If we jump to conclusions without proof, we'll cause more problems. Jonas's idea is the best we have at this point. We will all participate in this effort." She looks all around the circle. "We're done here."

I open my eyes and see Marketa across the room. She hasn't stopped bi-locating yet. I think I'm beginning to like her.

The gathering with Jonas took place over a month ago. Since then, Marketa received a laptop from Maetha and I've been teaching her how to use it. Jonas has sent us several files and pre-written comments to add to various pages on the Internet. I figure he must not be sleeping much these days.

My grades are holding. I sometimes have a hard time

going at the slow pace of the professors. But a credit is a credit and I need a certain amount of them to get my degree, so I plod on.

Chris has been busy lately. He's been tailing Max as often as possible. The blog hasn't released anything new for several weeks and has begun to slide in rank. Jonas's multiple websites that debunk alarmists, UFO fanatics, doomsday preppers, and government conspiracists have really taken off. I know he's proud of himself, as he should be.

Staring out the window of my dorm room contemplating the last month's activities, instead of studying for my chemistry exam, probably isn't a good use of my time. The leaves are nearly gone from the trees as Thanksgiving approaches. I can't believe how fast the time has flown.

Marketa has done her job well, protecting my behind—from what, I don't know. More than anything, I figure she's just trying to show Crimson she's dedicated to remaining a Diamond Bearer. But in the back of my mind, I feel it's pointless for her to follow me around everywhere. I sometimes wonder if she feels the same way.

Presently, she's sitting on the other bed reading a book by Clara Winter.

I hear Jonas in my mind, pulling my wandering thoughts away from the window. He bi-locates to my side. "Calli, we have a big problem, with a capital 'big!'"

"What's wrong?"

"The blogger just posted about two individuals with magic diamonds in their hearts. Two young people, a girl and a boy. Us."

"Does he give our names?" My heart races.

"No. Not yet. Most of the info talks about super-powers, super-healing, and stuff like that. It's definitely moving in the Diamond Bearer direction, though. The only people who know you and I have a diamond were in the room at General Harding's compound. The question is who was in the room?"

"Max was one," I say with certainty. "I'll ask Chris who the others were."

"All right, I'll get back with you."

"Thanks, Jonas."

"No problem."

I throw a worried glance to Marketa.

She says, "You communicate with Chris. I'll alert the others."

I nod and close my eyes. I imagine Chris's diamond, but don't try to connect with it. I only send a message that we need to talk.

What is it Calli? His voice fills my mind.

I have news from Jonas. It's important.

Come to me, he says.

I get up and lock the door, not wanting someone to walk in on two Diamond Bearers deep in meditation and vulnerable. Sitting on my bed cross-legged, eyes closed, I connect with Chris's diamond. As his location comes into view, I find him lying in bed, a sheet pulled up to his waist, his naked upper half resting casually with his arms behind his head, propped up on the pillow. The fact he didn't cover up before I arrived doesn't escape me.

"Chris, um, hi." I stumble over my words, unable to keep my eyes on his face. I blink and clear my throat. A wide grin spreads on his face. Is he amused with my inability to think straight in the presence of so much skin? I need to focus. This is important. I look him in the eye and say firmly, "The blogger posted about two people with diamonds in their hearts."

He shoots straight up into a seated position. "He named you?"

"No, he only said a boy and a girl have magical diamonds in them. We figure the only people who would know that would be those who were in the room at the compound. Do you remember who was there?"

"Max! I knew it! That son-of-a—"

"Who else was there?"

Chris stares off at the far wall for a second. "I'm not sure. I'd have to see the files again."

"Do you think you'd recognize their pictures?"

"Yes." He looks up into my eyes. "Why is he toying with us? Is he asking for anything yet?"

"Nothing yet. Maybe he won't."

"No, I know Max. He's the type to ask for something in return for keeping his silence. I'll set up another meeting with him."

"But, remember, the blogger might not be Max. When you set things up, can I come along, too? Invisibly, of course."

"You're too far away to get here in time."

"No, I mean bi-locate."

"Can you do that? Invisibly?"

"Yes," I admit, cautiously.

"I didn't know you could. How come you never told me?" He acts nervous, as if he's wondering if I've seen him in compromising positions, which I have.

"We haven't had a lot of time together, to . . . you know, experiment." I don't want to tell Chris I've used it on him, so instead I say, "I tried it out with Jonas." As soon as I say the words, I realize I've made a mistake.

"Jonas?" he asks. His eyebrows come down.

"Well, I needed to know if I could do it, and I couldn't experiment with you."

An obvious change of attitude comes over Chris. Half of his mouth curls in a smile as he lies back and stretches his arms up and behind his head. He looks pleased with himself, as if he's figured something out. "Okay, I'll let you know when the meeting will be so you can come along. But make sure you don't make any noises, you know, like snickering."

"Wha—?"

His smile turns devilish all the way up to his eyes. "I knew someone was there, but I didn't know you could bi-locate invisibly yet. So, I thought I'd try to lure it out of you by not telling you I had lunch with Kikee. I thought for sure you'd get angry and fess up that you were there. You didn't. However, admitting just now that you can bi-locate invisibly tells me that was you."

"Chris, I . . . " I don't know what to say. I don't know how to react.

"Goodnight, Calli."

My mouth is still hanging open as I end our connection.

I'm sitting in class when I receive a message from Chris that he's meeting with Max in one hour. I respond, letting him know I'll be ready. Class will end soon and I'll have enough time to get back to my dorm.

Marketa waits outside the classroom door and walks with me. "I sense a bi-location in your future. What's happening?"

"Chris is meeting with Max again. I want to attend." I conveniently leave out the part about being invisible. Then I realize a big flaw in my plan. The last time I bi-located invisibly I was at the Denver house. When I reappeared, I scared the crap out of Brand. I'm not going to be able to go with Chris after all. Otherwise Marketa will become aware I have a Blue shard.

Marketa, being the intelligent woman I've come to know, asks, "Won't that be a problem for Chris if you're seen with him? You're not supposed to be affiliated."

I lie. "I'll be hiding nearby."

"Oh. I'll make sure you're secured in your room, and then I have some errands to run. Is that all right with you?"

"Okay." I keep my poker face even though I'm ecstatic to hear she won't be in the room with me.

We arrive at the dorm and I lock myself in and get ready to bi-locate. First, I communicate with Chris. Once he gives me the okay, I activate my invisibility and connect with his diamond.

The surroundings begin to appear around me, similar to when Chris shared his first meeting with Max. I see Chris sitting at the same table as before, his elbow resting on the windowsill. Max hasn't arrived. A glass of iced tea sets before Chris. He's not aware I've arrived.

I speak to his mind, *I'm here, Chris.*

His head snaps to the left, his eyes moving about, looking for me. The little bell on top of the door jingles lightly as Max enters the building. He nods his head in Chris's direction when a waitress asks how many in his party. He walks away from her and heads toward us.

"Chris, why the urgency?" Max sits in the chair and stretches his back.

"Do you know about the recent post on the blog?" Chris asks him pointedly.

"No."

"They basically name you."

Max laughs and leans forward. "What? Me? Why would that matter? I don't have powers."

A waitress stops at the table and Max asks her to bring him whatever Chris is having.

Chris insists in a hushed whisper, "It matters because the blog states a boy and a girl have diamonds in their hearts. There are a limited number of people who know that fact and you're one of them."

"Are you accusing me of being the blogger? Guess what? You also have that information. *You* were there, too."

They pause their conversation while the waitress delivers his drink.

Chris resumes. "I know the other three guards had their computers checked out already. You're the only one left."

"You can look over my files, Chris. I'm not hiding anything."

"Are you willing to let me look right now?" He stares without blinking at Max.

Max returns the serious stare. "Yes. My computer's in the car. I'll be right back."

"I'll come with you."

"Fine. I don't have anything to hide."

Chris throws a twenty-dollar bill on the table and the two of them leave.

Max walks confidently to his car and pops the trunk. He pulls out his laptop bag and closes the door. As he unzips the bag, Max says, "You're not going to find anything, but you're welcome to try."

"You make it sound like you do have something to hide and you know you've hidden it so well I won't find it."

We wait a minute while the computer boots up. Then Chris looks it over and opens file after file looking for anything related to the blog. I stand behind Chris, looking over his shoulder at the computer. I prompt him to search a couple files he skipped over. After an exhaustive search of finding nothing that connects Max to the blog, Chris says, "Just know you're the main suspect in this. Agent Whitman will be calling, you can bet on it."

Chris speaks mentally. *I'll come visit you, Calli.*

I take his words as an invitation to leave. I end my connection and open my eyes. Glancing around the room to make sure I'm alone, I deactivate my invisibility. If Max isn't the blogger, then who is? It simply must be him.

I wait and wait for Chris to bi-locate to me. It seems like forever before I see his shape form in front of me. Jonas's does as well.

Chris speaks to Jonas. "What do you think? His computer was clean."

Jonas says, "You'll need to follow Max to see where he's accessing the Internet. I suspect he's using a flash drive to upload files through the laptop onto the Internet. He's not storing the files on the computer. He's probably uploading from an open WiFi. If you can catch him in the act, or get your hands on his flash drive, then you'll have your proof."

Someone knocks on my door. Both guys vanish as I get up to open the door. It's Marketa.

"Anything new?" she asks once the door is closed.

"No. Max's computer is clean. We'll have to keep investigating."

Marketa gets a break from being my protector for the Thanksgiving weekend. The break goes both ways. I didn't realize how much I missed my privacy. I like Marketa. I mean, she's a polite, formal person. She doesn't try to boss me around or "mother" me. However, I'm still going to enjoy a few days of vacation, relishing in disorganization.

The blog has remained unchanged since the last post,

and Max isn't behaving in any unusual ways.

I spend Thanksgiving with my parents at a restaurant. My father has to go to work at five o'clock this evening and he wants to spend as much time with me and Mom as possible. He said he didn't want her to be tied up in the kitchen all day only to then be alone that evening with a pile of dishes to clean up. I have say, I agree with him.

My mother and I spend the evening talking about Chris and relationships in general. I've never had a conversation like this before with her, mainly because I've never had a boyfriend before. However, my mom keeps referring to Brand as my first boyfriend, to which I sharply disagree. She just smiles and raises her eyebrows with a confident, borderline-smug expression.

She says, "Did Brand ever kiss you?"

"Well, sort of," I sheepishly admit. "But it was not that type of a kiss."

"On the lips?"

"Yes, but—"

"Calli, I watched you two together. You liked being around him. You don't want to admit it, and that's all right, but Brand was your first in-depth relationship with a boy."

"That's different than a romantic relationship. I never wanted to be near him like I do with Chris."

"You learned how to communicate with a boy."

I'm not getting anywhere with my mother. I decide to read her mind. She's wishing I was with Brand instead of Chris. She reasons he's closer to my age, from the same town, and we obviously have a lot in common.

"But he doesn't make me feel the way Chris does," I say.

"I've told you before that feelings can lead to bad decisions."

"Well, that was before I could see the future, Mom.

Chris and I will marry down the road."

She lets out a defeated puff of air. "Are you at least using protection?"

"Protection? We're not even having sex, Mom!" I don't know why her assumption upsets me so much.

"That's good, at least."

"You're clearly worried I'm getting mixed up with an older man. You don't need to worry. Try to remember I can read his mind," *sort of,* "and I know what he's truly like."

"I do worry, Calli. You're my daughter and I don't want him to take advantage of you."

"Chris isn't like that."

"Have you asked him what he likes about you?"

"Well, not in those exact words."

"You should."

"What would you consider to be an acceptable answer?"

"It's not what *I* consider acceptable, but what you do. When I asked your father that question, he was at first flustered, then he listed off my personality qualities, my strengths, and a touch of physical attributes, too." My mother's whole countenance changes as she recollects the events of years ago.

"I think what you're saying is to find out if Chris is attracted to *me*," I point to my head, "or to *me*." I wave my hand down the length of my body.

"Exactly. He should be attracted to both but leaning heavier to your mind and personality."

"Okay, that's good advice. I'm going with him to Portland tomorrow. I'll find a time to ask him."

"Why are you going there?"

"He and I have some investigating to do for Maetha." I give my mother a short answer that she'll understand. I don't give her details of the coming blast.

"You'll be back in time for class on Monday, won't you?"

"Yep."

Chris speaks to my mind. *Calli, I need to talk to you.*

I reply, *Give me a second.*

"Mom, I need to go make a few calls," I say, providing a description she can wrap her mind around. Telling her I can speak telepathically would make her head spin.

I go up to my room and sit on the bed. Chris's diamond comes into focus. *What is it, Chris?*

Do you want to go on a date with me?

Uh, yeah! When?

Tomorrow.

We're going to Portland tomorrow . . . to work.

We won't be working the whole time. I'd like to take you to dinner.

Yes, I'd like to go out with you.

Okay, I'll see you tomorrow at 8:00 a.m. at the airport.

The morning comes with a biting-cold wind and large, wet snowflakes. A cold front has moved down from the north overnight but does nothing to dampen my excited jitters for my first official date with Chris. I think about the talk my mother and I had last night and am glad I never mentioned Chris hadn't actually taken me on a date yet.

I have my mother drive me to the airport. I'm relieved the snowflakes aren't sticking to the ground. The ground temperature is too warm. Our flight won't be delayed.

As we pull next to the private hangars, I see Chris striding toward us. He wears a thin parka and blue jeans that fit his athletic body in all the right places. His blond hair is matted and disheveled slightly because of the wind and massive snowflakes. The feelings rushing throughout my body are completely raw and primitive. I can honestly admit I've never felt like this for anyone else in my whole life. Good thing my mother cannot read minds.

He opens my door and leans down to speak to her. "Good to see you again, Dr. Courtnae."

"Likewise, Mr. Harding." She's polite, yet curt.

I jump out of the car, a little frustrated with my mother's attempt to point out his age. Chris opens the back door and takes out my suitcase. I say, "Thanks for the ride, Mom. I had a great Thanksgiving with you and Dad. I love you." The wind whips my hair around in crazy circles, making it stick to my face.

"I love you too, Calli. Bye. Good bye, Chris." She waves and Chris closes the door.

He wraps his arm around my shoulder and pulls me close to his side. "You're not properly dressed for this weather." He quickly unzips and removes his coat and wraps it around me before I can protest. At least he's wearing a long-sleeved shirt underneath. And even better, the waiting plane isn't too far away. I thought my clothing choice was good enough. I had checked the weather for Portland and packed for a thirty-percent chance of rain and fifty-five-degree weather. This snowstorm here at home wasn't on my radar.

I glance back over my shoulder and find my mother watching Chris's chivalry. She has an appreciative smile on her face. I wave my hand and she waves back. Chris and I hurry to the door of the plane.

Chapter 14 – First Date

Once we're seated and buckled in, Captain Rutherfield announces, "We're going to have a bit of a bumpy ride till we're out of this storm."

I look to my future to make sure this flight will be safe. No death today.

Chris turns and wraps one arm behind me, pulling me close. With his other hand, he turns my cheek and brings his lips down to mine. His warmth and sensitivity are like magical ingredients added to my near-boiling relationship soup. My stomach growls. I guess I shouldn't have thought of my feelings as food. I smile and giggle before we break the kiss.

"I'm hungry, as you probably noticed."

"Not to worry. I've brought food. Real food. We'll just have to wait till we're in the air."

"Oh, okay. What time did you arrive here?"

"Last night at midnight."

The plane rolls forward and we taxi to the end of the runway, then accelerate and lurch into the sky. Or maybe that was only my stomach lurching. Before long, we break through the storm and enter clear skies and smoother flying.

Captain Rutherford announces, "All clear. We have five hours of beautiful skies to Portland, Oregon."

I turn to Chris. "Where are we staying tonight?"

"Don't worry, I've arranged everything."

"I'm not worried," I say, with my shaky voice betraying me.

"Let me bring you breakfast." He gets up and walks to

the galley. He returns with a covered plate and sets it on the stationary table in front of us.

I slide forward in my seat and remove the warm cover. Underneath, I find a breakfast special similar to something straight from a diner: two eggs, toast points, hash browns, and sausage links. I inhale the delicious aroma and look over at Chris. He's watching me intently. "Thank you!"

"You're welcome. Made it fresh this morning."

"You did?"

"No. I forgot to add 'the restaurant' to the first part of that sentence." He steals a sausage link, plopping the whole thing in his mouth.

"Do you have a plate?"

"Yeah, mine's a little different, so we can mix and match." He retrieves a second plate which contains assorted sliced fruits and a couple pancakes.

We eat and laugh and talk about topics that don't really matter. I find I'm enjoying any time I get to spend in his company. I've even catch myself unconsciously touching his arm or knee while talking. I notice it because I realize he's doing the same thing. When I would watch people at college as Matchmaker Calli, this kind of body language was a definite determination of attraction. I shake my head and try to stop over-analyzing the situation.

We watch out the windows at the ground far below and experiment with our Hunter's super-sight. We play a kind of "I Spy" game to pass some time. After a while, we settle onto the long couch beside each other.

"What do you like about me, Chris?" I ask.

"What do you mean?"

"It's not a trick question."

"Uh, this kind of question is always a trick question, in my experience. I'm not sure what you want me to say."

"I don't want you to say what I want to hear, I just

want to know why you're with me. Why not some other girl?"

"The answer is no other girl is like you, and not because you have powers, either. I saw a difference in you before you were given the diamond."

"My aura? Oh wait, no, you saw the girl from your vision."

"Both. In Clara's office, I saw the woman from my vision in the girl on the couch. I'll admit, I wondered why I felt such strong feelings toward you, but as I watched you progress through the delivery journey, I saw all the qualities I've ever wanted in a girl. I like that you're an individual and not from the same cookie cutter as everyone else. You're beautiful, smart, independent, and determined. I can't be with a girl who needs me to be the strong, authoritarian-type of man. That's not who I am. Too many girls want guys to be that way but then complain when they actually are. You don't. You seem happier to have me walk beside you, not behind, not in front. I don't think you like weak or overly strong men. Your parents modeled that kind of relationship for you—working together, not in opposition of one another. My parents' relationship is the reason I feel the way I do. I can't have a girl who's weak and frail or who needs a man to feel complete. My mom is a wonderful lady, but she always thought she needed to be led, that she needed to be a shadow behind my dad's figure. I am determined to not be like my dad. If you were too much like my mom, I'd constantly be afraid of becoming like him. If you were like my mom, well . . . have I answered your questions?"

"Yes." My voice cracks.

"Have I upset you?"

"No. I'm touched."

Chris smiles. "Now it's your turn. What do you like

about me?"

I'm really relieved I thought this through earlier. "I like that you're not self-absorbed. You're dedicated. You have conviction. I've always pictured myself with a guy who encourages me to excel. You do that. I've always wanted someone willing to get bloody to defend me, but not go looking for a fight. That's you, too. You're not afraid to take charge of a situation and you don't need my approval for every little thing. I love that you're not perfect, but how perfectly we fit together. I love your smile and how my soul is warmed by your touch."

"What about my stunning good looks?" he teases.

"Well, it's been difficult to deal with, but I'm handling your gorgeousness as well as I can."

The plane touches down in light rain alongside the Columbia River. By the time we de-board and rent a car, the sun has broken through the clouds, illuminating the lush green area. I find it interesting how green everything is, even though many of the leaves have fallen. Crisp blue sky opens as the small shower moves off to the northeast.

"Where are we headed, Chris?" I ask, as we pull out into the departing traffic from the airport.

"Nowhere in particular right now. Let's grab a bite to eat for lunch and then do some driving around."

"Sounds good."

We find a locally-owned restaurant and go inside. A nice server seats us and gives us menus. I promptly choose a bowl of Pacific Northwest clam chowder and side salad. Chris orders a Rip City burger and fries. Strange.

After the server leaves with the menus, Chris looks at me and asks, "What?"

"Nothing." I smirk and put my thoughts out for him to read. *Since when do you eat burgers and fries?*

"They're good."

"What does Rip City mean?"

"It's to do with the Portland Trail Blazers' basketball team. An announcer used the term years ago and it stuck."

"Oh." I change the subject. "Are we going to go downtown to find the city's government offices?"

"No, we can look those up online. We wouldn't be able to talk with anyone anyway. It's a holiday weekend. I thought we'd drive the main freeways and look at the possible evacuation routes."

"That's a good idea. I already mapped out the roads."

"Do you know yet where the blast will hit, Calli?"

"No, nor how big of a radius will need to be evacuated."

"Have you heard from Crimson lately?"

"No, she hasn't communicated with me. She set me on my path and will intervene if I make a bad choice . . . or something like that."

Our meal is served and we eat while scanning the bodies of nearby customers, searching for illnesses. Neither of us decides to heal anyone; no one's illness fits the bill of being healed.

We leave the restaurant and drive around, crossing one bridge over the Columbia bringing us into Vancouver, WA. Then we travel to the other bridge and cross back into Oregon, heading in the direction of downtown Portland. After a while, we pass a sign that says, "Keep Portland Weird."

"Did you see that?" I ask.

"Yeah, it's great!"

We travel downtown to the banks of the Willamette River.

Chris says, "Let's go check into our hotel and head to dinner."

"It's only three o'clock."

"Well, we have to drive a bit to get to dinner. By the time we get our rooms and get cleaned up, we'll be right on schedule."

I note the word "rooms" is plural. It sounds like Chris is still gravitating to the safe side. I decide I'll follow his lead.

He pulls the car up to the lobby entrance of The Nines hotel and we get out and enter with our luggage while the car is parked for us.

The associate behind the counter, whose nametag says James, is well-mannered and professional, however I can't decide James's gender, not that it matters really, I'm just curious. I've become more aware of the world around me and the uniqueness each person brings to the table. This individual is one such person.

I've noticed several individuals since we arrived in Portland who didn't fit the typical mold of people I knew back in Ohio. Airport workers, rental car employees, restaurant staff, many of whom had unique and sometimes brightly colored hair, facial piercings, and tattoos come to mind. Keep Portland Weird, indeed. I find a certain comfort being in such a tolerant, accepting place. James's mind reflects that, too.

James's future opens up in my mind. I see him among many other sick people, his arms wrapped around his middle and doubled over in pain. Chris helps to heal him. I pull out of his future, knowing James will be sickened by the cosmic blast.

"Here you go," James says as he hands Chris the room keys.

Chris takes them and we head for the elevator for the

short ride to our floor. Once the doors close, I say, "I just had a vision of that hotel employee. He's going to get sick when the blast hits."

Chris says, "I've seen several different people's futures since we arrived. I didn't want to say anything to you just yet, but they're all going to get sick. But hey, that's why we're here. We're going to figure out how to help. Right?"

"Right."

The elevator doors open. Chris leads me down the hall and opens my room door, then ushers me in. The first thing I notice is the adjoining door on the wall.

"Where's your room?"

He points to the adjoining door. "In there." His eyes search mine for signs of fear, at least that's what I figure. He adds, "We don't have to open them, you know."

"How about we cross that bridge when we get to it? Now, if you'll excuse me, I need to get ready for my dinner date." I playfully nudge him out the door. After it closes, I focus my thoughts away from the depressing, impending doom of the coming blast and move them to the romantic evening ahead. I then unzip my bag and remove the clothes I've packed. I change quickly and refresh my makeup and comb through my hair.

When I'm ready, I knock on Chris's adjoining door. He opens the door, looking ravishing in dark jeans and a black, long-sleeved dress shirt. My eyes travel the length of his body. "You clean up nice."

He says nothing, only stares—like, jaw-droppingly stares. "This is the vision I saw when you chose that green dress for the funeral. I just didn't know where we were located in the vision." He closes the distance between us and places his hands on my shoulders. He slides them down my arms, moving his hands midway to my sides and down to the top curve of my hips and then back up to rest at my waist. His nearness is intoxicating. Not that I've ever been drunk before, but my head spins and my thoughts muddle as if I am. His mouth moves to my ear and his hands slide around my back. He whispers, his hot breath caressing my ear. "I told you it would fit. But, you need to wear something else."

"Huh?" I squeak.

He pulls back and lays his hands on my shoulders again. "I should have told you before you changed. You need warmer clothes for where we're going." His strong arms turn me around and lightly push me back into my room.

I walk to my bed where my clothes are strewn about. I pick up a long sweater and leggings and turn around for his approval. He's leaning against the door frame, nearly filling it with his six-foot frame. He doesn't speak, only nods, then walks into his room and out of sight.

Whew, I think, *that stare of his is still sizzling on my skin.* I hurry and change and present myself at the doorway.

"There you go," he says. "I just don't want you to get cold."

"Where are we going?"

"Uh-uh, not telling. Let's go."

We drive across the Willamette River on some historic bridge Chris feels I need to know about, but my mind is still in the hotel room and I miss his history lesson. He effortlessly merges onto I-84 heading east and I force myself to pay attention and get my mind back on track. I'm amazed at the heavy traffic for being the day after Thanksgiving. I would expect to see this kind of traffic in two days when everyone heads home from their vacations, but not today. Then again, it is a busy shopping day. We travel beyond Portland's boundaries and into Wood Village, then Troutdale.

I say, "These areas will probably need to be evacuated too, Chris."

"Probably. We're not that far away from the center of Portland.

"Where are we going, Chris?"

"Like I said, it's a surprise."

"Not even a hint?"

"Nope."

I admire the dense forested area butted up against the rising Cascade Mountains as we travel east along the Columbia River. We pass a sign indicating we've entered the Columbia River Gorge scenic area. Moss grows everywhere, and water falls from the cliffs above. We pass a sign announcing an exit for Multnomah Falls.

"Oh! I've always wanted to see those waterfalls, Chris. Do we have time to stop?"

"Yep. That's where I'm taking you."

"What? Really? This is so exciting! How did you know I like waterfalls?"

Chris glances over at me and smiles. He changes lanes and takes the exit as my nose is glued to the window. I try to locate the falls. The trees part, allowing a partial view of the upper portion of the falls. Chris parks the car in the packed lot and we get out. He takes my hand, interlocking our fingers in a firm grip as we walk on the sidewalk toward a pedestrian tunnel. A freight train rumbles by on the tracks above as we walk with many other tourists through the tunnel to the lodge at the base of the falls.

The roar of the falls and the mist dancing in the air, coupled with the smell of fresh-roasted candied almonds, melds together in a thrilling sensory experience. We climb the stairs to the main viewing area and wait for a few people to move so we can get a front-row spot.

"Calli, I wanted to take you to Cave Falls for our first date, but we've been too busy to be able to get away for a few days. When Crimson told me we would be going to Portland over the Thanksgiving holiday, I decided I'd take you to this waterfall."

"It's breathtaking, Chris. I'm really happy you brought me here."

"Come on, let's hike up to the bridge." He points to the narrow walkway that crosses above the crest of the lower falls and pulls me up the stairs and onto the paved trail.

I'm so excited to be by his side, hand-in-hand, with the sound of the waterfalls in the background. The only other time he and I have been together in a situation like this was at Cave Falls when I read his mind for the first time and discovered he viewed me as his soulmate. I remember how stunned I was to learn he already knew me. So much has happened since then.

We weave in and out among the slower tourists, most likely Thanksgiving weekend visitors, and complete the quarter-mile hike to the bridge. The view is incredible. We can see all the way across the mile-wide Columbia River to Washington. I lean over the edge slightly to see the water falling away beneath me, then turn and look all the way up to the top of the upper falls where I see people standing near the crest.

"There's people up there," I say, pointing up.

"This trail goes all the way to the top."

"Can we go?"

Chris looks up, then back to me. "I don't think we have enough time before our reservations . . . dinner reservations at the lodge restaurant."

My heart melts even more. "You made reservations for us?"

"Yeah, a month ago. Did you see the line of people outside the entrance?"

"I did, but I didn't know why they were there. How's the food?"

"The salmon is raved about, but I wish they served rabbit holes."

"What? Oh, right." I remember telling him at Cave Falls there were rabbit holes nearby. He'd said he didn't think he'd get filled up on rabbit holes. Chris's sentimental side is so darn cute! I didn't know he was like this. I didn't know I'd be so drawn to the fact that he remembers such little details.

A few larger drops of water hit my mist-moistened face. Rain.

"Come on, let's go eat." Chris lets go of my hand and places his palm on the small of my back, directing me across the narrow bridge, weaving in and out of gawking tourists. I notice one of the females has an Unaltered aura.

I turn to Chris. "Did you see her?"

"Yes. That's strange."

We get across the bridge and stop. We both watch the girl with the aura. I look into her mind but don't find anything that causes alarm. She's simply a person who wasn't affected by cosmic energy during development in the womb. Chris shares the same deduction and we continue down to the lodge for dinner.

We arrive back at the hotel after dark. Chris follows me into my room and walks through the adjoining door to his to take his jacket off. I take my jacket off and change into my night shirt with a cartoon character brightly colored across the front. Even though the night shirt covers more of my legs than the green dress did, I feel more exposed.

Chris saunters into my room, having changed into more comfortable clothing as well: loose-fitting jogging pants and a snug tank top that exposes his defined, muscular arms. He walks directly to me, wraps his arms around my waist, and buries his face against my neck below my ear.

"Thank you for a wonderful dinner, Chris," I say softly, wrapping my arms around his shoulders. In a swift movement, he tightens his hold on my waist and lifts me off the ground.

A squeal escapes my lungs from the surprise. "Okay, put me down. I've already determined I don't like flying."

He sets me down again, maintaining his firm hold on my body, and glances over to the bed. "Do you want to lie down?" His invitation lingers in the air.

"Um, okay, I guess."

"Don't panic. I just want to hold you close, Calli."

"I wasn't panicking," I lie.

Chris walks me backward till the backs of my knees hit the bed. I sit down, then crawl up so my head rests on the pillows. He lies down on his side, beside me, and props his head up on his palm, his elbow supporting his weight. His other hand finds mine and clasps onto it.

He says, "When Maetha told me I'd be accompanying you to Portland over the holiday weekend, the first image that popped into my head was this right here." He looks down the length of my body and back up to my eyes.

"You imagined me in a child's cartoon nightshirt?" I make light of the tense position between us.

"You could be wearing your grandma's nightshirt and I wouldn't care. I just want to be close to you. We've been so close, yet so far away for too long. It's deceptive being able to bi-locate because you feel like you're right there, but you're not."

"I know what you mean. I always feel empty after bi-locating to you."

"Touch is a powerful sensation." He moves his hand away from mine and drags the back of his finger along my cheek and over my lips. "Everyone needs human contact. It's science." He brings his lips to my cheek.

"Are you a scientist now?" I say rather breathless as he kisses closer to my mouth. A million fireworks explode and goose bumps prickle all over body.

"Mmm, no," he whispers. "I'm a delivery man."

"I thought you said you only wanted to hold me," I remind him. I don't want him to stop kissing me, but I also don't want to miss out on the opportunity to be held in his arms.

"Yes, I did say that." He sits up and grabs the remote control for the television, then lays back down and pulls me closer to his body. He hands me the remote. "How about you find a movie or something."

"Oh, dinner *and* a movie." I accept the remote and snuggle closer while I click through the channels. I find a slasher movie. Not that I like scary shows, but I figure the frightening scenes will give me an excuse to retreat further into his arms. I twist my head around and kiss him quickly on the lips, surprising him. "Thank you, Chris. Our first date will be something I'll always remember."

"Me too. And, you're welcome."

"You've made it very special for me." I pause and put my hand on his chest. "Ever since I saw the vision of you becoming an Unaltered, I've been a bundle of nerves. In my mind, it meant you could become a Bearer like me . . . like Jonas did. The thought of outliving you hasn't set well with me. But now I know we'll have forever if we choose."

"I choose to."

"I do, also. For tonight though, can we just cuddle? I'm not . . . um, ready."

"Absolutely. I'm not ready either. I just want to be close to you, like I said earlier."

"Well, being that I can't read your mind, I didn't know if you meant something else when you said, 'hold me.' I just wanted to make sure we're on the same page."

"Yes, we want the same thing. But, I might kiss you some more before the night is over, be warned."

I giggle and relax in his arms—such a wonderful place to be.

I didn't mean to fall asleep, but apparently, I did. I'm awakened by Chris as he's trying to get up without disturbing me. Too late. The movie is over and he turns off the television. I don't remember a thing about the movie.

He speaks in little more than a whisper. "I'm going to my room."

"You don't have to," I say, eyes halfway open.

"Yes, I do. Goodnight, Calli." He comes over and kisses my forehead. "I love you." Then he stands and walks to the dividing door.

"I love you, Chris." I'm left feeling a little confused. Did I do something wrong?

I return to school following my romantic weekend with Chris in Portland. He and I accomplished a lot concerning the logistics of what will be needed during an evacuation. By driving on the actual roads and bridges, it was easy to see where the potential problems will crop up.

Marketa is back on duty. She's mastering her computer quite well. Jonas continues to send assignments to flood the Internet, which we dutifully post. I keep researching how city governments work.

I think it will be better to have the city officials handle the evacuation, rather than the clansmen or the Bearers. Keeping the details of what Bearers can do, and how many clansmen there actually are, will be beneficial in the long run. Down the road, once the Elementals die off, perhaps the rest can go down as legend or myth, allowing Bearers the cover they need to do their jobs.

A few weekends have passed. Chris has visited me twice and I've gone to him once. We talk in our minds quite often when Marketa isn't around. I'm really happy with my relationship with Chris. I feel comfortable around him, yet am still so easily excited.

My classes are winding up for the holiday break and I couldn't be happier. Holiday break equals time with Chris. Hopefully.

I think back to August and the crazy, non-stop events that took place shortly after my nineteenth birthday and lasted nearly two months. Learning I'm the one to unite the clans and pull the Bearers together really threw me for a loop. So far, I haven't done that yet. My first meeting with Jie Wen and company went horribly sour and Crimson said she'd arrange more meetings, but that hasn't happened. It will, I'm sure.

Yesterday, I called Clara Winter and set up a time to visit her in early January. I'll be asking her to put together a meeting of the clans so I can address many of them at once. I know Beth's brother, Nate, is staying with Clara. It will be good to see both of them.

I pack up my things to head home for Christmas. Marketa will be staying at my parents' home as well. Although, she'll be in-and-out periodically.

Maetha has assigned several tasks to Marketa, since Maetha can't do them herself. She's still in hiding.

The blogger seems to have dropped off the map. Halleluiah!

Perhaps Christmas break will be peaceful.

Chapter 15
The Diamond Bearer's Secret

It's New Year's Eve and I'm in Denver with Marketa.

The decision to leave my parents' home came after a new post showed up on the blog. Additionally, the blog post was picked up by some much bigger bloggers with millions of followers. The blog post claims that pictures and the names of two Diamond Bearers will be released today. Chris heard Max was heading to Denver, so he and Maetha are flying here as well. I'm excited to see Chris again, especially on New Year's Eve to welcome in the new year. But if the blogger, whom we believe is Max, releases my name and picture, my whole world will change. I don't think I'd be able to return to college, and I'd most certainly have a target on my head.

At least Christmas break was nice and quiet . . . well, up to this point.

Marketa comes into the living room. "Max's plane lands in twenty minutes. Let's go. We don't want to lose visual on him."

"Okay."

We leave the house and get in the car. I'm thrilled with the prospect that when we get back, Chris might be here waiting for me. I've really missed him.

Marketa drives to Max's home address, according to General Harding's files, and parks along the road by the apartment complex.

Max arrives forty minutes later. He parks his car, gets out toting a laptop bag, and enters his apartment.

He comes out after fifteen minutes, carrying a large

suitcase and the laptop bag.

I say, "That's a big suitcase. I wonder where he's planning on going?"

After he leaves the parking lot in his car, Marketa follows him from a distance.

"He's too far ahead of us, Marketa. We're going to lose him."

Marketa shakes her head. "It's fine. I'm following his scent."

I wonder what she's talking about, because Max told Chris he was run through the power-removing machine, the same as Chris. He wouldn't have a scent. Perhaps Marketa is talking about a cologne or particular smell of his vehicle.

Crimson's voice enters my mind. *I'm nearby, Calli. I'll be by your side. Marketa won't know. Just stay calm.* I am relieved to hear her instruction and to know she's nearby. I take a deep breath and calm myself.

We follow Max to a big chain bookstore, the kind with a coffee vendor inside and free Wi-Fi service. This must be where he's going to access the Internet, like Jonas supposed.

He enters the building, carrying only the laptop case, and turns toward the coffee bar.

"Let's go," Marketa says, parking the car and shutting off the engine.

"What are we going to say to him if he's actually uploading?" I ask as we jump out of the car.

"We'll deal with the situation as it presents itself."

We position ourselves behind a tall rack of magazines, out of his sight. Max has his laptop case slung over his shoulder while he waits in line for his coffee. At the checkout stand, he speaks with the male cashier and places his laptop bag on the counter. The cashier takes the bag and places it down at his feet where another identical bag is then picked up and placed on the counter. Everything happens so smoothly, nothing looks out of the ordinary. I have to assume they've done this many times. Max takes the bag and his coffee and sits at a table. He removes the laptop and turns it on, sipping on his coffee as he waits for the system to boot up.

Marketa directs me to a closer location where we can see Max better.

He sets his coffee down and pulls out a flash drive from his pocket, then inserts it into the slot on the side of the computer.

Jonas was spot-on about the flash drive, but even he didn't suspect Max might use someone else's computer.

I receive the eerie sense that my future holds obsidian. I tell Marketa with my mind, *We should run. I sense obsidian.*

I do too, but we need to stay on course. We have our charged topazes and will be able to run if we need to, she reassures me. *Come on.*

Crimson says, *You'll be fine, Calli. Don't use your topaz. Let this play out naturally.*

Marketa leads me toward Max. We're going to confront him.

Max sees us approaching and smiles—not the type of reaction I expected. I read his mind and find he's placing thoughts out for easy reading. *I didn't expect to see you here, Marketa. Why didn't you tell me you were bringing Calli?*

I'm floored by what he's saying to Marketa, but I try not to let my face give away the fact that I can hear his thoughts. I question Crimson in a panic, *Are you sure I should stay here? He knows Marketa.*

Yes. Let this play out.

I hear Marketa's telepathic conversation. *Do it, Max, shoot her.*

Now? he asks.

I plead with Crimson. *Are you sure about this?*

Marketa yells with her thoughts, *Yes!*

But I haven't posted the blog yet, Max responds.

If you don't shoot her first, she'll disable you. Hurry!

Max pulls a small pistol from the laptop case, trying to keep the gun low so other customers don't see it. My fight or flight instinct is to run, but Crimson seems to know something I don't, so I stay put. I watch in horror as he aims. I enter his mind to see where he's aiming exactly because I know the gun isn't a big enough caliber to blast my heart out. At best, he can only injure me. His sights are set on my shoulder. Why there?

He squeezes the trigger. Intense pain rips through my left shoulder as the blast of the shot deafens my hearing temporarily. Even more terrifying, the bullet must be made of obsidian because my powers have drained from my body. I drop to the ground, narrowly dodging being hit with the next round he fires. A rack of ceramic coffee cups is hit, sending bits of shattered mugs raining down on my head.

Bystanders scream and run, some yelling, "He's got a gun!" through the previously quiet bookstore.

I can't believe I've been shot. Crimson said I'd be fine. I still have my running topaz that works in the presence of obsidian, but I highly doubt I could run very fast with this amazingly painful injury.

Max continues to aim the gun at me but doesn't pull the trigger. Our eyes are locked for a second, then he lowers the gun a fraction of an inch. He looks at Marketa and shakes his head, then runs, waving his gun to make the frightened people get out of his way.

Marketa bends over me, not knowing I've heard her thoughts. "Are you all right?" she asks, expressing fake concern.

She wasn't following his scent earlier. She knew exactly where he was going. A memory flashes through my head of her saying she'd keep the blogger away from me while I attended college. Now I know she meant "literally." She and Max are obviously partners. I nod, holding my bleeding shoulder.

Her eyes travel over my shoulder area. "Looks like the obsidian bullet shattered and pelted you with a bunch of shards."

Interesting that she knows it's an obsidian bullet. She hasn't even touched me yet. I want to point that fact out to her, but Crimson stops me.

"Oh my God!" a male bookstore employee exclaims. "Is she dead?"

"No, just injured," Marketa assures him.

"Where did the gunman go?" he asks as he looks around frantically.

Marketa says, "He took off that way." She points toward the back of the store.

The employee anxiously issues instructions to someone at the coffee counter to call an ambulance. A female standing nearby tells him she's on the line with emergency services and help is on the way. Most of the other customers have fled the building.

My injury isn't life-threatening, so I decide to play along with Marketa's ruse. I ask, "Did Max leave his computer?"

She glances over to where he was. "Yes."

"We have to delete his blog, Marketa. Help me up."

She lifts me to my feet and helps me to the table. Max's laptop is logged on to the blog and the file is ready to go. My own face stares back at me on the screen. Another picture shows Jonas lying on the floor in the compound just after the diamond had been shoved against his chest by Freedom. Max must have gotten hold of the surveillance footage soon after the event took place. Our names are listed and Jonas's picture includes his faked death information. This is bad and must be deleted. I highlight the content and hit the backspace key. Then I go to Max's blog profile and change the login password so he'll at least have a struggle to get back into his account. I yank out the flash drive and put it in my pocket.

Blood drips from my elbow onto the floor. The shrill wail of approaching emergency vehicles catches my attention.

Marketa says, "Time to go. The police are coming." She takes my hand and helps me walk.

"What are you doing?" The bookstore employee points to the front windows, wiggling his finger, shaking his head. "The paramedics are here. You can't leave until the police come." Even though I can't read his mind, his facial expression tells me he's quite confused with our be-havior.

Marketa ignores him and takes me outside.

The paramedics are readying their equipment, waiting for the police to arrive to secure the building first before entering.

Marketa whispers, "Get on my back. We need to get out of here."

I do so and find it hard to hold onto her with only one arm. As Marketa jogs away from the building, the police arrive. I assume she's jogging because she doesn't want to be recorded as an inexplicable flash on surveillance, like Chris and I were. The motion is killing my shoulder.

"Hang on, Calli," Marketa says, then pours on the speed.

By the time we arrive at the house, I've lost a good

amount of blood. I'm light-headed and wobbly on my feet, but Crimson said I'd be fine, so I try not to worry. I'm saddened to find Chris hasn't arrived yet. To get my mind off the pain, I try to focus on finding out why Marketa is a traitor.

Marketa lays me on the dining room table and rips my shirt open, flinging buttons across the room. My shoulder is extremely sore and I really hope Crimson will show up soon and make me feel better.

Marketa asks, "Is there a first-aid kit around here?"

"Under the bathroom sink," I utter through gritted teeth. Being laid on my back on the hard surface makes my injury even more painful.

She leaves and then returns with the small metal box with a red and white plus sign on the top. She places the box by my feet and opens the lid, then removes the contents and places them carefully on the table in an orderly fashion.

I feel like shouting, *Hey, don't worry about me. I'm just bleeding out here!*

Finally, she moves up to my wound holding a pair of tweezers. Instead of going to work on removing the obsidian, she rips my taped-on topazes off my chest.

"You won't be needing these anymore." She separates the stones and clutches one of them in her hand and pauses for a moment, then says, "Oh, my. So, that's how you're able to do what you do. You have a mind-control topaz. Clever. You *definitely* won't be needing this." She sets the topaz down on the table away from me. She pushes my shirt over my injured shoulder and goes to work picking the easy to reach obsidian pieces out of my flesh with the tweezers. Each piece is dropped inside the first aid box with a barely-audible click sound.

I crane my head to look at my shoulder for the first

time. It's hard to see the full extent of my injury because my neck won't bend that far, plus doing so hurts badly. I see one larger wound and several smaller openings. I assume a piece of obsidian is in each of the smaller openings.

She digs deeper into my muscle and I scream in agony.

"Come now, Calli. Be the brave girl Crimson thinks you are."

I try to control my reaction to the pain. I'm not sure I heard her correctly, but it sounded like she just insulted Crimson.

Another clink is heard. This time when she digs into my flesh, she says, "Oh dear, this obsidian is sharp. I nicked a vein that time."

I feel liquid warmth trickle along my collar bone to my neck and slide down the back of my shoulder onto the table. I turn my head to see what she's doing and find my wound is much bigger. She's injuring me in the process of fishing out the pieces of obsidian.

I struggle to get up—Crimson's expressed wishes be damned. I've got to get myself out of this situation before Marketa kills me.

Marketa holds me down. "You're not going anywhere, Calli. I'm not finished." She retrieves another piece and drops it into the box.

My powers haven't returned yet. There must still be more inside my body.

She continues her ministrations while saying, "You know, we stopped Max just in time to prevent exposing your identity to the world. You were going to run when you sensed obsidian . . . run away like a scared child" — another piece lands in the metal box— "but if you had, your name and picture would be all over the Internet now.

I try to think clearly, figuring I might be able to get her

to talk. Through gritted teeth, I say, "Max didn't seem shocked to see us."

"Well, he probably knew you'd catch him at some point." Another clink. "It's too bad we're all alone in this situation. No one knows you need help. No one can even bi-locate to us."

"You're helping me." I wince with more pain.

"Not really. What I'm doing is helping Crimson and Maetha realize they've made a mistake by bringing in a teenager to do an adult's job. None of the other Bearers were sixteen when they got their diamonds. Why you?"

Searing pain rips through my shoulder, worse than before. I scream and try to get up again. What is she doing to me? I still don't have my powers back. I don't have my topaz, but I know it's not far away. She'd laid it on the table. If I can just get to it, I could freeze her and try to save my own life.

"You've got a lot of fight in you, I'll give you that," she commends while holding me down. "I'll have a good tale to tell of how you wouldn't hold still so I could get the obsidian out before you bled out."

"Why are you doing this?" I plead.

"Because kids are not Bearers! Giving all that info to Max did a good job of scaring everyone, but probably wasn't going to ever be as effective as just having you die. This is a much better solution. I'd rather have diamonds without Bearers than have children with diamonds."

"Why didn't you just kill me at college?"

"I could have. Thought about it a few times. But everyone would know it was me and I'd be punished. This is much better. An unfortunate accident." She drops another shard in the box.

I take a shallow breath, trying to ignore my pain and the swimming room. "Why are you still removing the pieces if you want me to die?"

"Got to make it look like I tried everything I could. I have to look convincing to Crimson."

"How long have you been against Crimson?"

"Ever since you were chosen," she says.

"How have you kept your feelings secret?"

"I learned a long time ago that the Blue Diamond allows the Bearer to hear other Bearers' thoughts. So, whenever Maetha or Crimson was around, I minded my mental tongue."

I say, "I bet you could still save your life if you'd recommit to the Bearers. You haven't been against nature for very long."

She laughs. "Listen to you. Acting as if you're not dying, thinking you still have a position as a Bearer." She raises her voice in exasperation. "You were wearing a mind-control topaz, for crying out loud. You didn't even have enough sense to use it on Max!"

I warn, "You're crossing the line, Marketa."

"I've crossed the line so many times that it's impossible to know where the line is anymore. All Bearers cross the line eventually. You already have," she accuses.

"I haven't crossed the line."

"Yes, you have. You killed Hunters and criminals."

"I had to."

"Exactly. In war, each side crosses the line and kills the other. Yet, each side believes they're in the right."

"I wasn't aware the Bearers were at war with one another."

"We don't think Crimson and Maetha are following nature's will by bringing in kids."

"That's ironic. I think Crimson feels you are out of line with nature."

As Marketa pokes her finger in my wound, she says,

"See, both sides feel they're right."

I writhe on the table as she swirls her finger around inside my shoulder. My mind becomes hazy.

"Can't have you clotting up, now can we?" She uses my shirt to wipe the blood off her finger and continues, "Maetha will be shocked, no doubt, to hear of your death. She selected you. We all thought your mother was the better candidate, but Maetha chose you. It's time Maetha starts listening to the group, instead of running things independently. Once you're dead, we'll take out Chris and Jonas and get things back to normal."

Oh, that's it! A surge of defiant energy rushes through my deflated veins. I say, "The only person qualified to decide who is capable of keeping a diamond is the Diamond Maker—your boss. You were hired to do a job. You've not only failed, you refuse to do the job."

Crimson appears beside the table.

Marketa takes a step back, completely stunned. "Huh? How long have you been here?"

Crimson says, "Long enough to know you don't deserve a second chance. Surrender your diamond!"

I turn my head to try to get a better view of what's going on. I notice a baseball-sized piece of regular obsidian from General Harding's collection rise off the shelf behind Marketa and float in a stationary position.

Marketa says, still astounded by Crimson's sudden appearance, "What? You expect me to hand my diamond to you? Now?"

"You've lost your right to be a Bearer."

"I disagree. You've lost your mind."

"This is not a debate. If you won't give it to me, I'll take it from you."

Marketa grabs onto her belt and pulls off one of the medallions, exposing a large piece of obsidian, and laughs.

"How are you going to do that?"

"With obsidian," Crimson states calmly. She raises her clenched fist to shoulder level and in the blink of an eye, pops open her hand, extending her fingers. The floating lump of volcanic glass rockets forward into Marketa's back, blasting her heart out the front of her chest. The obsidian continues flying directly into Crimson's open hand. Marketa's heart lands on the floor with a thud. Her body is a little slower to crumple into a heap.

"Hang on, Calli," Crimson says, hastily picking up the heart and setting it inside the metal box with the obsidian pieces. She also replaces the metal medallion over the large piece of obsidian on Marketa's belt to contain the effects. Then in one fluid motion, she reaches into my wound and removes the last obsidian piece. She places the final piece inside the box and closes the lid. My powers rush into my body like a battering ram.

Maetha appears the moment the obsidian is covered.

Crimson lays her hands over my wounds. "Let me heal you, Calli. Save your strength." She turns to Maetha, angrier than I've ever seen her. "This shouldn't have happened!"

"I'm as perplexed as you are. I thought she was strong enough," Maetha responds in an emotion-chocked voice.

"Who is nearby? Someone needs to come take care of Marketa's body." Crimson nods toward the floor and brings a shaky hand to her forehead.

Maetha must not have noticed Marketa when she appeared. *What happened? Was she shot?* Maetha directs her thoughts exclusively to Crimson, but I overhear because of the Blue Diamond. *How is this possible? Did she remove her own diamond?*

I am not able to hear Crimson's thoughts, but I don't need to. I am able to pick up on the conversation.

Maetha says, *You used the Primal Stone to remove her diamond. But why? Marketa was supposed to protect Calli. If I had any idea she could be injured I would have gone myself. I was certain she wouldn't be harmed.*

I mutter, "Max had obsidian bullets."

Chris bi-locates to my side, drawing my attention away from Maetha and Crimson.

"What's happening? Why are you bleeding?" Chris panics.

I reach out for him, but my hand moves through his form. "Max shot me and Marketa tried to kill me," I mumble. I'm really weak and just want to go to sleep.

Crimson taps my cheek firmly. "Stay with me, Calli. Keep your eyes open."

Stay with her? Where am I going to go?

I look at Chris and wish I could touch him, but he's just air, not real. I close my eyes for a moment. When I open them, he's gone. Crimson is still healing me.

"Why did he leave?" I ask.

"Their plane landed a half hour ago. They'll be here shortly." Crimson's voice is strangely quiet.

"Are you okay?" I ask, barely able to get the words out of my mouth.

"I will be, and so will you."

I notice the glittering blue mist around our bodies. She must not want anyone else to know what's happened. I wonder why.

Chris and Maetha come barreling through the front door. Chris doesn't stop running till he's by my side, stroking my hair and kissing my forehead.

Maetha takes over for Crimson and places her hands over my wounds. Crimson sits down right away, as if all her strength has gone.

Maetha says, "Chris, give strength to Crimson."

He reaches one hand to her, not wanting to let go of me.

"No," Maetha says sternly. "Both hands. I've got Calli covered."

Chris moves to Crimson and grabs both of her bloody hands.

The four of us sit in silence for several long seconds. My mind replays the events at the bookstore. I clear my throat and say, "Marketa knew where Max was going. He wasn't surprised to see her. That was my tipoff. Marketa seemed to know he had a gun and told him to shoot me." I turn my head a little and look at Crimson. "Why did you tell me I'd be fine?"

"Because you weren't supposed to get shot. I thought we were about to make a big point to Marketa about why you were chosen to be a Diamond Bearer. It went terribly wrong."

Chris asks, "What point? What do you mean?"

Maetha looks at Crimson and they exchange glances. Maetha says, "We should wait to begin this discussion. The Healers will be here soon to pick up Marketa's body." Maetha's thoughts continue, *If Calli doesn't make it, there's no point in discussing anything.*

"Maetha's right. We need to wait." She stands and drops Chris's hands. "Thank you, Chris. I'm good now. Take Calli in the bedroom and use your healing power on her shoulder. Maetha needs a break."

Chris closes my shirt over my chest and helps me sit up. I'd forgotten my shirt was wide open, exposing my bra.

Maetha's thoughts to Crimson are heard in my mind. *This could be over. All this planning will have been for nothing . . . my powers didn't improve her, only kept her hanging on, the same as yours. Why did you wait so long to intervene?*

Chris lifts me off the table and holds me in his arms. I

rest my forehead on his neck. His skin contact with mine infuses some energy into my weak body.

Crimson approaches us. She places a hand on each of our shoulders. "No one will be able to see or hear you." The glittering mist of secrecy enshrouds us. Chris carries me into the bedroom where my belongings are.

I remember when he helped me after Maetha tried to insert the diamond into my heart at Lake Patoka. Before that, he was the one to remove my lifeless body from the stone altar. Too many times Chris has been in this stressful position of caring for me. I'm tired of feeling so helpless. And I don't even know how to interpret Maetha's thoughts just now. She acts as though I'm dying. Maybe that's why Crimson is isolating us from the other Bearers' knowledge. She doesn't want them to know when I die.

"I was so afraid when you passed out earlier," Chris says. "So was Crimson and Maetha. They argued about your readiness and your alteration, whatever that meant."

"Crimson has said a lot of confusing things."

He lowers me down onto the bed. "Let's take that shirt off." Grabbing my good arm, he eases the shirt open and pulls my arm out. Then he brings the shirt around my back and pulls it off my left arm, leaving me sitting in only my bra and pants. "Lay back," he suggests, placing his hand on my back to support my body as I lay down. He sits on the edge of the bed, leaning over me.

I close my eyes and focus on his touch. He's not an apparition this time. He's real and his hands are like magical feathers moving across my skin, infusing me with much needed strength. His fingers travel to my blood-covered shoulder. "Your wound is not healed yet. If neither Crimson nor Maetha could heal you, how are you going to get better?"

"I don't know. Crimson told me not to use my powers, to save my strength. But I want to try to heal myself now. I need to try, at least."

"Together. Let's do it together." Chris takes my other hand and places it on top of his, on top of my wound.

I access the healing power within the diamond and focus the energy to my shoulder. What happens next is something entirely new. A tremendous, scorching-hot sensation emanates from my shoulder. I open my eyes in alarm and see Chris's eyes wide as saucers as he witnesses whatever it is that's happening. A brilliant blue-green glow lights the entire room.

I feel phenomenal! Awareness races through my body at lightning-fast speed, identifying every injured capillary and vein in my body, not just in my shoulder, but everywhere. My acute sense of healing focuses on every cell within me, repairing, rebuilding, and sloughing off at an incredible rate. Then my focus turns to Chris. I race through his body composition in my mind, doing the exact same thing. Once there is nothing left to fix, I let go of his hand.

"What the . . . Calli?" Chris exclaims. He points to my shoulder. "Not only are you healed, the blood is gone. It's as if it was never there."

I sit up, bringing our bodies close together. "I think we just accessed the healing power as two Bearers in love," I whisper, placing my hand on his cheek. My eyes drop to his mouth. After having performed an extensive search through his body, healing any and all of his ailments, I need to feel his mouth on mine to complete the connection. I pull his head forward and bring my lips to his. He must feel the same urgency because he wraps his arms around me and pushes his hand into my hair, holding my head. His other hand finds its way to my cheek as he intensifies the kiss. His hand slides down my neck and out over my bare, freshly-healed shoulder, then around to my back. Everywhere he touches vibrates intensely. It's the most wonderful feeling. I wrap my other arm around him too, feeling I need to be as close to him as possible.

I explore his firm chest and back and slide my hands along his shoulders as he explores my mouth. I move my hands down his sides and grab onto his shirt hem and begin to push upward. His arms shoot up and he reaches back and grabs his shirt from the neckline, pulling it off in one swift movement. Our lips part for only a microsecond while the material slides between us. Before I know what's happened, he's kicked off his shoes and is laying me back on the bed, his body length stretched out beside me. I roll toward him and arch my back so our chests and tummies can touch. Wrapping my arm over his body, I pull him closer because I want to kiss him again. But as I move to his mouth, he pulls away and props himself up on one elbow and smiles.

I remove my arm from his body and lay it on my side. I try to read his mind. He's blocking me. I look into his eyes and watch as they travel down my body and come back up stopping at my chest. I'm able to read his thoughts now. He wants to touch me, but he's afraid of overstepping his bounds. Instead, he takes his hand and slowly traces around my hairline. He tucks my bangs behind my ear while his feet stroke mine. Then he drags his hand lazily down my arm to my hand and intertwines our fingers.

"Your skin is so soft, Calli." He pulls our clasped hands to his mouth and slides the back of my hand over his lips. "Are you feeling better?"

"Mmm-hmm." I untangle my fingers from his and lay my hand on his chest over his heart. I feel his heart racing beneath my palm. The urge to feel his muscles overwhelms me and I begin touching his chest.

He lets out a heavy breath and lies on his back. "Your hands on my body feel so good. You have no idea." He closes his eyes and inhales deeply.

"I think I have a clue." I remember the day on the bank of the river when I massaged the water from his lungs and how muscular his body felt. Now, with his shirt off, I can identify each of his major and minor muscle groups. "Runners' bodies are truly amazing," I say in admiration as I follow the lines and planes of his torso. When I reach his sculpted abs, he snatches my hand from his belly and holds it protectively.

"We better let them know you're all right," he says.

I let out a long sigh. "I don't want this moment to end, but you're right."

"I don't either, Calli."

"I'm so glad you're here with me on New Year's Eve. I know you came because Max was headed this way, but now we'll be able to welcome in the new year together. I think this next year is going to hold some amazing things for us."

"Why do you say that?" He angles his head.

"I don't know. It's just a feeling. But I want to go find out. I want Maetha and Crimson to level with us. Then later, you and I can pick up where we left off," I hint, moving my body closer so I can kiss him. Before our lips touch, he rolls toward me and then halfway onto my body, causing me to lie back.

His mouth descends to mine and he kisses me sweetly. "I love you," he says. Then he gets up from the bed and pulls his shirt back on.

"I love you, too, Chris." I lay there peacefully. Letting the memory of our time together imprint on my mind, still feeling his body against mine.

He searches through my bag for a different shirt for

me. "You still have my jacket?"

I look over and find him holding the jacket he gave me at Lake Patoka. "Yeah. It smells like you, well, before you lost your scent." I feel kind of silly for some reason.

"Well, how about you wear it then?" He tosses the jacket to me and I put it on and zip it up.

I close my eyes and inhale the dwindling aroma of Chris. When I open my eyes, he's moved next to me. His mind says, *It's as though I'm still wrapped around you.*

We walk out of the bedroom and stop as we enter the living room.

Maetha and Crimson have wrapped Marketa's body in sheets and a dark blanket to mask the blood. Even though it's dark outside, I can understand a blood-soaked, white-sheet-wrapped body would not look good to anyone passing by . . . like Agent Whitman.

The memory of Marketa's body blowing open flashes through my mind. Then General Harding's gruesome death follows. Neema's was difficult to witness, as I considered her a friend. Thinking about her death brings back sharp feelings of betrayal, which I quickly dismiss. Justin Macintyre's death was violent, but I knew it was coming. Freedom's death was by far the most drawn-out and dramatic. I watched him die several times during Brand's attempts to get the bullet to hit Freedom's heart.

Then there's Chris's death.

I've watched him die over and over again in alternate futures. Someday, I'll be responsible for ending his mortal life and bringing him back to life.

Seeing Marketa's wrapped body brings thoughts and images to mind that I'd rather not see. Several other deaths replay in my mind. The poisoned Runners, Hunters being shot, the heart-attack guy . . . am I already becoming cold-hearted and numb like Marketa? Why am I not disturbed more by these deaths? Why am I not upset Marketa died a few hours ago? She's been by my side for nearly four months.

The dark blanket's edge is crooked and disheveled on Marketa's wrapped body. I leave Chris's side and walk over to her. I reach down and straighten the blanket's hem so that it lines up directly centered down her body, tucking parts of it underneath her body. I stand and look over her body. I think she'd be pleased.

"Why did you do that?" Chris asks, bringing Crimson's and Maetha's attention to us.

"She liked things in order."

"Yeah, but she just tried to kill you."

I look at Chris, not knowing how to explain that I feel sad for her. She chose to go against nature's will. She didn't need to die, but in the end that was her choice.

"How are you feeling?" Maetha asks.

I step away from Marketa and stand by Chris. "I'm all better." I open the zipper on the jacket enough to expose my shoulder. Both Maetha and Crimson move closer to inspect my skin.

"Unbelievable!" Crimson stammers.

"I knew it!" Maetha affirms. "You healed yourself, didn't you?"

"No, we did it together," I tell her, wrapping an arm around Chris's back. "Why would you think I'd be able to heal myself when neither of you could do it?"

"We're going to discuss that after the Healers get here," Crimson announces. "Sit down." She motions to the couch.

Maetha returns to scrubbing the table, cleaning up my blood.

"Let me help clean up," I offer. "That's my mess."

"Nonsense. You need to save your energy. Sit and I'll

get you a cup of tea."

"But I feel fine."

"Sit. You too, Chris." Crimson's finger shoos us away.

Chris and I follow her orders and sit together silently on the couch, his arm around my shoulders holding me protectively, his thumb gently massaging my arm.

I speak to his mind. *Do you want to see what happened when we met with Max?*

Yes. Yes, I do.

Okay, focus on the memory I'm putting forward.

Chris accesses the memory with ease. I pay attention to what I'm feeling while he does. I can basically see what he sees and it makes me wonder if this is a form of thought-extraction. The difference is, he's not forcefully removing memories, so he won't be exhausted when he's done. The same way I wasn't exhausted when I viewed his memory of meeting with Max.

Once Chris gets to the part of the memory where Max shoots me, he becomes quite enraged. Then he relives what I went through at the hands of Marketa, and becomes livid. Once he finishes, his says, *She tortured you, Calli. Why did Crimson allow her to do that? Why did Crimson think you'd be fine with obsidian in your future?*

I don't know.

Crimson brings me some chamomile tea. I cradle the mug with my hands, inhaling the soothing steam. Crimson sits in a chair across from us and activates her invisibility. I can still see her silently observing us. I wonder what she's thinking.

The two Healers arrive and Maetha issues instructions. I don't pay attention, though. My mind is occupied with memories of Marketa. I'd put my trust in her and she never gave me a reason to doubt her.

She knew, however, the Blue Diamond afforded the

Bearer the ability to hear other Bearers' thoughts. That would be why I never suspected her as one of the four dissidents . . . which in turn means I've tagged someone else as being a dissident who isn't. But who? Yeok Choo, Jie Wen, Kookju, or Chuang . . . or perhaps someone else entirely.

Not that I didn't understand the importance before, but now I fully understand why Crimson wanted me to keep the Blue shard secret and why I will continue to do so. Marketa thought she was safe. She thought she'd get away with my death. She thought wrong. She made a bad choice.

I notice I never received the strumming sensation that a diamond no longer had an owner after Marketa died. The exposed obsidian on her belt prevented that from happening. This would mean that no other Bearer, other than the four of us, is aware Marketa is dead.

Chapter 16 – The Altered Unaltered

Maetha sees the Healers off and comes back inside.

Crimson reappears, stands, and walks around our group, securing our conversation while Maetha makes a cup of tea.

I speak first. "May I ask a question that's weighing heavily on my mind?"

"Go ahead." Crimson nods.

"Will I ever become like Marketa? Will I have crossed the line so many times that I'll become insensitive and un-compassionate?"

"The fact that you're worrying means you will continue to evaluate each situation as it presents itself. The line Marketa spoke of was drawn by humans. Every human has a different idea of what constitutes crossing the line."

I correct her. "Actually, the courts have the last say in who is crossing the line."

"Not really. The lines are drawn in sand. They can be fudged this way or that to allow for different variables. Consider the laws governing this country. They are not identical to the laws governing other countries. All laws are made by man in each corresponding area of the world. Those in charge or in control have the power to alter a law—or move the line—to accommodate a situation. It has always been that way. It will always be that way.

"Way back before I found the Primal Stone, I belonged to a wandering tribe that lived in the area you know as the Middle East, specifically Iraq. We would follow the herds, follow the sun, move away from the ad-vancing cold, and make trades with other tribes. Everything we owned, we carried with us from place to place. My tribe was my family, and my family had order and structure. Two rules had to be followed: don't hurt others, and don't take their things. If a rule was broken, you'd be banished from the tribe. If you killed someone, you'd be killed. This way of life was simplicity at its best and we had a happy tribe. Then a stranger walked into our camp. He was a Healer, like me. Assur, he said was his name. He was welcomed and embraced. But soon after his arrival, mysterious deaths began to occur. I suspected him but couldn't convince the others. I followed Assur, prayed to my gods for enlightenment, waited to catch him in the act of harming someone, but I never did.

"Soon after, I heard something calling to me. I followed the hum, coming from inside a cave. A brilliant red stone sparkled in the dark, amidst the bones of skeletons. I picked the stone up and when I did, power upon power raced through me, scaring me to death. I tried to drop the stone but it was stuck to my skin. I shook my hand but it wouldn't release. So, I rubbed the stone against my chest to try to pry it off. You can guess what happened next. I woke much later, after dark. I had no fire and became afraid I'd get lost trying to get back to my tribe. However, I realized my sight was different, better. I could see at night. I looked down at my hand, remembering the red stone. It was gone. Then I noticed my dress was torn and bloody. I knew the stone was inside my body; I could feel it but couldn't get it out. Panic made me run back to the others, to my love, Kirkuk.

"Kirkuk thought I'd been attacked. He took me to Assur even though I said I was fine. As soon as I saw Assur, I read his mind and found he was going to kill me to secure his place with the tribe. Kirkuk wouldn't listen to me, didn't believe I could hear Assur's thoughts. I'm sure I looked crazed out of my mind to Kirkuk. Assur tried to take me away to heal me when I somehow harnessed lightning and shot a bolt out of my fingertip, killing him.

"I'd broken the rule. I'd killed. Even though it was self-defense, I'd crossed the line. Kirkuk led the pack to drive me off a cliff. I could have stopped them, but they were only doing what had kept the tribe safe for generations . . . and, I was heartbroken. That was the point in time where I became determined to stop any Healer who set out to harm others. To protect those who were being killed off unnaturally.

"As with all my Bearers, with the exception of Chris and Jonas, I chose you, Calli. I chose you because of, among other things, your compassion, your mind, your ability to look at a situation and make an immediate decision in nature's best interest. You thrive on learning, on figuring out solutions. The older Bearers do not think like you. They simply cannot. They can still serve nature, if they choose, but they will never be able to perform at your level."

Maetha nods her head. "It's true, Calli."

Crimson continues. "You've grown up in a generation that preserves life. Wars are not as deadly as they used to be due to new technology. Medicine keeps people alive longer. The older Bearers come from a time when death was common and came at a young age. Killing was necessary for survival. Wars were fought to acquire land and to assimilate cultures. My Bearers had to be willing to meet violence with violence.

"In today's time, the world is more civilized, for the most part, and the Bearers are not used to this type of peace. Obviously, some of the others worry that you, Chris, and Jonas won't have the guts to do what is necessary— kill. But I say the future belongs to your generation. Your generation will decide what kind of future they want to live in. Will you cross the line as Marketa stated? I hope so, but only in the proper way, as you already have." Crimson finishes and sips on her tea.

Maetha says, "You are wondering about some of the cryptic words we've spoken lately." She motions toward Crimson. "We've been working on a project for several centuries. Once the Death Clan formed, I began experimenting with my Unaltered line, making them stronger, so that one day an Unaltered could successfully pose as a Runner. Unaltered humans are not able to have the running power passed along to them by holding hands. Yet, according to the vision I'd seen, the only way a diamond would be accepted by the Death Clan would be from the Runners, who, unfortunately, cannot touch a diamond. An Unaltered needed to be placed with the Runners. Your mother's DNA alteration wasn't strong enough to pass. That's why she wasn't chosen."

I interrupt, "So, I'm *not* an Unaltered?"

"Technically, you are an Unaltered in the true sense of the word. However, I altered your DNA. When your eardrums burst in middle school, Crimson was able to evaluate your body thoroughly and conclude you would be strong enough for the task, both in body and mind. She saw the grim outlook for the future of mankind change once she inserted you into the equation. It was decided. We began moving forward with the plan. However, never before had a slightly-altered individual become a Diamond Bearer. We knew your body wouldn't reject the diamond, we just didn't know the diamond shard would move around as much as it did." Maetha turns to Chris. "Calli's attraction to you and your effect on her amplified the problem. I wouldn't have sent you two off with obsidian had I known she could die."

I shake my head and raise a hand. "Wait, hold up. Crimson, you said I was chosen because of my personality and characteristics. Now Maetha is saying I was pre-planned to be strong. What if I had turned out to be a spoiled child with strong DNA? What was your backup plan for the cosmic blast arriving in two years?"

They look at each other, then Crimson speaks, "I would not have chosen you if your personality wasn't in line with nature, regardless of if your DNA alteration was effective. We thought we'd failed when your mother's alteration didn't prove to be strong enough. The future concerning the blast was still ominous. Then there was you. I've never considered giving a diamond to a teen. But once I looked into the future with you in the equation, everything began to look optimistic."

"Oh, so it was for both reasons." I think for a second, then ask, "What was the point you were trying to make with Marketa?"

Crimson says, "That you're stronger than her. The bullet wasn't supposed to injure you. I thought the bullet would ricochet off you. It didn't. What's worse, the bullet was made of obsidian. Earlier, when you detected obsidian in your future, I did as well. I just didn't know it would be in the form of a bullet. I thought the obsidian would be like what Marketa had attached to her belt, and in that case, you'd be able to escape. But I was wrong. You were injured. I'm sorry."

"You thought I'd be bulletproof?"

"That's been the goal—to produce a Bearer with the ability to resist injury by healing incredibly fast, well, besides being able to pass as a Runner."

I shake my head and squeeze my eyes shut momentarily. This explains a lot. But bulletproof? Come on! "But, why did you want to make a point at all? Were you trying to save Marketa?"

"I'd much rather reform a Bearer than find a new one. I had no idea how far off the deep end she'd gone until she tried to kill you. However, I do want to commend you for trying to persuade her to change her thinking so she could still be one of us. I observed her behavior and choices while she worked on you. At some point, I looked to the future and found it was no longer optimistic. I couldn't fix the situation. Your shoulder injury was non-fatal initially, but Marketa had taken you beyond what could be healed because, ironically, Maetha's alteration on your body prevented us from fixing your damage. We knew from the beginning you'd need the full diamond before you'd become indestructible. We just didn't know how long it would take for you to achieve success. Then throw obsidian into the mix, and we were suddenly in over our heads." Crimson sips more on her tea.

Maetha says, "We could only keep you alive, and barely at that. Obviously, you harnessed the greater healing power that resides within the diamond. I believe you have now become indestructible, Calli."

"Why do you think that?"

"Because I cannot use my healing power on your body."

Chris says, "I can. Well, as much as she'll let me."

"Only because you two are in love."

Everything swims around in my mind, but something still doesn't make sense. I sit forward and say, "So, you worked hard to create an altered Unaltered, so I could pass as a Runner to bring down the Death Clan? But I only now became indestructible, if in fact I am. I don't understand why you went through all that fuss. Unless you have another reason you're not telling me. If there's only one thing I've learned about you two," I point at both of them, "it's that I never seem to get the whole story out of either one of you."

Crimson says to Maetha, beaming proudly, "She's perfect." Then she looks at me and says, "Besides uniting the clans and Bearers, and being their leader when the Elemental cosmic ray hits the earth, you will also assist me as I try to capture the ray within a diamond, similar to the Grecian Blue Diamond. To do that, you need to be indestructible. My Primal Stone protects me, but I alone can't capture the power. I need help. We need to capture the power to be able to use it in defense of those who will become altered from the blast. If we can't defend against the Elemental power, humanity will die off within a century and a half. Capturing the power is the end goal. That's the bigger reason why we created an indestructible Bearer."

I stare at Crimson and then at Maetha. I turn my head to Chris, who's looking at me with deep concern in his eyes.

"So, you're saying I can't be injured?"

"We think so."

"What does this mean for me? Will I still be able to have children?"

"Yes, your future still shows you with children."

"Will they be indestructible too? You said this alteration is handed down genetically."

"Yes. You are stronger than your mother, and your children will be stronger than you. But only a Diamond Bearer can become indestructible with the use of the Healing power. If your children become Bearers, they will be like you."

"Who else knows?" I ask.

"At this point, only the four of us."

"But you were going to show Marketa," I say.

"Like I said, Calli, I wasn't aware of her deeper

thoughts. As you've probably noticed, the Blue shard only gives us the ability to hear active thoughts of other Bearers when we're around them. You can't dig into their minds. This is the risk taken every time we select a Bearer. Will the individual turn against us? Take yourself, for instance. Will you turn against nature?"

"Never!" I declare adamantly. My own words fill my head of a time I told Chris to never say never. I revise my declaration. "I mean, I don't believe I'd ever do that."

"Just remember, you're only virtually indestructible, not entirely. Your future is in your own hands. I believe you'll continue to be yourself. In fact, I'm counting on it." Crimson smiles warmly, letting me know she doesn't doubt me. She continues, addressing Maetha and Chris, "Should anything ever happen to me, I want Calli to be the Bearer of the Primal Stone."

I sputter, "You'd put the fate of the world in the hands of a nineteen-year-old?"

"It already is. If only every young person would recognize the awesome responsibility they all have, that is, to do everything in their power to preserve this planet, our humanity, our progression. If humanity survives the coming cosmic blast, which looks optimistic, I see the potential for a cataclysmic event down the road, due to the deteriorating condition of the environment, one that would take many millennia from which to recover."

No one speaks. The room is eerily silent.

She continues, "But I also see the potential for humanity to bond together and win the battles that lay ahead. Not just against the Elementals and whatever else follows, but the battle for repairing the environment, the battle for a healthier human race, and the fight for progression to continue worldwide."

"I'm honored you believe I can handle this responsibility. I'm humbled, too." I pause, then ask, "Why can't I see the future the way you do?"

"You don't know how, nor do you have a Primal Stone. I recommend, like I have in the past, to not look for the future other than to protect your lives. You'll take away the joy of living. Don't live your life waiting for the destination, or you'll miss the journey."

Chris and I share a tender glance with one another.

Chris asks Crimson, "What is the Primal Stone made of?"

Maetha turns her head, curiosity written all over her face.

Crimson says, "It's a diamond, and it's red, but not like the red diamonds found in nature. Every time a new red diamond is discovered, and that's not very often, I personally examine it to make sure it's powerless. Something not everyone knows is natural red diamonds are actually clear. They are pure carbon, like other pure white diamonds, without any impurities. However, they have rearranged atomic structures that bend light, displaying a red color. Even though the Primal Stone is pure carbon, it glowed in the darkness of the cave without a light source. No other stone like it has been found."

Maetha asks, "Why did everyone think you have red spinel?"

"I took a shine to spinel for its ability to be charged, similar to topaz, and because I did, others did too. Spinel became the immortality stone that everyone sought, including Freedom. I never corrected any of my Bearers concerning the true nature of the Primal Stone. And by the way, you three will be the only ones who know." She looks at all three of us. "I've withheld the differences of crystals and rocks in an effort to prevent the obsessive behavior as with spinel. Just look at what has happened with the knowledge of what certain obsidian can do? However, I do regret not sharing with Maetha the information about the Imperial topaz."

Crimson looks directly at me, "I haven't told you everything, which should come as no surprise. I want you to process what you've learned before we go further. We will host a Diamond Bearer gathering tomorrow where Marketa's death will be announced. I have Jonas searching for Max Corvus and his assistant at the bookstore to help the authorities capture them. Hopefully Jonas will have word by tomorrow morning. The bookstore shooting is already on the wire. We'll have that to deal with, too. Just so you know, you don't have to worry about containing the information concerning Calli's indestructibility, Chris. I've blocked that information within both your minds." Crimson stands and removes the blue mist over our conversation. Maetha joins her and together they walk into the kitchen.

I lay my head back on Chris's shoulder and say, "Is your mind as blown away as mine?"

"Yep."

"Are you afraid?" I ask.

"Are you?"

"No," I declare.

"Then neither am I." He squeezes my shoulder lovingly and kisses the top of my head. I move closer to his body and let out a deep exhale.

Learning exactly why Crimson has protected my life up to this point boosts my confidence and clears the last remaining self-pity cobwebs from my head. However, knowing some of what lies ahead brings apprehension like I've never felt before. She wants me to process what I've been told, but how am I supposed to do that? My life, my world, my purpose has been completely turned on end.

These secrets Crimson and Maetha have kept for decades are nearing the end. At least, I hope they are.

One thing that hasn't changed is my love for Chris, and his for me. Having Chris by my side tonight, on this New Year's Eve, brings tranquility to my soul. I realize Chris is sending me healing energy. I gladly accept his offering. My worries and concerns melt away and I only feel peace. What a sweet guy! I'm in heaven . . . for tonight, anyway.

Thank You!

Thanks for reading my books!
I hope you'll take the time to leave a review on
Amazon or Goodreads. I'd really appreciate it.

Also, drop on over to my website,
www.LorenaAngell.com,
and let me know what you thought of the series
by using the Contact Me form.

While you're visiting my site, sign up for my
newsletter to be kept updated on the progress of
upcoming books in The Unaltered series, and to receive
exclusive freebies and news.

Thanks again for reading my books. --Lorena

The Unaltered series continues...

Book Six: *The Diamond Bearers' Rising*

Now that Calli understands more of what's expected of her, she needs to figure out how to achieve success while keeping friendships and relationships in place. The future of the human race is dependent upon her choices and the pressure is mounting for Calli. How long will Max stay off grid? How will she win over the respect of her fellow Bearers? Is she really invincible?

Find out in *The Diamond Bearers' Rising*, book six of The Unaltered series.

Available now on Amazon, Barnes&Noble Apple Books, Kobo, and Smashwords. Audiobook coming soon!

ABOUT THE AUTHOR

Lorena Angell is the internationally bestselling author of the YA fantasy series, *The Unaltered*. Inspired by an interview from J.K. Rowling, Lorena began to write and published her first book in 2011. Since then, she's earned over 4,200 reviews (average of 4.5 stars), has been a #1 bestseller in over 11 countries and wants nothing more than to write more books for her readers.

Connect with Lorena Angell at:
www.LorenaAngell.com
Twitter: @LorenaAngell1
Facebook: The Unaltered Diamond Series
Instagram: the.unaltered.series